The danger was real . . .

Rick pulled up next to a telephone kiosk. He had a phone in his car, but he didn't want Molly listening in.

The policeman was slow to give out information, so Rick missed seeing the Caddy that had been behind him turn back into the street. He was just about to hang up when the car drew alongside his Camaro.

"Duck!" he yelled to Molly.

A hand holding a gun emerged from the Caddy's window. Molly was horrified but followed Rick's warning. The bullet flashed through the open windows of the Camaro and hit the kiosk. The Caddy roared off. Rick jumped back into the car and held a trembling Molly in his arms.

"I'm okay," she said. "But they were trying to kill me!"

ABOUT THE AUTHOR

Eve Gladstone believes that romance and adventure are a constant challenge, and *Operation S.N.A.R.E.* marks her third exciting foray into Intrigue. Since she began her writing career, she has had a number of books published, both fiction and nonfiction. Eve lives in a New York City suburb with her husband and a compatible assortment of dogs and cats.

Books by Eve Gladstone

HARLEQUIN INTRIGUE
23–A TASTE OF DECEPTION
49–CHECKPOINT

Operation S.N.A.R.E.

Eve Gladstone

Harlequin Books

TORONTO • NEW YORK • LONDON
AMSTERDAM • PARIS • SYDNEY • HAMBURG
STOCKHOLM • ATHENS • TOKYO • MILAN

To: Estelle Gleit
and Sharon Cowen

Special thanks to:
Eve Brandel
Ethel Kirsner

Harlequin Intrigue edition published October 1987

ISBN 0-373-22075-8

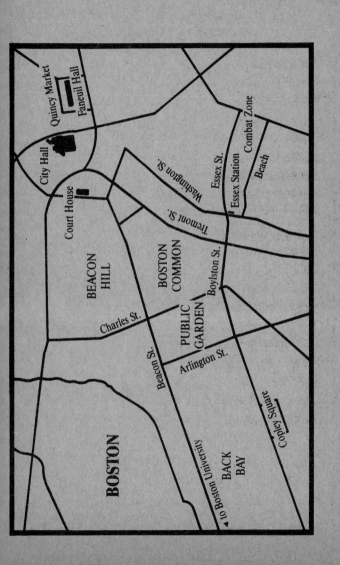

CAST OF CHARACTERS

Molly Ryder—Being the judge's niece put her life in danger

Rick Boulter—He would leave no stone unturned to reveal the truth

Judge William Ryder—Was he an innocent bystander—or part of the conspiracy?

Serena Ryder—Her gentleness belied a shrewd business sense

Tinky Marin—His pickpocketing days were coming to an end

Gentry Perot—The sophisticated—and silent— partner of Daniel Halloway

Daniel Halloway—The president of Halloway Construction—now reported missing

Elliott Lawrence—A poker-playing buddy of the judge's, and a top union official

Tom "Buzz" Beam—An able assistant to Lawrence who also played poker

Jason Loring—His work as a TV news reporter was his undoing

Prologue

The train door closed between them. She was inside, indignant and wide-eyed, shouting something at him that he couldn't understand. For a moment Tinky Marin stood there grinning back at her, his hand wrapped tightly around the tape recorder. Then he turned and ran. The train started to roll as he jumped over the railing and dashed for the stairs.

When he hit the street he took off in the opposite direction, the train going one way, Tinky the other. Well, that would put the entire city between them, he thought. Fool, leaving her bag open like that. He remembered her eyes— big brown eyes that made her seem both tough and smart— and how for the briefest second he'd wavered. She was the kind of woman who never gave him a second glance, who thought she was too good for him. Well, that was her tough luck.

The whole thing had been a cinch from the word go, although at first he'd figured Buzz was putting one over on him.

"Pick some dame's bag? Why don't you do it, Buzz?"

"You ask too many questions, friend. It's because she may have seen me with the boss."

The boss. Tinky had no idea who the boss was, but the notion was enough to strike fear in him. They'd been standing near the Essex Street station when Buzz had pointed her out.

"That's the one, the brunette. Look, she has her bag open—you're in luck. Just pick it out nice and easy and bring it back to me, and there's another fifty for you. I'll be waiting for you on the corner of Beach."

"Fifty. Right."

Tinky had taken off after the brunette. She'd been so preoccupied she hadn't seen him closing in. A quick hundred bucks just for sticking his hand into her bag and pulling out a tape recorder. He could do it with his eyes shut. Only he never shut his eyes, not Tinky Marin.

He was still running when he hit the corner and turned onto Beach. Then he slowed down and checked the small, slick instrument he had just filched. A Panasonic micro-recorder, maybe the most expensive model there was.

But where the hell was Buzz? A police patrol car came cruising down the street. Tinky took in a nervous breath. That was it. With the cops haunting the neighborhood, Buzz wasn't keeping any dates. Tinky commenced whistling, his eye on the patrol car as it moved south. He wondered why the hell his hair was standing on end.

He stared curiously at the Panasonic, which was voice activated. There was a tape on the reel.

"Hello there, folks," Tinky said jauntily into the recorder, but then realized a cop was heading toward him. Man, they were coming out of the woodwork today. He switched the tape off, picking up his pace as if he knew where he was going and was late getting there. He passed the cop, keeping his gaze straight ahead. He was in his usual guise now: a small, slight youth in jeans and a denim jacket, on his way to work. Work? Listen, it was a living.

Where the hell had Buzz taken himself off to? What was going on? Tinky had an awful premonition. What if they were setting him up, planning something with the broad and he'd be the fall guy? They'd have him nailed with his fingerprints all over the recorder. Did they think he was dumb or something? He glanced nervously around. Still no Buzz.

Tinky was having one of those hunches he always played. *Get rid of this thing, and fast.* He could always make excuses later, tell them she didn't have it or that somebody got there first. There were too many cops on the streets. It could be a setup. He knew just the place to unload the Panasonic.

Powers Pawn Shop was in a seedy section of Boston, not far from where Tinky Marin lived. Old man Powers was shortsighted and complained about needing glasses, but he'd never gotten them and he never asked too many questions. It was the kind of place to call home, Tinky decided, pushing the door open and sniffing the familiar smell of dust and leather and cigar smoke. In some ways, old man Powers was his boss, considering the amount of money that had passed between them over the years.

But Tinky was in for his second shock of the day. "Hey, where's the old man?" He asked the question warily of the short, squat fellow who stood behind the counter and grinned at him.

"What old man you referring to? My old man?"

"Mr. Powers," said Tinky, approaching the counter tentatively. He didn't like surprises.

"Retired. I'm his son. His *oldest* son. Harv, that's my name."

Tinky squinted at him. Something about the eyes, maybe, looked familiar. Small blue eyes under heavy lids. That was it. He hadn't seen the resemblance at first. The same shortsighted eyes as old man Powers had. He relaxed a bit. "Hey, Harv, where'd he retire to?"

"Florida. That's the law." Harv waited, and when Tinky didn't laugh, he explained it was a joke.

"Right," Tinky said, although he failed to see the humor.

Harv leaned his burly arms on the counter and asked Tinky in a friendly way, "Can I help you?"

"Right." Now Tinky was all business. He put the Panasonic down on the counter.

Harv whistled admiringly. "A beauty. A real little genuine beauty. Don't get to see many of these in here."

"Hate like hell to part with it," Tinky said, "but something's come up and I need the money."

The man behind the counter looked hard at Tinky and then smiled. Tinky had to suppress the desire to cut and run. "Your kid sister needs an operation, right?"

"You a comedian or something?"

"I'll give you twenty-five bucks for this."

Tinky wavered. "Listen, that cost me a helluva lot more. I mean, I'm parting with my life with that thing."

"Take it or leave it."

Harv flipped the tape on, and Tinky first heard his own words, "Hello there, folks," which ran over the beginnings of a woman's voice announcing the day, a time, a place. It came to him in a flash. Buzz had had him steal the recorder for the tape. A terrible fear washed over him. "That's my sister. School project," he said, reaching over and switching the recorder off. "Maybe I'd better take it back...."

Harv smiled and put his hand firmly over the small machine. "You just made a sale. I'll need your name and address."

"Hey, come on, your old man knows me."

Harv picked up a receipt pad. "But you see, fella, I don't. That's why he's in Florida and I'm here. Family decided he needed a long vacation from knowing too many people."

For once Tinky lost his head and gave his real name and address. He thought about grabbing a bus out of town before Buzz came looking for him. He took the money, two tens and a five, and left with unseemly haste.

Sergeant Harvey Klein smiled, turned the tape recorder on and prepared to listen to the warm, inviting voice that told the time of day so engagingly.

Chapter One

She'd kill him. She'd *kill* him. She'd track him to the ends of the earth if it took her entire life and all of her money, time, energy and brainpower.

Leaving her bag open like that. *Inviting* him to steal the tape recorder. If only she could rewind the tape of her life and push the start button. Or at least go back to when she'd begun to climb the station stairs, her hobo bag wide open and filled with notebooks, corrected student papers, the tape recorder, a red Delicious apple, a makeup case and an engagement calendar. In other words, the detritus of her daily life, including her wallet, which contained two tens and a twenty.

How had he managed it? By what schooled touch had he picked out the Panasonic? Why a recorder whose principal value was the strip of magnetic tape containing conversation so dull it could be of interest only to a linguist, namely hers truly, Molly Ryder?

She was aware of half the passengers in the train staring surreptitiously at her, the other half pretending to read their newspapers. If they were clucking, the sound was lost in the rumble of wheels along the track.

"You shouldn't have left your bag open like that, dear. It's an absolute invitation." The woman standing next to Molly was full of motherly advice.

"I've lived in Boston all my life," Molly said, "and that's never happened to me before."

"There's always a first time."

Molly resisted the temptation to grind her teeth in response. Before the train pulled into the next station, a baker's dozen of her fellow passengers had surrounded her with a carload of advice and admonition. She didn't need any of it. She could write the book on advice, admonition and regret. Molly got off the train and ran down the stairs into the street. What she wanted was a sympathetic officer of the law who'd listen to her story of woe.

It was nine o'clock on a Monday morning in May, and suddenly, after a relaxing weekend away, she had become the victim of a petty thief. Where was a policeman? Where was a station house in this section of Boston? She had no idea. Did it pay to look for help when the end result was a fait accompli? Her story would be repeated to a series of bored official faces. She'd be handed a stack of forms to fill in. There would be mug shots to be examined. At last she'd be treated to a lift of the shoulders and perhaps even a suggestion that her tape recorder would show up in a pawnshop sooner or later. In other words, *Don't call us, we'll call you.*

She could pull rank and mention her uncle Willy, Judge William Ryder, and deal with his I-told-you-so's later. Or she could make the rounds of local pawn shops herself, after she taught her last class at Boston University. She decided that was what she'd do.

Molly hailed a passing cab and told the driver to take her to the Boston University campus on Commonwealth. At least she wouldn't have a trainload of people staring at her

as if she'd just stepped off a turnip truck. And she point-
edly ignored the friendly chatter of the cabdriver, simply
because she wanted desperately to tell him what had happened. *Calm down, Molly,* she told herself, *and look at the
positive side.* The man could have stolen her bag with
everything in it, and her right arm up to her shoulder besides. She was lucky. It could have been worse.

But that thought didn't help one bit. Pollyanna wasn't
her middle name. Her glass was not half full, it was half
empty. All that time she'd spent on Friday at a beer-and-
sawdust bar, explaining that she was a linguist and that her
doctoral dissertation was on Boston accents, coaxing four
people to unburden themselves unself-consciously on tape.
They might not have understood what she was about, but
at last they had entered gaily into the proceedings. One of
them had even recited fractured Yeats for her. Now it was
all gone and she was running short of time. Having asked
for and received one extension on her dissertation for a
year's study at Oxford, she couldn't possibly ask for another.

Molly brushed an errant twist of hair from her face and
stared out the cab window. She had grown up in this town,
knew its streets and its people, and felt immune to its vices.
But on a Monday *morning*! She could hear her uncle and
aunt now: "Serves you right, Molly. How many times have
we told you it's *dangerous*, a good-looking woman alone at
any hour of the day or night..."

Mother hens, both of them. They had taken her in, six-
teen years before when her parents had died, treating a
stubborn, scared twelve-year-old as their own. One might
say she'd been her uncle's late-in-life child, as she had been
for her parents. On the other hand, her aunt Serena had
been barely thirty at the time, twenty years younger than
Willy.

They had spoiled her, worried about her, and couldn't for the life of them understand why she wanted to study linguistics instead of law, like Willy, or business, like Serena. But Molly loved the music, the tone and the possibilities of language. Willy had thrown up his hands at last. "Linguistics. Where will that and ten cents get you?"

Serena, though, had come to her defense: "Willy, she'll do what she wants, so stop hounding the girl."

As the cab made its way along Boylston, Molly admitted to herself that she had asked for trouble. Keeping her bag open in a public conveyance was an invitation to the unsavory to go to work. Calmer now, she made up her mind how to proceed. After class, she'd organize a tour of the local pawnshops. She had to find her tape recorder.

RICHARD BOULTER SAT IMPATIENTLY on the hard wooden chair opposite his chief, Alex Creedon, district attorney for the city of Boston. Creedon, on the telephone on a long-distance call, was giving him one of those have-I-got-something-for-you looks.

"Shall I come back?" Rick—he hadn't been called Richard since grammar school—mouthed the words. He practiced containing the scowl he knew Creedon would pick up, then thought better of it and offered a crooked smile instead.

Creedon shook his head and mouthed back that he'd be just another minute, Rick should stay put.

Rick ran a hand absently across his chin and eyed the container of coffee on Creedon's desk that he had brought in with him. There was a pile of paperwork waiting for him in his own office. Operation S.N.A.R.E. had been set in motion; everything was in place and ready to go. He wanted no last-minute problems. Glancing curiously at the tape recorder sitting at Creedon's elbow, he wondered what the

D.A. had come up against and if it would put a crimp in S.N.A.R.E.

The chief's end of the telephone conversation was all yeses and noes, spoken in an agreeable, accommodating voice. He was anointing someone, part of the honors of his job—that and the long lunch hours with the city's honchos.

Rick glanced restlessly around the familiar office. There was an American flag in the corner, any number of awards and citations on the pale cream walls and a map of Boston facing the window, which offered a good view of the very same city. Also, in the office—and casting furtive, longing glances at the assistant district attorney—was Creedon's decorous secretary, Fran, her steno pad and pencil at the ready. Rick caught her eye and the blatant invitation in her direct gaze. He looked away. Not a good idea.

He unfolded his long legs, stood up and sauntered over to the window. He was a lean man with light brown, unruly hair and an expression of impatience in his brooding, dark brown eyes. Boston was Richard Boulter's town, and he knew it inside out. He had turned down several offers after law school, some in exciting places complete with paychecks to match the high cost of living. Instead, he had chosen the public sector. Ever since he'd been a small kid watching the good guys catch the bad guys on television, he had known what he wanted. And it wasn't a shiny, well-furnished office with a gold sign on the door stating that in order to make a buck, he'd take any case that came his way. A small laugh was in order. He was an assistant district attorney, *not* making a buck, and taking any case they threw at him.

Operation S.N.A.R.E. was different, however. It would blow the town wide open, with Rick right there setting off the dynamite. S.N.A.R.E. The mnemonic was his: Strike-force to Nab and Arrest Racketeers and Extortioners. Admittedly it would look good in the media accounts of the city government's sting, but Rick had never been more serious in his life. This was the good guys versus the bad guys, all grown up. Maybe later, when riding to the rescue of the milked and bilked was out of his system, he'd opt for the gold sign.

"Call me whenever you have a minute. Right. Love you, kid." The district attorney replaced the receiver. "Okay, Rick, let's get to work." He nodded at his secretary, which she understood as a sign of dismissal. "And, Fran, hold my calls until I tell you."

A smile for Rick and her boss, and then the office door closed behind her. The notion struck Rick suddenly that perhaps she had something going with Creedon, but he kicked it quickly to the back of his mind. The D.A. was a straight shooter with an attractive wife who was an asset to his career. Whatever had put that thought into Rick's head? Maybe having to share a dour, well-married secretary with a couple of other assistant D.A.s had something to do with it.

Rick took his seat on the hard wooden chair. And that was another thing: if he ever made it up the ladder to Creedon's job, the first thing he'd do would be to get rid of these instruments of torture. The district attorney believed in punishing his visitors by moving them quickly in and out of his office. He said hard wooden chairs and decor that had never seen betters days kept business brisk.

Rick had been an assistant district attorney for two years and he still couldn't get the backslapping part of the job down pat. If he wanted to become the district attorney, he'd have to learn, and there was no better teacher than Creedon. He rearranged his lanky frame on the chair but was no more comfortable than before. And *that* was one of the particular rewards of *his* job—hard chairs, cramped offices, too much work for too little money. He loved it.

"The police department has mounted an interesting operation of its own in a number of pawnshops in and around the Combat Zone," Creedon said at once and without preliminaries. "I expect I don't have to go into details."

Rick nodded. The Combat Zone was a small, seedy area of Boston that the city's lesser lights called home.

"It's proving to be a gold mine of stolen goods," Creedon went on. He tapped the tape recorder. "This little nugget was handed to Sergeant Harvey Klein over at Powers Pawn. The sergeant had the good sense to listen to what was on the tape and pass the whole thing to his superiors. Since the department is interested in prosecuting for stolen merchandise and not what's on a piece of tape, in no time flat his discovery made its way over here." Creedon smiled in anticipation. "Pay close attention, Rick. I'd like a little input from you."

"Go ahead. I'm all ears. What am I being treated to? A bad rendition of 'America, the Beautiful'?"

The district attorney laughed. "Maybe that's what it is," he said thoughtfully, "a bad rendition of 'America, the Beautiful.'" Creedon was a big, gruff man who ran a tight ship and was fair and honest; this was his third term in office, and he had every intention of having a fourth and maybe even a fifth. After that, he'd think seriously about retirement. Upstarts like Rick Boulter were eyeing his title, and the day would come when they'd begin pushing.

He told Rick about Tinky Marin, whose description of the recorder's owner had been reluctantly given when he'd been picked up for questioning.

"Listen," Tinky had told his interrogators earnestly, "a brunette with these big brown eyes. Smart, though, you know? I mean, pretty, maybe five five, but, like *clever*, like she'd figure everything out about you.''

No, Tinky didn't know her name. She'd left the tape recorder on a park bench, but by the time he retrieved it and took off after her, the lady was gone. In a cab going north maybe. No, he couldn't catch the license plate. Of course he'd tried. What did they think he was, anyway? So he didn't have any choice but to go over to Powers Pawn with it because he needed a couple of bucks, what with the rent being due and everything. The thing was safe at Powers Pawn, like being in a bank vault. He was thinking of putting an ad in the papers, even.

The district attorney reached over and switched on the tape.

''Hello there, folks.''

''That's Tinky Marin,'' Creedon informed Rick.

Then, Rick heard a voice with a sultry undertone that the speaker tried to disguise by clipping the ends of her words. So there she was, Rick thought, in full recording array, *possibly* a brunette with a clever, pretty face—*if* it were she giving the time, day and place. He wondered if she was aware of the throaty, husky quality of her voice and its soft promise. When was the last time a woman had whispered into his ear with such a voice? He stared past the window to the Boston landscape beyond. A tempting May afternoon with a sky blue enough to go swimming in. *Pay attention,* he warned himself.

The place was a nameless bar on the south side, so she said. Then her voice took on a gently chiding manner. ''Now, I don't want you to be self-conscious. Just go on the way you always do. Forget this little apparatus. It doesn't bite. It can't even talk back.''

There followed a long, aimless conversation between a couple of men and a woman, self-conscious in spite of the prodding. Then it warmed up, as if everyone were talking just to hear himself talk.

The subject of baseball slid without rhyme or reason into somebody's uncle's recipe for Texas hot chili and was followed by an argument over clam chowder. Someone recited Yeats badly and was applauded for his efforts. After ten minutes, the owner of the sultry voice thanked the patrons of the bar and disconnected the tape. A moment later she introduced a new time, a new date and a new place identified only as an upper-class house party on the north shore. A lot of disjointed conversation, again making no particular sense. Cocktail-party talk in educated, mixed-bag accents: I said and then she said and then he said and then we all said; plenty of high-pitched, unconnected laughter. Maybe she was a writer interested in the way people disported themselves in groups, Rick thought. So far he hadn't learned a thing that could help S.N.A.R.E.

The district attorney nodded across the desk at him and pointed to the tape, letting him know that the interesting part came next.

Again her voice: "Right. Just let me get rid of this thing, and I'll be yours until the end of time. For the next hour, anyway."

A man's voice in response—deep, resonant and somehow familiar. He was young, perhaps in his thirties. Rick smiled. Young, in his thirties. Rick's own age, dammit. Then why did he feel so old most of the time?

"That thing can be a real pain in the butt, kiddo, and I'm the one to talk," the voice said. "You're going to take it to the grave with you."

She: "Hey, it's my living, so don't knock it. Wait, wait, I'm coming. Don't run away, you heartless beast. I'm famished. If I don't get something to eat . . ." She laughed. A door opened; the clicking of the lock was remarkably clear. Then her voice again: "Whoops! Oh, hi. Sorry, I didn't see you." She gave an embarrassed little laugh. A door slammed shut, then silence. Someone coughed. There was a faint sense of the tape whirring on, of some presence, someone prowling a room and breathing as if with a slight catarrh in the throat, just enough noise to keep the tape running. Eerie, Rick decided.

He stood up and went over to the window for a breath of fresh air. What the hell was the point? He thought of going outside for a cigarette. The chief didn't allow smoking in his office, but then Rick was trying to cut down, too. He went back to the desk, threw himself into the chair, picked up his cup of cold coffee and took a sip. The chief cautioned him to relax.

He tuned in impatiently. Creedon's sharp nod told him something was coming. The recording was remarkably clear. Rick could hear the door being opened once again with the familiar clicking of the lock, and closed, this time more softly. There was a distant noise he couldn't make out, perhaps laughter from an open window, then at last, voices.

"So, what do you say?" Male, mature. Rick had the impression the speaker was overweight.

"Bad news." The man with the catarrh cleared his voice, then said, "The D.A. is beginning to look through the proverbial magnifying glass. I got that right from the horse's mouth."

"He won't find anything."

There was a hard laugh. "Not even under the rocks."

"The mayor has his constituency to worry about, and cost overruns make him a very nervous man. First thing he does is cry to the press. The press cries back, and everyone asks for an investigation. The thing is so clean, I'm telling you, you can see your reflection in it. We've covered our butts every which way to Sunday. There's no chance it leads back to us.''

"Halloway didn't figure on union raises, cost of living, the price of bananas. He was a very stupid man.''

"Halloway *is* a very stupid man. Watch it, friend. We use the present tense at all times.''

"Correct in every way. *Is* a very stupid man playing the crap tables in Monte Carlo.'' There was a gruff laugh. "What I need right now is a good stiff drink to his health.''

A cabinet door was opened and closed. "Mine host being a teetotaler, there's only sherry here and Dubonnet. Your choice, *m'sieur*.''

"Forget it. We'll get something later. Right now I want to make sure we're operating from the same starting point.''

"Shoot.''

"Everything has to be run tight as a drum from now on. This job is too big to screw up.''

"How can we possibly screw up? We've got everybody but the cleaning lady in our back pockets.''

A laugh ended in a cough. "If you want to get down to the nitty-gritty, I have a little more than the cleaning lady in my back pocket.''

"Talk about screwups, let me point out, pal, you drink too much, for one thing. I want you to put a lid on it.''

"Hey.'' Indignation was written into the word.

There was the sound of the door opening again and a faint and unidentifiable click-clicking, a voice cut off at the first syllable—perhaps a greeting—then nothing.

"That's it,'' Creedon said. "The tape ran out. Those bastards are talking about the northeast sewer project. Who the hell are they?''

"Another question is who is the horse's mouth?''

Creedon frowned. He picked up a rubber band and pulled it taut. "Think there's a leak in this office?''

"We're playing S.N.A.R.E. so close to the chest, I don't see how." Rick shook his head slowly. "I don't think it's S.N.A.R.E. he's referring to. It's our curiosity about the way city construction deals are made and Halloway's sudden departure from the scene. *Is* and *was* and crap tables in Monte Carlo. They sound like two very nervous men to me."

"Any guess about who they might be?" Creedon asked.

"Principals in Halloway Construction, I'd say."

"That's what I've been wondering about," Creedon mused. "The owner, Daniel Halloway, is away on permanent leave for his health, according to his secretary, a rather snippy, short-tempered piece, incidentally. It's just what we've been talking about all along," he said, leaning across his desk and fixing Rick with a satisfied smile. "Daniel Halloway, president of Halloway Construction, came in as low bidder on the initial northeast sewer construction job. Innocently enough, he calculated his costs without including a payoff to the powers that be."

"Foolish man," Rick interposed. "Obviously born yesterday."

"And maybe died yesterday, too," Creedon added, repeating the story they both knew by heart. "He wins the job and according to the terms of the contract has to put a lot of cash up front. He eventually takes in a partner, Gentry Perot, who's everything Halloway isn't: suave, experienced in dealing with union contracts, wealthy and well connected. Before Halloway is ready to start work on the project—the way we figure it, before Perot—he gets a visit from a couple of big guys with hands like sides of beef. They're amiable enough. They explain where the poor man went off in his calculations. They explain how they do business. X amount of dollars, and they'll see that the job gets done on time with no problems, or dot-dot-dot, fill in the blank spaces. Connections, they tell him; to get the job done on time and with a profit, you need connections. That's a euphemism for a consortium of union bosses, businessmen and, I'm sorry to say, bankers. Plus their assistants, the guys with the hammer hands.''

''Let's not leave the assistants out of it,'' Rick said.

''Either Daniel Halloway refused to go along and they killed him, or he decided that the best way to stay alive was to leave the country. The official ticket, just like his secretary said, has him on permanent leave for his health. Halloway Construction is left in the hands of its new partner, one Gentry Perot. Gent Perot has an impeccable reputation. Old family, Harvard, wife and four kids, angels all of them, and plenty of service to the community.''

Creedon thought for a moment and then, with an abashed expression, handed Rick a fresh bit of gossip. ''Womanizer, incidentally.''

''Imagine his wife likes that.''

''Friend of judges, mayors and governors,'' Creedon went on, ''plus plenty of experience in dealing with city construction projects. The union runs smoothly in tandem with this new setup. Perot has been known to have dinner with the construction union's big muckamuck, Elliot Lawrence. Perot's record is absolutely clean. So far. So is Lawrence's. It's all hands-across-the-sea stuff, too true to be good.''

''So far,'' Rick echoed.

The two men stared at each other, both thinking the same thing. ''Where do we start, Rick? Your guess about who they are.''

''Could be Perot, could be a couple of union men, could be just about anybody in Halloway Construction or on the periphery. And who the hell was 'mine host,' the teetotaler? Possibly someone not at all visibly connected with Halloway, some string-puller.''

"Or influence peddler.''

"Or racketeer,'' Rick added.

"Suppose we can get a voice pattern on this and on Perot?'' Creedon asked.

Rick nodded. "We can but try. It'll take time, and we'll have to be very careful.'' He narrowed his eyes and put the tips of his fingers to his lips. He was thinking about that other voice on the tape early on, the one that told a woman with an attractive, husky voice, *You're going to take that thing to the grave with you.* A familiar voice, but he couldn't place it. Who was the man?

Creedon slid the tape recorder across the desk. "Maybe this patch of tape will make S.N.A.R.E. a little easier for us. Nothing like hot merchandise, I always say.'' His smile turned serious. "I'd like to know who she is, where she is, and why these voices are on the tape,'' the district attorney said. "I've got a funny feeling in the pit of my stomach that tells me we'll meet Halloway Construction over the upcoming bids for the *extension* of the northeast sewer project.''

"Sure,'' Rick put in, "I'll bet it does tie in with S.N.A.R.E. We've rigged the bids on the extension of the sewer project so that Georgia Boston Construction will win the contract. If the manager of GBC has a visit from the same hamfisted heavies, we'll be able to catch them in the middle of an extortion attempt. We can write finis to that kind of thing once and for all.''

"As for Halloway himself—'' Creedon began.

Rick finished the sentence for him. "I'm still willing to bet Halloway is at the bottom of the bay trying to do the dead man's crawl to Monte Carlo.''

"I'm not arguing with you there," the district attorney said.

"The recorder is voice activated, and the starter button was left on by mistake," Rick said, examining the machine. "The red light indicator is broken. Defective merchandise. The lady ought to get her money back."

"I wonder if she knows what she has on it."

"Dynamite," said Rick, "is what she has on it."

POWERS PAWN. Molly Ryder stood outside the loan emporium and gazed up at the old sign and the three golden balls hanging from it. She turned to her best friend, Liz Gerard, and said, "If I weren't so angry, I'd spend a little time contemplating the age and worth of that sign. It's certainly in good condition."

"Wonder it hasn't been ripped off," Liz said.

"You're so right. Unless the denizens of the neighborhood consider it a kind of shrine."

Liz laughed. "Since when do they feel sentimental about shrines?"

"True. I keep forgetting what I'm here for."

"We're here because you refuse to go to the cops and report the theft."

"The reason, dear Liz, as I explained before in some detail, is that they'll file the complaint under S for Silly. Woman has her tape recorder stolen and actually expects us to find it for her. Silly, silly, silly. Now, vast experience and my little gray cells tell me that stolen recorders are hocked shortly after being stolen. Therefore, go the hockshop route, which is what we're doing and why we're here."

"And the sooner we remove ourselves from the neighborhood the better I'll like it," Liz said truculently.

"This won't take a minute," Molly said. She had already dragged Liz through an unsuccessful trip to a half-dozen loan parlors and contemplated this one without much hope. The thief had probably destroyed the fruits of her labor, anyway.

"Listen," Liz said, putting her hand on Molly's arm, "I hate like hell leaving you in your current state and in this neighborhood, but I'm teaching a class in an hour. I've got to go. Why don't you let me drop you somewhere, and we'll start again tomorrow right after class? Could be your young thief is still sitting on it. Give him a day to make up his mind to unload his ill-gotten gain."

"It doesn't matter," said Molly. "I've left my cards all over the place. The important thing is to touch base with every pawnshop in the city."

Liz sighed. She was a tall, elegant, impeccably dressed blonde with a very practical nature, exactly the opposite of Molly, which was why they got along so well. "Molly, you're insured. You'll get another tape recorder."

"I'm not about to do those interviews all over again. Anyway, I'm furious, Liz. For some tiny, inconsequential reason, I don't like being mugged. My plan is to find the tape recorder," Molly went on, warming to her subject. "Then I'm going to have the pawnbroker arrested as a receiver of stolen goods, and under tough grilling—tough, Liz; I mean thumbscrews and the works; he's going to reveal who sold it to him. Thanks to my persistence and detective work, they'll find the thief, arrest him, and I personally will see him through the entire court system until he's put away for life." Then she added, grinning, "After all, I'm not without contacts in our system of jurisprudence."

Liz sighed once again. "Molly, I can't stand here and argue with you. Are you coming?"

"Sorry, I'm being stupid, but I want that tape recorder back." She put her cheek to her friend's. "You've been an angel. What are you doing for dinner? Maybe I can cook up something for the two of us.'' She spoke halfheartedly, yet as if not wanting to see the last of Liz, either.

Liz shook her head. ''I'm having dinner with Al.'' She broke off, the look on her face telling her friend not to press the issue.

''Thanks for coming along with me. I really needed the moral support. I'll see you tomorrow.'' Molly waited while Liz stepped into her car, put the engine in gear and moved cautiously away from the curb. Molly gave a quick wave, then squared her shoulders and marched into Powers Pawn Shop.

She had the routine down pat by now and began at once. ''I'm looking for a tape recorder,'' she said to the man behind the counter.

''Well, we have those in spades.'' He gave her an appreciative smile.

She was used to that, too, and took advantage of it to speed things up. ''I figure if I'm going to buy one secondhand I ought to get the best, and I've heard the voice-activated Panasonic microrecorder is it.''

''We don't have one in the place. How about an RCA?''

''Panasonic. I'm treating myself.''

''Have you tried the other pawnshops around here?''

''Yes,'' Molly said, ''but they didn't have exactly what I want.''

''I don't recall one coming into the store in . . .'' The sergeant raised his shoulders, as though giving a date were beyond him. Hers was the voice on the tape, all right. ''But give me your name and address, and if one shows up, I'm going to call you before anybody else.''

''Listen, would you? I'd be *so* grateful.'' Her smile was earnest and genuinely charming.

Sergeant Harvey Klein surreptitiously checked out her left hand. No wedding ring, if that meant anything. He toyed with the idea of asking her for a date, then remembered the hidden camera recording the scene, not for posterity but for the benefit of the district attorney's office. He was also a married man. "Name?" His pen was poised over his address book.

"Better than that," she said with a burst of enthusiasm, "I'm going to give you my card."

"Hey, a driver's license will do."

"Driver's license! I haven't bought anything yet." She reached into her hobo bag and extracted a very worn card case. "Here's my card."

While Sergeant Klein checked the card, Molly obligingly read the information out for him. "Molly Ryder, linguist. Forty-five Dartmouth Street, Boston, Massachusetts. That's my telephone number, but you need a magnifying glass to read it."

"A linguist," the detective said. "That means you speak in tongues."

"Funny. No, it means I study language and all its permutations. Call me if a Panasonic microrecorder shows up, voice activated." She smiled in a friendly way, gathered up her bag and made her way out of the shop, mentally checking off Powers Pawn.

The sergeant went quickly to the rear of the shop. "She's the one, all right," he said to a man adjusting a video camera, which had been running the whole time Molly was out front. "Imagine her marching in here. That dame is the one or I'll eat my hat, and I don't wear hats." Klein looked at her business card. "Ryder's a pretty important name in this town, but then again, maybe it doesn't mean a thing."

"Judge William Ryder, that who you mean?"

"You take over out front," Klein ordered. "The camera will run by itself. The word's down from on high that if anyone shows up looking for that tape recorder, let the D.A.'s office know posthaste. I always like to make points with the D.A.'s office." He scribbled Molly's name and address on a scrap of paper. "You make the call for me and tell them I'm following the lass."

"Harv, we got an operation going here. I'm supposed to be on the video camera."

The sergeant rubbed his hands. "Take it easy. I'll be back as soon as I find out for sure she's who she says she is."

It was late afternoon by the time Molly, exhausted from her fruitless search, stepped out of a cab in front of the renovated town house near Copley Place where she rented a three-room apartment. She should have headed straight for her uncle's apartment on Arlington, but without thinking had told the cabdriver to take her home. If your uncle, Judge William Ryder of the state supreme court, can't help you find your stolen tape recorder, then who can? She should have gone running to him first thing, instead of playing detective on her own. He counted the police commissioner a good friend, and in fact, Molly had often chatted with the man over dinner.

Molly took the last two steps in one, pulled out her keys and, after picking up the mail, went through the hallway to her apartment. There she stopped dead, frowning, because her door was open a slit. She experienced a nameless fear and realized it was composed of the outrage and shock that had been with her from the moment the train door had shut on the grinning thief. Was there anything on the tape by which she could be traced? Names? Addresses? No, of course not. She'd always been very careful about that. Names and addresses were for notebooks, not tapes.

There was no sound from within her apartment. She stood there indecisively, thinking of various reasons that might account for the open door. None augured well. She turned on her heel and made her way to her landlady's apartment.

"My door is open," she began at once, aware of the panic underlying her attempt to appear calm. "I know I locked it when I left on Friday morning."

In a moment, the good woman bravely offered to accompany her back to her apartment.

"Maybe we ought to call the police," Molly said.

"Nonsense. I know everything that goes on in this building. It's the wind." Then she reminded Molly that the entrance to her apartment was in line with the French doors leading to the patio out back. "My dear, the force of the wind could blow both doors open."

It was a crazy idea, but, still shaky with indecision, Molly obediently followed the landlady back and pushed the apartment door open. A breeze floated out, bringing with it an odd, sweet scent. Molly, her heart battering against her chest, remained with her landlady on the threshold, looking through the small entry hall to the familiar living room beyond. Her gaze swept past the couch to the wide-open French door that led to the patio. "Maybe it was the wind," she murmured.

Then her landlady gave a little scream and clawed at Molly's arm. "Oh, oh, my dear—look!"

Molly saw it then, the spill of blood on the pale carpet. With increasing horror her gaze slowly, hesitantly, followed the trail of red drops past her cocktail table to the crumpled, bloodied body of a man lying on the floor, his eyes open in death.

Chapter Two

The Public Garden at that time of year was a pale, new-born, leafy green, filled with flowering rhododendrons and pink azaleas. It had, under the deepening blue sky, the look of a very elaborate Easter basket. Neither of the two men strolling along the path, however, had the interest or the imagination to feel himself uplifted by the beauties of spring in Boston. The discussion they held, in fact, concerned a green of a very different kind.

One of them was talking in a low, urgent voice. "That clever game of football with the tape recorder. Molly Ryder was having a fit, and the more she complained, the more they got into the spirit of the thing. That was the time to destroy the damn tape. Anyone with an ounce of brains would've dropped it on the terrace floor and then made a mess of the tape, trying to retrieve it. All you'd have had to do was push the erase button before handing the thing back. Finished, done, the end. Nobody the wiser until it was too late."

"So why didn't you do it?"

"I was offside, Buzz, to stay with the football image. Too far away from the central action. When I was ready to go into action, the play was over."

"This whole conversation smacks of Monday-morning quarterbacking. Molly Ryder has the tape recorder, and I didn't erase the tape and you didn't erase it. We hire somebody to grab the recorder from her bag, only she doesn't have it on her person." Buzz dug his hands deep into his pockets, contemplating the ways of taking out Molly Ryder and making murder look like an accident.

"Not to be. The word is lay off Molly Ryder."

Buzz made a face. "She listened to the tape, she knows, and it's only a matter of time." But more than that, Molly Ryder had caught him heading into the library, information he was keeping to himself for the time being. "The lady's a linguist," he said aloud. "We're talking experts here. We're talking about a lady who can read the commas in your voice."

"We don't know if she even listened to the tape."

"We're talking big bucks here. We can't let anyone stand in our way, no matter who she is."

"The conjecture is she didn't listen to the tape. Molly left Marblehead early Monday morning after a late night. She had a couple of errands to run and then a class to teach. When would she have had time to listen to the tape? Tinky Marin didn't find it in her bag, which means either she left it in her apartment, and we'll know about that soon enough, or it's still in Marblehead. The scenario is first we find out what she knows and then we act accordingly. The order from on high is no more bodies. One dead cop is enough to open up every door in town. Now leave it, Buzz, and that's an order."

However, Buzz danced to a very simple tune. She had bumped into him going into the judge's library. The tape was voice activated. All she had to do was put two and two together.

Oh, hi, she had said, *I didn't see you.* The tape had probably caught those words, too—words given with a big smile, as if reserved just for him. There was no doubt the judge's niece was a charmer. Then, a couple of minutes later, while he had been waiting in the library, his voice or even a cough would have reactivated the tape.

Too bad. She was a problem. An accident happening to Molly Ryder was the best way to solve this particular problem. Accidents happened every day. The devil of it was that cop showing up unexpectedly and ending facedown on her carpet. That had been an accident, too, but it made things very complicated.

RICK BOULTER FLICKED THE VIDEO TAPE ON. He had rolled it once earlier, right after it had been dropped on his desk. Then, because of constant interruptions concerning a sensational murder case about to go to trial, he hadn't been able to get back to it before now. Rick glanced at his watch. Nearly 7:00 p.m. His stomach reminded him he'd been living on coffee since lunch.

At five-thirty he'd been alerted to the news that Sergeant Harvey Klein, who had been tailing her, lay dead in the apartment of one Molly Ryder, purported to be Judge Ryder's niece. Only this Molly Ryder hadn't pulled rank on anyone when they'd invited her to the local precinct for questioning. She had, in fact, gone along willingly. She had not called her uncle or asked for a lawyer. She was extremely cooperative and entirely too interested in the proceedings.

That made the whole thing curiouser and curiouser. Rick reread her statement, delivered to his office not fifteen minutes previously. In theory it all added up neatly. Her movements that day had been clocked up to the precise moment of finding the body. In fact her landlady, who fancied herself a concierge, had watched Molly leave her cab and march up the front steps. Molly Ryder had spent the day very visibly as far as the police were concerned.

She had taught a couple of classes at Boston University and then after lunch, in the company of a friend, had made the rounds of Boston pawnshops until she reached Powers Pawn. After that she was on her own, tailed part of the time by the sergeant. Somewhere along the line Harvey Klein had stopped tailing her. Her movements, however, read like a map of the city. She had pawnshop personnel to vouch for her, as well as a friendly cabdriver. When she arrived home, she was every bit as surprised as her landlady to discover the body of Harvey Klein.

There was no doubt of her innocence in terms of this murder. Klein was tailing her and he was a smart-enough cop not to give himself away. How he had ended up in her apartment, and why, were questions they had yet to find an answer to.

So far Molly Ryder hadn't supplied a clue, only admitted to seeking her stolen tape recorder with all the purpose of a Crusader trying to make the shore of the Mediterranean before sundown. To Rick, however, she was the lady who had lost a hot tape, and the story all added up to an irreducible sum: she was involved, someway, somehow. There was one other thing to be considered: she was Judge Ryder's niece and, according to her statement, "didn't want to bother him with it." A dead cop, and she didn't want to bother Judge Ryder with it. *Well,* he thought, *sleep tight, Judge, because tomorrow's going to be a busy day.*

A lid was being kept on the sergeant's murder for as long as possible. Conversely, the news could break in the next ten minutes. Someone would let the cat out of the bag, someone seeking personal publicity or paying back a favor, or maybe a disgruntled character who liked making trouble. A cop killing was hard to keep quiet, even though the pawnshop sting operation as well as S.N.A.R.E. would be in jeopardy once the news was out. Klein's picture all over the dailies would send every pickpocket in town running for cover, and that included Tinky Marin.

Rick wanted to check the videotape of Molly Ryder at Powers Pawn in slow motion once more, to study every move she made. There were always the telltale signs: a shrug of the shoulders, a flick of an eyebrow, a shifting glance. He was fascinated by how people gave themselves away with unconscious gestures.

He hadn't realized that merely from the sound of her voice he had formed a picture of her in his mind. She fitted that picture exactly. The videotape was hardly quality stuff, but then it wasn't stolen merchandise, having been ordered by a city purchasing department with no money to spare. But even in the indistinct black-and-white image on the small screen, he could admire the woman Tinky Marin had so colorfully described. High marks for Tinky; the kid was a poet.

She was smiling at Sergeant Klein, whose right shoulder was caught in the corner of the picture. Implicit in her dark and clever eyes was the order *Don't fool around with me, I can get the better of you any day.* To quote Tinky, who must have taken a psychology course somewhere, "She was smart, I could tell, like she'd figure everything out about you."

Molly Ryder was smart except for one small thing: she had kept her bag wide open in a seedy section of town, inviting a mugging. And what was Judge Ryder's clever niece doing around Washington and Beach, the Combat Zone?

Rick squinted, bringing Molly into sharper focus. She was leaning on the counter, giving the sergeant a look that was pure charm. Rick shook himself when he realized that he had stopped paying attention to what she was saying. Her hair was dark and spilled around her shoulders in a careless manner, as if the wind had arranged it for her. She had a sensual, expressive mouth and a small nose that was a little sharp. A pretty woman, a very feminine woman who could take care of herself. She wore a voluminous jacket with a stand-up collar that framed her face. Her bag, which was large and still wide open, rested on the counter. She hadn't learned anything on that account.

She smiled, picked up the bag, slung it over her shoulder and marched to the door, her voluminous skirt swinging well below her knees, the camera's eye following every movement. She looked back once, throwing a quick, unreadable glance at Sergeant Klein.

Rick replayed the tape, this time determined to keep his mind on her words and actions and not on the woman herself. When he finished, he remained thoughtful. They had brought her down to the precinct around dinnertime. He wondered if she was still there. He could do with meeting the judge's beautiful niece in person, but casually at the precinct, as though he had just stopped by and figured as long as he was there, they'd have a chat. He reached for the phone, smiling. Clever lady. He doubted she'd buy it, but it was worth a try.

"SIT DOWN, MISS RYDER."

It was eight-fifteen when Rick arrived at the station house and had Molly Ryder brought to him in a small, anonymous office belonging to the absent chief of detectives. It was not exactly the kind of place he'd have chosen in which to interview Judge Ryder's niece. It smelled of a year's worth of stale cigar smoke, and the cleaning people hadn't yet been in to clear away the mess of papers, dirty ashtrays and paper cups strewn around.

Tired as she was, Molly Ryder entered the room with her back straight, her head held high, knowing full well she could walk out anytime. Why a meeting with the assistant district attorney was necessary at this time of night she couldn't say, but she hadn't dared refuse. She glanced around the room and then selected one of two worn leather-seated, hard-back chairs facing the desk. Her object was to question Rick Boulter about why the district attorney's office was questioning her. Her object was to find out what in the world was going on. Her object was to keep her uncle out of it because he sat on the state bench and the breath of scandal had never touched him.

Rick studied her through narrowed eyes. She sat down, the skirt that flared below her knees sliding up to reveal a bit more of her leg. She wore the same jacket as on the videotape, and beneath that a white silk blouse that was open at the neck in an attractive, flesh-revealing V. Up close Judge Ryder's niece didn't disappoint, although the brilliance of her eyes showed a hint of weariness and her lids drooped slightly at the corners. She gazed steadily at him, however, and he returned her gaze, not resisting a small smile.

"I'm only doing this on sufferance," she began in her husky voice. "I came down voluntarily to the station house because I'm—"

"Curious?" he interposed.

They stared at each other for a long moment, Molly suddenly pulling back when she saw the light of interest in his eyes—nice eyes they were, too, dark brown and self-assured. His face was angular and his chin determined, although made boyish by a deep, attractive cleft. His light brown hair was cut a little shaggily and was rumpled, as if he had combed through it with his fingers just before she had come into the office.

The station was quiet, with only the muted sound of some piece of machinery churning in the basement. The silence between them held a little longer. Then Molly spoke up. "I didn't expect to have the honor of being interviewed by an assistant district attorney." She was aware of a certain aggressiveness in her voice that was unusual for her. "I'm not quite certain I understand why."

"Things always get a little sticky when a cop is murdered," he stated quietly.

"With no thought whatsoever to the headlines, I imagine. JUDGE RYDER'S NIECE QUESTIONED IN COP KILLING." She drew her lips together determinedly and then said, "I don't want my uncle brought into this. That's why I'm being so cooperative."

"I appreciate it. You're right, Miss Ryder, it does make good front-page headlines. Still, the public has a right to know the police department is in there, working its collective butt off." Rick pushed his chair back and stretched his legs out. "If a case hits the public fancy, then TV reporters, print journalists, everybody but your aunt Fanny turns detective. We're putting in a little overtime so we can head off some of the pressure early in the game. Fair enough? With your cooperation, maybe the police department can save you and your family a large headache. The trouble is the precinct is a popular one with reporters and there are always one or two hanging around."

"I'm afraid I can't help you very much," Molly said. "I came home, went to my apartment door, which was ajar, and because I knew I'd locked it when I left, called my landlady and together we discovered a stranger dead on my carpet."

"Not exactly a stranger," Rick put in.

"A stranger. I had a few words with him earlier, when I stopped at Powers Pawn. He was behind the counter and didn't introduce himself as a police officer."

"Harvey Klein," he reminded her. "Sergeant, Boston police force."

She did not look away. "I don't know Sergeant Harvey Klein, I never heard of Sergeant Klein before tonight and I've no idea what the unfortunate man was doing in my apartment."

"The fact is, a police officer is dead on your carpet in your apartment."

"*Is* dead, *was* on my carpet," she corrected him, flushing suddenly at the memory that she had been vainly trying to suppress from the moment she had stepped through the door to her apartment. "Is no longer, I hope."

"Miss Ryder, why don't you want your uncle brought into this?"

She frowned. "I thought I'd made myself perfectly clear." Was he waiting for her to use her connections to impress him? She couldn't tell, and his calm infuriated her. "My uncle is a very distinguished jurist," she said at last. "I don't want him involved in any way. It isn't fair," she added, aware of the change in her tone and angry with herself because of it. "I live apart from my uncle and aunt. I don't want him subjected to scrutiny and stupid, idle speculation. I don't want reporters or television personnel hounding him from morning to night. Dammit, he has a bad heart." She stopped and clenched her fists. The words had slipped out. His bad heart was something Willy had wanted kept a secret.

The assistant district attorney gave her a reasonable smile, one that only served to infuriate her further. She didn't like being catered to, either, or dismissed as a featherhead.

"I understand perfectly," he said in a smooth voice. "We really appreciate your cooperation, Miss Ryder."

The way Boulter was looking at her, in fact, was new, disconcerting. He was studying her closely, as if something about her confused him and he was waiting for the right moment to catch her in a lie. Somehow Molly knew he posed a much greater danger than the police and even the reporters.

"I've offered my cooperation willingly," she said stiffly, "because I don't see any reason not to." The only thing she hadn't counted on was being questioned in such a superior way by this annoyingly polite man from the district attorney's office. It was possible she'd made a mistake in not calling her uncle, after all. She had foolishly believed that by being open and honest she'd end up walking away and being able to forget the whole thing. What would the head of her department say, and her colleagues? She was in a mess, and it wasn't her fault at all.

"About this tape recorder you ran all over town looking for," Rick pursued. "Why were you so desperate to recover it?"

She stared unbelievingly at him. "Because of what's on it. I've said that a dozen times tonight."

There was a half second's beat before Rick asked the question. "What *was* on it?" He watched as surprise sent a crease across her forehead.

"My work."

"Ah, that's right. You're a linguist." Rick found himself wanting her to smile, but he was out of luck. He settled for admiring her skin, which had a luminous quality. A slight flush on her cheeks heightened the delicate cheekbones and soft, full mouth. Yet Rick was certain that she was stubborn, even over unimportant matters.

"I'm a linguist and a pretty worn-out one."

His look softened at her words. They'd been playing cat and mouse. She knew it as well as he and had acquitted herself nobly. She'd managed a suitable amount of indignation and no information at all. Rick was impressed. More than that, Molly Ryder wasn't on trial. She was nowhere near guilty of anyone's death. She was a very tired lady who had lost an incriminating tape; a tape he couldn't tell her he had. "Come on," he said, springing into action. "I'm taking you home."

"Home?" Her husky voice was raised, incredulous. "Home has blood on my carpet. I'm not going home."

"Wherever it is you intend to spend the night."

His half smile told her that he expected her to spend the night with a boyfriend. No such luck, and not with Jason Loring, certainly. "My uncle's," she said in a resigned voice. "No, wait. By the time I got there, they'd probably be in bed." Willy reading, his glasses perched on the edge of his nose; Serena on the telephone as usual, cream on her face, her blond hair pulled girlishly back in a ponytail. "Besides, I'm not certain I want to face them first thing in the morning. I wonder if they already know."

"We've been cautious about letting out information, Miss Ryder."

Was he talking about a news blackout? She got shakily to her feet. "Why? Usually the death of a cop stops the presses, doesn't it?"

He looked at her for a long time without answering. The lid was down tight because of the long threads that led from a lost tape to a dead cop to a very important project on the books: S.N.A.R.E. "What was on that tape," he asked carefully, "that made you go tearing around the city trying to recover it?"

"Dammit, nothing that's of the least interest to you. The tape! What in the world does it have to do with anything?'' Molly came over to his desk and leaned on it with her fists. "Work was on it, pure and simple. Work. And now," she added, feeling the heavy beating of a heart that warned her they weren't finished, not by a long shot, "if you don't mind, I'm going . . . home." She needn't answer one more question. She had no idea what he was getting at, but she might put her foot in her mouth and ought to consult with her uncle before saying another word. She turned, hoisted her bag and with a quick "Good night," marched out the door.

The meeting with Rick Boulter had been decidedly off-putting. With those looks, he must play havoc with female suspects, only she wasn't a suspect. There was a moment when she had found him focusing on her with a look as piercing and knowing as any she had ever received. She had left just in time. She didn't need any dark, soulful pools to fall into.

She'd take a cab over to Liz's apartment. No, no good. Liz was with her boyfriend and her apartment was a one-room studio. A hotel, then. That was easiest and could be managed without fuss.

The corridor was quiet at that time of night, although somewhere, incongruously, a baby was crying. She ran down the flight of stairs that led to the lobby and the front desk. The place was absolutely empty but for a lone man asleep on a bench in the corner. The air was chilly with the breath of damp, peeling plaster walls and marble floors slopped clean with disinfectant. If there were reporters in the station house, Molly guessed, they had been put into a room somewhere to be kept happy with the promise of news that would be slow in coming.

She hurried outside, running down the stairs and across the sidewalk without stopping. There were half a dozen police vehicles parked along the curb. The precinct house was on a main road and she stepped tiredly between two of the cars to hail a cab.

"Miss Ryder."

She turned. It was Rick Boulter coming up behind her. "Come on, I'll give you a ride," he said. "Can't let you go wandering off into the night alone. That's not exactly the style of the Boston Police Department. Where to?"

"But—" she began, then stopped. He was smiling warmly at her, and his eyes held only concern. Maybe influenced by the time of night, maybe by the pileup of the day's events, suddenly she wanted desperately to trust him, to believe his smile.

"Come on." The words were whispered as he took her arm. "Where to?"

"A hotel, the Meridien. I've always wanted to stay at the Meridien," she told him, glad to be relieved of the necessity of finding a cab, and worse than that, of being alone.

They were seated in his old blue Camaro heading downtown. Rick said in a tone as conversational as if they were on a first date, "I suppose you go around recording people's speech patterns, is that it?"

"I'm afraid so."

"For which you need the top-model tape recorder?"

"Obviously you don't need your car for your work, or you'd be driving a Mercedes-Benz."

He laughed. "Insult me, but don't insult my car. This little animal is lovingly pasted together."

"Well, I deal in nuance, Mr. Boulter. Paste doesn't come into it. Anyway, it didn't cost the world. I want the tape more than the recorder."

"Incidentally, they call me Rick."

"I deal in nuance, Rick. Speech patterns, colloquialisms; why you say tomayto and I say tomahto—not to put too fine a face on what I do."

"So your desperate search for the machine was not just because of the expense involved, but for what you had on the tape."

"Time, that's what I also had on the tape." Her voice dropped away and she was silent for a while. He thought she had fallen asleep. "I'm starved, I'm absolutely starved," she announced suddenly. "I haven't eaten since lunch."

He smiled and glanced at the clock. Neither had he. "Say the word, and I'll buy you a sandwich. I know a diner that's open all night, a truckers' rendezvous out on the highway."

She sank against the seat and contemplated his offer. His motive was certainly not altruistic, but since she didn't know anything, she had absolutely nothing to lose by accepting. Besides, she dreaded facing a long night alone in an anonymous hotel room. "You're on."

THE LIGHT IN THE DINER WAS MERCIFULLY DIM, without the usual blue cast of such late-evening places. They were the only customers. The music issuing from an old-fashioned jukebox was something mellow out of the forties. They took red leather seats near the windows overlooking the parking area and the road beyond.

After glancing briefly at the huge, confusing menu, Molly ordered a cheese omelet and home-fried potatoes, and dug into the food as soon as it was served, first bathing the potatoes in catsup.

Rick stuck to a hamburger and coffee. The idea was to stay clearheaded about Molly Ryder. It wouldn't be easy. She had a way of lifting one eyebrow when she spoke that seemed the most blatant invitation he'd ever had, and then she was spearing a potato and popping it into her mouth. He couldn't figure out if she knew the effect she was having on him or not. He watched her as she chewed. She flicked her tongue out and ran it along the edge of her lips. It was pure provocation. He had a sudden urge to reach for her, and then realized she was saying something and he hadn't even been listening. He shifted in his seat and wondered what the devil was happening to him.

"Mind telling me what you were doing near the Combat Zone today getting your pocket picked?"

She laughed out loud, and Rick caught the light in her eyes as though it were a reward he'd earned. Dammit, she looked good. He had a sudden flash, a momentary image of her naked with her arms outstretched, welcoming him.

She threw him a canny glance that seemed to accuse him of thinking exactly what he'd been thinking. "To begin with," she said, "I'd just boarded the train when my bag was invaded. The station's around the corner from a bar I had stopped in. The owner had agreed to let me spend a little time there later in the week, interviewing some of his patrons. My work, remember? The doctorate? My dissertation concerns the cluster of accents in a small community within a larger community—in this case the Boston working class. You're interested in the tape," she added after a moment's pause, "not in my work per se. Mind telling me why?"

"Molly," he began patiently, "you spent the day looking for a stolen tape recorder—a rather counterproductive way of doing things. If you added up your worth in time for the whole day, my guess is that had you brought your problems to the police in the first place and then gone about your business, you'd have money in the bank and no surprise package waiting for you when you came home."

"Or waiting for me and I'd be the body on the floor." She beckoned to the waiter. "Boulter, you don't know what you're talking about. I think I'm going to have a large chocolate malted with an extra scoop of ice cream.''

When the waiter was gone, Rick said, "You're a very odd number, Molly.''

"Am I?" She looked curiously at him. "In what way?''

"Nice. I'm about to congratulate myself on the perks my job has to offer. Sitting here watching you OD on diner food is one of them.''

She seemed about to smile and then checked herself. "I surrender, but I'm not going to forget that you're sugaring me up so I'll tell you what dreadful thing is on the tape that ties me in with what happened in my apartment today.''

"Molly, either there's a linkup with the murder or there isn't.''

"There isn't," she stated flatly.

"Why don't you let me be the judge?''

His eyes, shaded by dark lashes, had a way of shutting down just when Molly thought she might be able to read something in them. He gave her a crooked, encouraging grin, as though he enjoyed her careful appraisal and was perfectly willing to sit still until she had had her fill of him. Molly colored, aware of a sudden jolt in the pit of her stomach. And then she let the thought in that he was entirely too attractive for her to allow her guard down for an instant.

"Time's up, Molly," he said. "Tell me what you remember.''

"Nothing more than the usual sitting-at-a-bar talk. Maybe ten minutes in length. By the time I had the tape set up and everyone talking freely, I realized I was late for another appointment and cut them short with a promise to come back. It was everyday talk by everyday people, which is why I was there in the first place.''

At Rick's skeptical look, she added somewhat huffily, wondering why she was being so defensive about them, "They were hardworking people relaxing after hours with a couple of beers. I took their names down in my little notebook, and if you insist upon having them, I'll give them to you, after consulting my uncle. I promised these people anonymity, not a session with the police. Incidentally," she added, "I never tape anyone unless I let him or her know what I'm doing." She stopped, remembering yesterday, Sunday, at Windward, her uncle's house in Marblehead Neck on the north shore. Well, it was a small-enough lie and not worth going into.

"I'm curious about why the niece of Judge Ryder wouldn't have pulled strings to recover an important piece of work like that."

She leveled a sharp gaze at him. "Are you being superior again?"

"It's a reasonable question," he remarked, "under the circumstances."

"I spent years getting out from under the label Judge Ryder's Niece." She paused, pursing her lips together. "No, thanks. No special favors. And in a case like this—murder, I mean—I want him kept out of it."

"His bad heart."

"Forget I said that," she told him evenly.

The waiter brought over the malted milk shake and Molly began sipping it at once. The forties song came to an end, and the silence in the diner was unexpectedly acute. The manager came out from behind the counter and stuck in a few coins, and the same record started again.

"I asked you to forget what I said," she remarked. "It has nothing to do with anything. You don't have to play the ambitious assistant district attorney every minute of the day."

"Is that what you think I'm doing?"

"Isn't it?"

He smiled and then picked up his coffee cup, studying her thoughtfully over the brim. It was his experience that people, innocent or otherwise, used whatever help they could get. Molly Ryder claimed independence of one of the most influential citizens of Boston. Maybe. Claimed he had a bad heart. Maybe. She hadn't cleared up the matter of the tape, not by a long shot. There was also the little business of her having bumped into someone on the way out of the room.

"Do I pass inspection?" she asked quietly, poking at the malted with a straw.

"With flying colors."

They exchanged a long, silent look. "I wonder," Molly said at last, then glanced at her watch. She had an early class to teach and doubted she'd get much sleep that night, but had better try. "I've got to get going. Have you learned everything you wanted to learn the easy way?"

"So far I've heard what you want me to hear." He leaned forward, elbows on the table. When he spoke, he hoped he conveyed concern. The last thing in the world he wanted was to scare her off. "Molly, I've learned a few things about you, but they add up to very little in the crime-solving department."

"But you're not supposed to solve the crime. You have a police department to do that," she said.

"One," he went on, ignoring her remark, "your tape recorder was stolen. Two, a man was found dead in your apartment. Three, unfortunately, he was a police officer. Four, he was a police officer you'd met earlier today."

"Five," she said. "I'm Judge Ryder's niece. If he were handling a criminal case of some kind and . . ."

Rick shook his head. "Anything's possible, Molly. We could sit here all night and list them one by one. Go on about the tape. What else?"

"Nothing, that was it. The taping at the bar happened on Friday. Later I went to—" She paused, made a grab for the malted again. She had packed her gear, left the bar and met Jason Loring at Donovan's in Faneuil Hall for a drink. She'd invited him to come sailing with her on Sunday and he'd agreed to it readily. Then she'd picked up her car and headed along the north shore to Windward for the weekend. She hadn't used the tape recorder again until Sunday, and then more as a matter of routine than anything else. Serena was throwing one of her all-day parties to which twenty or thirty people were invited. Molly had activated the tape and recorded some nonsensical stuff just for the fun of it. That was all.

"You went to...?" Rick prompted.

Molly examined him frankly. *He knows something,* she thought, *and for some reason he thinks I'm caught up in it.* Granted that a policeman was dead, the death had nothing to do with a tape that held nothing more than idle chatter.

"A party on the north shore," she said, smiling carefully at him. "I kept the recorder on, as I usually do. If the talk adds up to nothing, I wipe the tape clean."

"Did you? Wipe the tape clean, I mean?"

"I never got around to it." She stopped again, troubled by what had actually happened. She had hit the rewind button the moment she realized the tape had run out.

"Without listening to it," Rick prompted, interrupting her thoughts.

"Without listening to it," she reiterated.

"The north shore stretches all the way to Canada and beyond." He seemed to be waiting for her to enlighten him. "Where exactly?"

"Fifteen or so miles up the coast. I don't have to say anything more. I take it I'm not on trial." What she did on weekends was none of Rick Boulter's business. After a moment she said, "I think we ought to get going."

"Imperative?"

"Imperative. I'm exhausted and I really need time to sort everything out."

Rick decided that she really had a most expressive face. If he were on a jury, he'd believe anything she said. They were only human, after all, just as he was. It was his experience that juries were suckers for women like Molly Ryder. "I'm interested in that party, Molly, and you know it. Maybe you caught something on tape someone didn't want overheard."

He watched carefully as a mote of light was reflected in her eyes just before she got to her feet. Rick thought he saw a streak of fear shoot through her features, and then it was gone, replaced by cool resolve. She was lying through her teeth. She remembered all right, and if it took him the rest of the night, he'd find out what she was holding back. Getting the truth would be easier in a small room with an overhanging light and a couple of cops standing around. She wasn't a suspect, however, and anyway, he didn't really want to take that route. No, indeed. Quietly winning her trust was the way to go. The only trouble was a dichotomy that one moment had him wanting her shaking under his questions and the next moment just wanting her.

Back in the Camaro, Molly knew she had caught herself just in time. Before she told Rick Boulter one more thing, she had to see her uncle.

The scene at Windward flashed back in its entirety. She had come in from sailing with Jason Loring and had headed straight for the library and her tape recorder. Because the red light indicator was broken, she hadn't even noticed that the start switch was on. The tape had wound itself out. She automatically hit the rewind button as she came onto the terrace.

There were perhaps a dozen and a half people sitting there, including her aunt and uncle, Jason Loring, Gent Perot and his wife. She tried to remember who the others were. All she knew was that they were friends of both Serena and Willy—who came and went with the political climate or the latest sale of an office building or estate.

The Ryder guests were wealthy and influential. Willy and Serena understood the power of money; it was there in the way they lived, the people they courted, and who courted them. It was there in the comfortable old weekend house at Marblehead Neck. It was there in the luxurious Back Bay apartment on Arlington Street, in the cars they owned, in Serena's passion for jewelry and furs, and in the parties they gave.

She had come onto the terrace waving the recorder aloft. "Would you believe it?" she announced to the startled gathering. "I left the tape on in the library by mistake and it's all run out. Somebody's been talking. It's voice activated, although frankly, any kind of noise might have got it going."

There had been a long, stupefied silence, and at last Gent Perot had spoken up. "Tell me, wordsmith, do you realize that's the most irrelevant remark that's been made all day?"

"Oh." Molly had flushed. "Is it?"

Perot had shaken his head as if amazed by her guile. He was a handsome man in his late thirties with the flip, confident manner of a married man who was attractive to women and made the most of it from behind the safety of his wedding ring.

"Non sequitur," Jason had remarked lazily to Molly. "That's the operative term. Unless you're leading up to something, after all."

"Really, Molly," her aunt had said with a despairing sigh, "perhaps your friends have had quite enough of you and that instrument of aural torture. Serve you right if it ran out and ran away."

Molly had laughed. She had flopped onto one of the deck chairs, the tape recorder in her lap. "Come on," she had announced, winking at her uncle, who'd been eyeing her rather sternly, "I'm doing this in all seriousness. I've a dissertation to finish, remember?"

"I'm afraid we remember nothing else," her uncle had said in a dry, measured tone. He was a bear of a man with a prudent, yet determined manner and had a habit of blushing red to the roots of his white hair whenever too much fussy attention was paid him.

"You've been talking about me and my work, haven't you, Willy, while I was out sailing. Unfair, and I wasn't even around to defend myself." Molly hadn't been angry, although she'd pretended to be. The day had been too beautiful, and the conversation comfortably banal. At her remark, Jason, who'd been sitting closest to her, had picked the tape recorder off her lap and held it up as if it were a football.

"Catch," he'd said to Perot.

"No!" Molly had cried, trying to grab the recorder back, but it had been already out of reach. She'd found herself entwined in Jason's arms as the recorder was passed back and forth in a rather gentle mock-football game by half a dozen people. When the noise had subsided, her uncle was in possession of the recorder.

"Okay," he'd said. "Enough of this nonsense." He'd held the small machine out to Molly. "With one proviso, my beloved niece—that you take this, keep it to yourself and not force our friends to be guinea pigs without their express agreement. Agreed?''

"The judge speaks," Molly had said. "Do I have a choice?"

"Not much of one." His tone had been final, but tempered as usual with a loving smile.

Molly, chastened, had accepted the tape recorder and tucked it into her bag. After that she and Jason had left the party, heading for dinner with some friends in a small, charming restaurant in Salem. She'd returned to Windward for the night, flopping tired and happy into bed.

The Panasonic had gone straight from her uncle's hand into her bag and from there, the next morning, into the hands of a thief.

Someone had been in the library talking and later had been on the terrace when she made her announcement about the tape having run out, someone who had ordered the tape stolen. She felt fear drain through her. Who was it?

Surely not Serena or Willy. Jason, a television reporter who was working on a story about corruption in local government, had spent the afternoon in Molly's company. As for the others, they were Serena's and Willy's cronies. She had no idea, with the exception of the Perots, who they were.

Rick's voice broke through the quiet. "What do you remember, Molly?"

She glanced over at him and snapped, "What makes you think I remember anything special?" He should have smiled but didn't. He knew nothing, she told herself, merely surmised that she had a story to tell.

"I can add and I'm not crazy about the total—a stolen tape recorder, a dead cop, and your own remarkable silence," he said.

Molly blanched. Someone had come into the library whose voice had activated the tape. Whatever had been said was meant for no other ears. The speaker didn't know whether Molly had listened to the tape or not. But what she knew didn't seem to matter much. It was possible that the word was out to get rid of Molly Ryder first and ask questions later. That notion was chilling, to say the least.

Chapter Three

Rick came to a stop at a red light and turned to Molly. "The air is thick with speculation. Want to share some of it?"

She managed a laugh. "I was thinking about having to check into the Meridien at midnight without luggage."

"Don't give it a thought. I'll be right behind you."

"That's what I'm afraid of."

For a moment they remained quiet, regarding each other. Then he reached out and took her hand in his. "You have choices, you know. I mean about where you want to bed down for the night."

She thought, feeling the warmth of his touch as his fingers brushed her skin, that she was beginning to look at Rick Boulter in a disquieting way. Why wasn't he some sixty-year-old with a beer belly and a sly manner? She could have handled him easily then. She extricated her hand gently from his. "You're right, of course," she said. "I do have choices. They consist of a hotel and a motel."

The light turned green and he eased the Camaro across the intersection. "My suggestion is infinitely better than either. A rather comfortable little place with a view. How about it?"

"You don't expect me to answer that, do you?"

He started to say something and then changed his mind. "Pity," he said finally. "I have a feeling we could've become better acquainted."

"Just what is it you want of me?" she asked, feeling a small shiver of apprehension slide down her spine. The light at the next intersection perversely turned red. He pulled up short.

"What do I want of you?" he asked. "Everything, Molly. Before we're through, everything."

He couldn't be serious. It wasn't possible. Had she been giving out signals she wasn't even aware of?

"Mr. Boulter, with that remark I think you've just lost me as a passenger. I can go on from here by myself." Molly hitched up her shoulder bag and stepped out of the car, making certain to slam the door behind her. Her heels clicked smartly on the concrete as she headed for the telephone kiosk at the opposite corner. She found change without too much trouble but when she reached for the receiver, discovered it swinging on its cord like a hanged criminal. There was no dial tone. The coin box had been tampered with.

The perfect end to an absolutely incandescent day in which nothing had gone right. She looked back at the Camaro. Rick had pulled up to the curb and was leaning against the car, watching her, his arms folded across his chest. She turned and marched away from him toward a gloom of trees and closed apartment buildings. She was halfway down the block, contemplating the utter emptiness of this part of the world and the risk she was taking, when the Camaro caught up with her. Rick leaned across the seat.

"Need a lift, lady?"

"Rick, you're beginning to try my patience."

"Come on, get in."

She sighed and slid into the car. "You *are* taking me to the Meridien, aren't you?"

"All the way."

"I just feel so disjointed," she declared after a moment, "or maybe displaced is the word. This has been one crazy day. First the robbery, and then a body on my living-room floor, then hours of questioning in the police station, and now to top it all off, I'm going to sleep in a hotel in a city I've lived in all my life. You'd think I could call on a lot more people than Liz and my aunt and uncle at this time of night." Then she added, "Actually I do, but I hate the thought of having to explain myself. Talk about not planning ahead!" She was silent for a moment and then said, "I don't see how I'm going to continue living in that apartment. And I love it. Plants, furniture, all my work." Her voice fell away. One moment was all it took to change her life irrevocably.

"There's no law saying you have to tough it out. You can always move."

"I don't want to tough it out. I want it all to go away. I want the world to be just the way it was when I woke up this morning—a sunny day with a schedule of pleasant work ahead. Semester ends this week. I'd been contemplating a long summer bout with the dissertation blues. I want the tape of my life rewound. Oh, damn! I thought all that this morning."

"Everybody wishes the tape of his life could be rewound," he said. "Even yours truly. I'd like mine rewound to that point where we might have met under better circumstances."

She laughed and put her head back against the seat. "We wouldn't have met, Boulter. You and I travel in entirely different circles."

"Do we? I'm willing to bet your circle and mine were destined to meet."

"Never. I live a structured, academic life, not an exciting one like yours, filled with murderers and assorted madmen."

"I don't deal in murder—or rarely, at least. I do a lot of boring paperwork in preparation for a trial and then spend a lot of even more boring time hanging around the courts. You only read about the exciting parts in the papers. I'd say it's fascinating two percent of the time." He glanced briefly at her. "I'm afraid I've used up my two percent today."

There was a slight pause, and he thought with relief as he concentrated on his driving that she hadn't heard him. But she spoke up, her question catching him off guard again.

"Why the interest in this particular murder? I mean the interest that keeps you wide-awake at this hour, ferrying me around?"

Rick stiffened slightly. He hadn't expected her to keep after him. "Molly, believe me, the early-morning edition is already full of what happened. So are radio and television."

"Fine time to tell me."

"I didn't have to tell you. You've known all along. You've been trying to avoid the inevitable."

She clasped and unclasped her fingers in her lap. "It's true, of course. I really don't want to face what's going to happen tomorrow morning when my uncle opens his front door or when he answers the telephone."

"All hell has broken loose. Count on it, Molly. The world looks relatively calm from here, but it isn't—far from it."

"So reporters will be camped on my uncle's doorstep," Molly said, her voice sleepy. "I'm being given the gold credit card because I'm Judge Ryder's niece—Judge Ry-

der, friend to mayors, governors, presidents. It'll look aw-
fully good when it turns out you've been keeping me under
wraps—wonderful for your career, terrible for my uncle
when he wakes up and doesn't know where I am.''

"We'll get to him," he told her. He could feel her eyes on
him. "Now, if that's what you want."

"No. Let me think.... He's a big boy," she stated after
a while. "A wonderful man, solid, secure. You can put
your life in his hands."

Rick's mind slid to that party full of people who were
having a good time. Judge Ryder, a good man, the only
problem being a couple of chatty people Rick would bet
were his friends, friends with connections in all the right
places.

"Your uncle a teetotaler?" he asked.

She turned on him sharply. "Why do you ask?"

He feigned a laugh. "The kind of man you can put your
trust in."

"He is."

Sooner or later, Molly would learn that he had held out
on her, that he'd known a lot more than he'd admitted.
Down the drain would go any kind of trust she now had in
him. Too bad. Of course, it might be that she knew exactly
what was on the tape and was just about the coolest number he had ever met.

Molly placed a hand on his arm. "Rick, do you think we
could go back to my apartment? I'm not mad about the
idea, but I really should pick up a few things. After all, I
don't know when I'll get back there again."

"I'll have to make a phone call," he said. "If the search
team has finished its work, we can probably stop off. You
won't be able to go in alone." He pulled up alongside a
telephone kiosk. Rick had a telephone in the Camaro but
didn't want her listening in.

The precinct was slow in coming up with the information, and he had to dig into his pocket for another coin. He glanced at Molly through the open door of his car and saw her going through her bag. Then his attention was drawn away when the precinct came back on the line. He was in the middle of a sentence when he noticed a slow-moving Cadillac cruising dangerously close to the Camaro. The Caddy rolled past. There were two men in the front seat and by the look of it they were having a heated conversation. Something clicked, some elemental sense of danger he couldn't explain. Rick's gaze shot to Molly still rummaging through her bag. She certainly hadn't noticed the Caddy. The cop's voice in his ear droned on, but it didn't register.

"Dammit," Rick called into the phone, "I think we're in trouble." He dropped the receiver, which dangled, squawking, and edged the door of the kiosk open. His idea was to get Molly's attention, but she wasn't looking at him. He knew immediately that his timing was off. The Caddy quickly reversed and in an instant was abreast of his car. Rick didn't wait to find out what might happen next.

"Duck!" he yelled to Molly.

"What?"

The hand that came out of the Caddy window held what he took to be a Smith & Wesson .38. Molly's head jerked around. Rick crouched and made a grab for the car door. Molly threw herself down across the seat. The bullet flashed through the open window and pinged against the kiosk. The Caddy's engine roared as it went speeding down the street.

"I'm okay," Molly said breathlessly when Rick pulled her up and held her trembling in his arms. "They were trying to kill me."

"Possible. Feel up to joining the chase?" He might get reamed out for taking her on a joyride, but he wasn't about to lose the two men if he could help it.

"Count on it."

He threw the engine into action and the car took off, wheels spinning.

"They tried to kill me." Molly grasped the door handle as if her life depended on it, as if only that would stop the shaking. "There were two of them, looking straight at me, and then one, and then one . . ."

"Take it easy, pull in a deep breath." The Caddy managed to increase the distance between them. Another car slid out of a side street into his path. The Caddy turned right. Once it was off the main road, it would be lost in Boston's maze of side streets. The light changed to red. Rick tore through the intersection and up the block and turned right on two wheels. The Caddy was gone. For all he knew, it might be sitting in an alleyway waiting for them, and he didn't like the idea at all.

The men who had taken the shot were on top of things. They knew about the tape, they knew Molly Ryder had been at the precinct, knew when she left and where she had gone.

What if he hadn't chased after her outside the station house? The thought of what could have happened sent a chill through him. He realized one thing, though: the shot lacked the earmark of a serious attempt at murder. Whoever they were, they'd been obvious and sloppy, which meant they weren't about to add another killing to that of Sergeant Klein. Which also meant that the shot was a warning, but a warning delivering what message?

He reached for his car telephone and called the local precinct. He had nothing to give the front desk about the car but the year, make and color, and two men in the front

seat. He turned to Molly. "Any description of the assail-
ants?"

She was shaking, her skin noticeably pale. "No. They
wore hats, and their coat collars were turned up. I didn't
even see them until you yelled at me to duck. The hand that
held the gun looked waxen, but that was the light, I guess."

"Get a couple of men over to her apartment right now,"
Rick said into the receiver. "I want the place, both building and apartment, shaken inside out before we get there.
I'll call back in twenty minutes." When he hung up, he said
to Molly, "You okay?"

"No. What am I going to do?" Then Molly added angrily, pointing to his car phone, "Why didn't you use that
before?"

"Because I didn't want you to hear what I had to say.
Simple enough." And stupid. She wasn't a child, not by a
long shot. He reached over and pulled her into his arms.
"Take it easy. They didn't mean to kill you, just throw a
scare into you."

"It worked," she said into the warmth of his jacket. "If
they want something from me," she remarked at last, "why
don't they ask for it? I'm pretty reasonable, particularly
because I've nothing to hide."

"'Why don't they ask for it?' That's a dumb question
and you know it. You're not thinking. They already know
you don't have it."

She stared at him, her eyes wide. "I don't have what?"

"Hasn't it occurred to you that your tape recorder wasn't
stolen by a random thief but was deliberately liberated from
your bag?"

She was silent for a while. "I've thought about it, and the
idea frightens me."

"Good. Now maybe I can expect some revelations."

"If it was stolen, then they, whoever they are, have the tape, Rick. And if they have it, they know there's nothing to be heard but some desultory chatter." She stopped, aware of a feeling of fear like a slow draining of every ounce of blood from her body. Was there something on it, after all? She expelled a sigh. The situation was getting too complicated. She needed to be alone to think.

"They may not have the tape," Rick was saying, surprised at how uncomfortable he felt with the lie. "Or if they do, they believe you know what's on it. Not only what, but who."

"Stop hounding me. How do I let them know they've succeeded remarkably well and that I've given up the search right now, this minute? Shout it from the top of the John Hancock Tower?" Her mind whirled. She longed to talk to Serena and Willy.

"Molly, relax. A deep breath, remember?" His hand was on her cheek, tracing a long, cooling trail.

A deep breath helped. She had kept her silence about Marblehead; a few hours more couldn't make that much difference. Of course, in a few hours she could be lying on a rug, just like Sergeant Klein, with a bullet in her head.

"Let's see about your apartment." Rick reached for his car phone.

As he spoke quietly into the receiver, Molly thought that if she didn't trust him now, she never would. He had saved her life—or at least had given the appearance of it.

He hung up. "If our friends were planning on greeting you when you got home, they've given up the idea. There's an unmarked police car outside the building. You can go in and pick up some things."

"And the car will follow us to the hotel," she finished quietly.

"That's the idea."

"And a policeman will stay outside my door for the night."

"Or inside with you, if that's what you want."

"No," she said abruptly.

"A nice, safe, married man."

"No."

"Then you'll be stuck with me."

She sighed. "This is one game I can't win."

He switched on the ignition. "I'm afraid you're right, Molly."

They were silent during the short drive to her apartment on Dartmouth near Copley Place. There was a blue sedan parked across the street, its lights turned off. A match flared briefly and then the interior was plunged into darkness. Flashing his lights as a signal, Rick backed into a parking space just past the front entrance. He jumped out and came swiftly around to Molly's side without taking further notice of the blue car and its shadowy occupant.

When Molly stepped out into the cool evening air, she had already made up her mind exactly what she would do. Without looking around, she'd quickly pack a bag and then leave. At the hotel, she'd sleep fully clothed and with her eyes open.

"I never asked," she said to Rick, "is it gone? The body, I mean."

"Gone. The search team dusted and vacuumed for trace evidence, but it'll be a couple of days before you can move back."

"I'm not moving back," she stated quietly.

"Sorry." He took her arm and guided her up the steps to the front door. It struck him suddenly that she had been refreshing her lipstick while he was in the telephone kiosk, which was why she hadn't seen the Caddy when it bore down on her. The notion of her putting on new makeup at that time of night was pleasing for a reason he couldn't quite define.

"They didn't find any clues, then," she said.

"Give them time."

"I haven't dusted lately, either, and I've a cleaning woman who certainly doesn't know what the word means. The search team could pick up prints of my friends, of anybody who's been around in the past couple of weeks."

"They'll put a postscript at the bottom of their report stating that you're a lousy housekeeper."

"A *busy* housekeeper who knows her priorities. Are you trying to be funny for my benefit, so that I won't concentrate on the fact that someone just took a shot at me?"

When they reached her apartment door, she handed him her keys. "You open it." Then Molly saw the sign across the door announcing that the apartment was the scene of a crime and temporarily closed. She stepped back, appalled by the cold reality of the notice.

"How horrible!" she said.

Rick placed his hands on her shoulders, steadying her with a firm grip. "Molly, I want you to go in and gather up your things and march out of there. It won't be easy, but that's exactly what you're going to do." For a moment she leaned into him, reluctant to move, feeling his warmth. He pushed her gently away and unlocked the door, running his hand down the interior wall in search of a light switch. The sudden brightness illuminated a room that looked undisturbed but for the red-brown stain in the middle of the carpet. Rick drew her inside, feeling the tightness in her body. Molly stopped just past the threshold, sobbed and turned aside.

"Come on," Rick told her. "Get whatever it is you want and let's make tracks out of here."

"Give me a minute, will you? I feel as if it isn't mine anymore."

"You'll react differently when the whole thing is over." He touched her arm and then, without meaning to, held her close. She uttered a deep sigh and sagged against him. He could feel the rise and fall of her breasts as she struggled to keep calm.

"I'm all right," she said at last, moving away from him.

All his instincts told him to play it cool, to keep an objective view. He could just see himself telling Creedon, "Look, I've taken a tumble for her, and you'll have to believe me, she's as innocent as a babe in the woods." He could almost hear Creedon's low bellow.

"I'll get my things," she said crisply, but then stopped when she caught sight once again of the stain on her carpet. It was a long while before she spoke. She was aware of Rick standing behind her. "Did he have a family?" she asked at last. "Sergeant Harvey Klein?" She pronounced his name with deliberate care, this stranger whose life would be bound up with hers forever.

"A wife and a couple of kids, college age. He was nearing retirement."

"Damn." Hearing about the family made the reality even worse. Mrs. Harvey Klein, a real person somewhere in the city, deep in grief. Then the thought came uninvited that sometime soon someone would whisper: *This Molly Ryder, a single woman. What was he doing in her apartment, anyway?*

"No more questions," Rick told her curtly, as though he'd read her mind. "Just get your things. Take enough for a few days. You might want to stay away until you have someone come about the rug."

"I'm throwing it out." She made the statement defiantly, somehow expecting Rick to tell her she needed permission.

He shrugged. "It's your rug."

There was a tiny bedroom off the living room that had once perhaps been nothing more than a generous utility closet. Molly did not have to cross the rug to get there; she could turn her back on it completely. She decided to be grateful for small things.

Rick followed her into the bedroom. He had expected frills, but the room was stark white, the bed covered with a simple cotton spread. He watched while she opened drawers, taking a gown from one and a few lacy things from another. There was a closet with a sliding door, and she stood in front of it for a moment before pulling out some garments and a suitcase.

As she began to pack, she remarked, "I can't say I'm looking forward to my classes tomorrow." Her mind slid to the head of her department, a stern, unbending woman who at the best of times thought that Molly was a bit too frivolous. What would she have to say about all this?

The bag packed, Molly brushed past Rick and puttered around in her bathroom, coming out with her toothbrush and a small leather makeup case. "Keeping me under surveillance, Counselor?" she asked as his eyes swept over her.

"Every minute of the way."

She clicked the bag shut and swung it up, depositing it in the small foyer. She stepped into the living room, and after a moment's hesitation made her way around the edge of the rug to her desk. "I have another tape recorder, an old one, but it'll have to do. Oh, and my work," she added. "I'll need a couple of things."

Her desk sat catercorner to the French doors leading out into the back garden. There was something disorienting about the arrangement of her possessions on the desk, but at first Molly couldn't imagine what it was. Then she uttered a small cry and clapped a hand to her mouth in disbelief.

"What's the matter?" Rick asked, coming up to her.

"My cassettes—a year's worth of work—they're gone!"

Chapter Four

Rick looked blankly at her. "What cassettes are you talking about?"

In spite of the heavy pounding of her heart, Molly's voice was calm. "Rick, I had something like a dozen cassettes stacked on my desk right here." She absentmindedly picked up one of the bookends, a hefty bronze Art Deco figure in the shape of a clown. "Don't tell me the police liberated them while they were at it. That's a whole year's worth of work. Dammit, they had no right."

Rick took the figure out of her hand and placed it firmly on the desk. "Molly, the police don't remove property for no reason at all."

"Call them," she demanded. "Ask them."

He gripped her arms, and when he spoke there was an edge of distrust in his voice. "Molly, what's on the cassettes?"

"My work, Counselor, my *work*; what I do for a living, remember?" She tore herself away from him and turned to stare at her bookshelves. "Not there, either." She turned back to her desk and began pulling drawers open and slamming them shut. "Not here. They're gone. They were on my desk, between the bookends, where they belong, period."

"Molly," Rick said in a careful voice, "I have to warn you. This is still the scene of a crime. I've let you get away with too much already."

She faced him, clenching her fists, trying to stop the shaking. "What's going on? I'm scared, Rick. A dead body on the floor, a shot fired at me, and now my tapes are missing. All right, I get the point. I'm mixed up in something and I don't know what it is and I'm *scared*."

Rick put an arm around her shoulder. He could feel her trembling beneath his touch. "Come on," he said. "Pick up what you need and let's move."

"My dissertation, don't you understand?" Her voice was now deadly quiet, her hands still clenched into tight fists. "All the work I've done for the past year is missing. *Missing*. That's an English word, adjective or present participle, take your choice. I'm not being hysterical, because I'm past it."

Her face had paled visibly beneath the frame of thick dark hair; even the crimson of her lips was a bright, unnatural color. Rick gripped her for another instant and then went over to the telephone. In a few minutes he had confirmation. The police hadn't taken any of her property, nor had they moved anything unnecessarily.

"What was on the tapes?" he asked Molly once more, when he had hung up.

"Nothing. Everything. How do I know? People talking, being themselves, saying what came into their heads. Let me think. Oh, Rick, the police don't have them," she added in a dull voice, gazing entreatingly at him.

"Molly, it's possible that's why Sergeant Klein was killed."

She closed her eyes and swayed against him, but when he attempted to hold her she pulled herself away. "There is *nothing* on them that would be of the least interest to you or anyone but my peers," she said. "I've played them all through, I was there when they were made, and...and oh...damn." She backed up against the fireplace.

"You're protecting someone. Who is it?" Rick wanted to shake her and he wanted to hold her, aware of both emotions surging through him. "Molly, whoever he is, he isn't worth it."

"I'm not protecting anyone. I don't *know* what's going on, don't you understand?" She threw the words at him, but knew that she didn't want a fight, that she wanted to be gathered into his arms, held tight, told that the nightmare would go away.

He was talking rapidly, smoothly, very convincingly. "Maybe I understand, but I can think of a couple of gentlemen who don't. When they weren't trying to put a bullet through you, they were busy looking for a tape they think you have. As soon as they find out the truth..."

"What truth?" she said. "There is no truth."

"You recorded something you may not even be aware of. Someone wants it back, wants it badly enough to murder for it. Don't be a fool. Try to imagine what might have happened if you had come back to your apartment early. You'd be lying on that floor with a bullet in your chest."

She acknowledged the possibility with a faint shudder. "I would have come home early, except that I was making the rounds of the city's pawnshops. Remember? You told me I'd have been better off going to the police right away."

"Point made. Got everything you need for a couple of days?"

She nodded, suddenly too tired to answer.

"Come on, we're splitting. We've been here too long."

Once outside, Rick went over to the driver of the blue sedan, but when he came back to Molly, he had bad news.

"They're short of men tonight. The police escort's off. Molly, come to my place. You'll be safe there."

Molly stared at the sedan as it pulled away from the curb. "The Meridien," she told him firmly.

THERE WAS AN AUTOMOTIVE CONVENTION IN TOWN, and the Meridien was booked solid. It was after midnight when an exhausted Molly Ryder found a room at a small, elegant hotel on Charles Street. Rick, over her objections, managed to obtain the adjoining room.

"I'd rather you sleep outside my door," she said, hoping her sarcasm wasn't wasted on him. Still, she was too tired to object strenuously and too worried about being alone. This was a compromise of sorts and one she wasn't anxious to dissect.

Rick went a step further when he opened the door between their rooms and, leaning against the doorjamb, smiled in at her. "I could've used a change of clothes and my shaving equipment."

"Opening that door isn't part of our contract," she said.

"I'm only interested in your safety."

"Really?" She raised an eyebrow. "My safety or what I know?"

"Ah, then you've remembered."

"Rick." She sighed with exasperation. "Look, there's an invisible wall between your room and mine, as well as a solid one. You stay on your side, and I assure you I'll stay on mine. Now, if you'll excuse me, I'm ready to take my shower and hit the sack."

Her room was old-fashioned and rather pretty, with plenty of pink ruffles and flourishes and wallpaper resembling dimity. A scent of roses and spearmint came from a dish of potpourri on the dresser. A romantic room, she thought, casting a glance at Rick, who was still leaning against the doorframe, his hands dug deep into his pockets. She opened her overnight case and took out a nightgown, tossing it on her bed.

"Where do you usually hang your hat?" she asked.

He came into her room uninvited and sat down on a wooden rocking chair. "I've a sublet for a year, overlooking the Charles River."

"And then what?"

"I don't think that far in advance." Not the little things, anyway, like where he'd live and what he'd eat for dinner.

"In other words," she said, hanging up a blouse and skirt but leaving the rest in her case, "I can't read you from the way you purport to live."

"Ask me anything you want to know. I'm an open book."

"Married?" The question slipped out, but suddenly she knew it had been on the tip of her tongue all evening.

He gazed at her in surprise, and for the first time in memory such directness pleased him. "No."

"Not now, not ever?"

"Not now, not ever. As for the future . . ."

"Where were you born?"

"Boston. Went out of state to college—University of Michigan—and then after many fascinating adventures, returned to home ground. All very routine."

"Being assistant district attorney can't be routine." Molly picked up her nightgown and then was aware of the way his eyes dropped from her face to the length of pale blue silk. She put it down, as if she had been burned. "I'm the local product," she went on hastily to cover her confusion. "Boston U. My uncle's a populist, and since he was paying the tab, that's where I went."

"Parents had nothing to say in the matter?"

"I went to live with my uncle and aunt when I was twelve. My mother died, and then my father a year later. Willy and Serena never had kids, and suddenly there I was on their doorstep. Serena is Willy's second wife, incidentally, a businesswoman pure and simple, and she treated me as if I were a delicate new product she had to market properly."

"But your uncle's a tough old bird, which accounts for the Molly Ryder we see, part lady, part street fighter." He watched her, a crooked smile on his face. At this hour, with her tousled hair and sleepy eyes, she made a pretty luscious package, one he'd buy without too much quibbling.

"If that's what I am," she said slowly. "I love them dearly and owe them everything."

All at once he understood. The party had been at their house somewhere on the north shore, and it was Judge William Ryder she was protecting. *Molly,* he thought, *you've bitten off more than you can ever chew.*

"Rick," she said, her eyes revealing how serious she was, "I can't begin to put a value on the loss of a year's work. I realize that when a man's life has been taken, I shouldn't even mention it, but . . ." She stopped and briefly drew her lips together. "I guess you think I'm talking nonsense."

"No, I don't think you are."

She was quiet for a moment, feeling her tiredness envelop her like a heavy woolen blanket.

"Okay, I get the point," he said.

She came up to him and held her hand out, which he took and pressed warmly. For a moment they were friends. "Molly," he began, uncertain what he wanted to say.

"Good night, Rick."

"Right." He pressed her hand once more, this time feeling the pressure returned. Once he retreated into his own room he thought she would close the door between them, but she didn't. He went over to his bed, smiling at the charming inappropriateness of the decor: country farmhouse in the middle of Boston, calico and cute. He heard Molly moving around and then after a while the sound of the shower. He threw himself fully clothed onto the bed. It was going to be a long night.

Rick picked up the telephone just as his eyes began to close. He ought to report to Creedon now, if only to force himself to stay awake. Creedon would have a fit, but he'd be able to slip right back to sleep once the telephone receiver was returned to its cradle. It was Rick who'd have to stay awake. He dialed Creedon's number, but his mind was on Molly in the shower.

In fact, Molly had stripped and was about to step into the shower when she remembered her nightgown. "Oh, damn," she said aloud, "it's on the bed and I'm here." Without a second's thought she wrapped herself in a bath towel and dashed back into her bedroom. She was about to scoop up her nightgown when, despite the shower running behind her, she heard Rick's voice quite clearly from next door.

"Don't worry," he was saying, "I have Molly Ryder under wraps. She's here with me now."

She caught her breath and stood stock-still in the middle of the room, listening.

Rick was silent for a moment and then said, "I've got a lot more to tell you, so keep your ears open."

Again silence, and then, "I don't want anyone getting at her, and I don't want her spilling anything, either. If she has information we need, I'll get it out of her. I have powers of persuasion I haven't even used yet."

The shower beat clouds of steam into the room. Molly didn't have to hear any more. She went back into the bathroom, proceeded to dress, gathered up her belongings, and with the shower running, carefully closed the bathroom door behind her as she left. Rick would get the point after a while, but by then it would be too late. Her only choice now was to call for a cab from the hotel lobby and head for her uncle's apartment on Arlington. She hoped she could get there in one piece.

THE STREETS WERE DESERTED, but Molly kept glancing out the back window of the taxi as it moved along Boylston. She was spooked about being followed by a Cadillac able to read her every move.

"You expecting company?" The cabdriver caught Molly's eye through the rearview mirror. He sounded as if he'd welcome a break in the long, boring night.

"Pardon me?" she asked.

"You keep checking the rear window."

"Oh, do I? Must be a reflex action."

He laughed, perplexed. "Reflex action?"

Molly didn't explain her remark but leaned back and closed her eyes, discouraging further conversation. Rick would have discovered by now that she was gone, and she'd have given anything to see his expression. Confusion, annoyance and at last the knowledge that he'd been bested. Good, serve him right, and she had no idea why she cared about his reaction. His words still rankled. *If she has information we need, I'll get it out of her. I have powers of persuasion I haven't even used yet.* Powers of persuasion, indeed. What a fool he had thought her. Now he knew better.

Molly had no idea whom Rick had been talking to. She had no idea what his real motives were. Except that he'd saved her life, she had no reason to trust him, absolutely none at all. In fact, he might have set up the whole thing just to gain her trust. She made up her mind to tell her uncle everything, particularly that Rick Boulter had appeared at the precinct, asking to see her.

"Arlington coming up," the driver said.

"It's at Commonwealth and Arlington, the Arlington Arms, driver." Yes, indeed, Rick Boulter had a lot to learn about Molly Ryder. A smile crossed her lips, then was quickly erased. She hadn't seen the last of him, nor did she want to, and her feelings had nothing to do with the events of the day. They had to do with rumpled hair, maybe, or the quickened look in his eye. His dependability had impressed her. She had wanted to believe he was a strong man, a trustworthy man, but she couldn't anymore.

"Just about there," the driver announced.

"It's the apartment building with the yellow awning." No, it was another kind of signal that Rick Boulter had sent in her direction, something very masculine, wild and yet contained. She groaned inwardly over her own foolish yearning. This had been a day like no other, and she was imbuing an assistant district attorney with a lot more romance than he deserved.

Arlington ridged the street opposite the Public Garden with fine old prewar apartment buildings containing huge, high-ceilinged rooms. Her aunt and uncle owned a sprawling penthouse in the Arlington Arms, an elegant Beaux-Arts building of gray granite with bow windows.

Molly leaned forward and was about to tell the cab-driver to stop when she saw a television van double-parked in front. The media hounds were camped out, and there could be only one reason why. "Listen, could you drive to the corner?" she asked the driver. There was no way her aunt and uncle hadn't learned about the murder. "I want to use the back entrance."

She caught a glimpse of half a dozen people at the door, including a cameraman, all turning in unison as the cab cruised slowly by.

"What the hell's going on?" the driver asked. "Reporters, looks like. You a celebrity or something?" He eyed Molly suspiciously through the rearview mirror.

"I just don't want to be jostled by reporters. Stop here," she said after he had turned the corner. She reached into her wallet for her money.

"You're the boss." He pulled up near the back of the building and gazed worriedly at Molly when she stepped out of the cab. The side street, bordered by trees and bushes in an urban landscape, was dark and empty. Ineffectual streetlights in the shape of turn-of-the-century lanterns flickered softly, adding an eerie cast to the lonely surroundings.

"Want me to wait until you're inside the building?"

"Thanks, I'd appreciate it." Molly shoved some money into his outstretched hand and reached for her overnight case.

Her heels clicked with an echoing sound along the stone path as Molly headed for the back entrance. The path dipped quickly under a canopy of leaves, and she knew the cabdriver would lose sight of her almost at once. Still, having him wait was reassuring. If she screamed, he'd hear her. She crossed a small courtyard that had been landscaped for the use of the building's tenants. During the day it was perfectly safe. Now it appeared dark and menacing. Past the square the path snaked under a row of thick-limbed sycamore trees. Faint light cast by the lanterns through young leaves threw a crazy pattern on the ground. Molly hurried toward the back entrance, hearing the sharp sound of her heels, certain she was making enough noise to wake the dead. She shifted her overnight case, which seemed to have grown heavier, from one hand to the other.

There was a small yellow light over the arched back doorway. She had to step into the shadowy interior in order to reach the door. She hit the buzzer hard, trying to rouse the guard. The cab's motor was engaged, and suddenly Molly was all alone in an intense quiet that not even the distant sounds of city traffic could break.

No one answered her ring. It was possible the buzzer was broken. She didn't relish walking around the block to the front entrance, nor did she want to meet up with the reporters waiting there. Molly was at the point of no return. The cab was gone. The way was dark and dangerous. If she broke for it and ran safely around to the front entrance, she'd end up in the arms of the media. From somewhere down the street she caught the heavy tread of someone who made no secret of his presence. There was little comfort in the thought. Molly punched the buzzer in a series of short, angry spurts, placing her ear to the door. It was ringing, all right. She didn't care if she woke the whole building. The sound of the heavy tread on the cement ceased and then started up again, slowly and deliberately. She couldn't tell the precise direction from which it came and pressed herself up against the wall into the shadow.

"Come on, come on," she said, pounding the buzzer.

"Hold your horses." From inside came slow, lazy footsteps. Then a bolt was released and the door was pulled open. The guard, trying to button his uniform jacket with fingers that refused to do his bidding, forced a smile. "Miss Ryder. What are you doing back here?"

"Trying to escape those reporters out front." Molly went past him to the service elevator. "Can you take me up?"

"Sure. They've been there all night." Once the door was closed and the elevator put in motion, the guard said,

"Man, you're not the only one using the back elevator tonight. And the reporters, too, trying to get in, trying to bribe me. Asking for the judge," he added with an air of importance, "as if I'm real impressed with them and I'm going to jeopardize my job for a few bucks. Heard it on the news tonight. Something to do with your apartment, Miss Ryder. A cop murdered. Is that the truth?" The elevator ground to a halt at the penthouse floor.

"Thanks," Molly said, stepping out. Well, that was it. Willy knew all about the death of Sergeant Klein in his niece's apartment. So did all of Boston. How clever of Rick to keep her incommunicado, insisting the police department would hold back the story for as long as it could.

"'Night." She hurried across to the penthouse door, aware of the guard still standing there watching her. She rapped softly at the door, knowing that she should have taken the time to call. Her aunt and uncle shared the same bedroom at the rear of the apartment, and it was possible they wouldn't hear her. The housekeeper, whose room was behind the kitchen, retired early and slept deeply. There was no doubt in Molly's mind that she hadn't been thinking straight when she had bolted from the hotel.

There came the soft slap of slippers along the highly polished hall floor and then the door was unlocked. Judge William Ryder stood there, his face drawn with concern. His eyes, which were usually sharp and direct, were red-rimmed and strained. Molly and he remained quietly looking at each other for a long moment, her uncle's face fixed in the same impatient expression as it wore in the courtroom when information he needed was late in coming. Molly dropped her overnight case and was about to say something when he pulled her close, crushing her against the soft flannel of his bathrobe.

"Well, the prodigal child makes an appearance."

"I didn't want you to know," she said from the comfort of his arms.

"She didn't want us to know," he exclaimed. "Where do you think we live, child, on Mars?"

"Child! Uncle Willy!" Molly was suddenly her old exasperated self, wanting him to know that somewhere along the line she had reached adulthood.

Her aunt appeared, dressed in a long rose-colored silk robe. Like her husband, she was wide-awake, and annoyed and worried at the same time. "For heaven's sake, Willy," she said, "this is no place for a reunion. Bring her in, bring her in."

Her uncle released her reluctantly, and Molly ran into the apartment straight into her aunt's arms. "It's been an unbelievable mess, Serena. My first thought was of you and Willy. You don't need this kind of notoriety."

"Come into the kitchen," Serena said, her arm across Molly's shoulders. "We'll talk about it over a cup of hot chocolate."

"Suddenly I'm a little girl again," Molly said, unable to resist a smile after all and letting Serena drag her along. It was good to have her aunt take over, and yet she thought, as she had often thought before, that their relationship had never been that of mother and daughter, but rather that of older and younger sisters.

All the lights were on in the large, well-ordered kitchen. It was an old-fashioned, cheerful room with glass-fronted cabinets edged in white and a newly laid floor of white ceramic tiles. There was a carafe of coffee on a counter and the scent of freshly ground coffee beans.

Her uncle said, "Molly, don't worry about my reputation. I learned a long time ago that if I have a public career, it's possible an occasional freckle might be exposed in the attending limelight." He helped her slip out of her jacket and then joined her at the table while Serena was busy making the hot chocolate. There were a couple of half-filled coffee cups on the table, and Willy reached for one. "We were worried sick about you," he said to Molly in a chiding voice.

"I knew you'd hear about it, but figured you ought to have a good night's sleep first."

"Have you eaten?" Serena asked, glancing back at her.

"Oh, Serena, you're wonderful. What a thing to think about now."

Serena laughed. "You're right, of course. Are you going to tell us everything or will we have to pull it out of you word by word?"

"Word by word. That *is* my line of work."

Serena Ryder was a slight, slender, impeccable woman whose straight, shiny blond hair even at this time of night allowed no strand to misbehave itself. Her makeup, as usual, was flawless, as though it never dared to smear or run or wear away. The loving smile she threw at Molly, however, held something girlish in it, closing the gap between their ages.

Serena had been born in Boston, a child of working-class parents, her beginnings as humble as the judge's were privileged. The common ground they met on was a law office, where William Ryder was a partner. When Serena was hired, Willy had been a widower for three years, not ready for a romantic involvement. Theirs was an unlikely union because of the difference in their age and social position, but they had fallen in love and were married, and when Molly appeared on the scene soon after, Serena had welcomed the frightened twelve-year old into her home.

No, Molly thought with regret, she doubted she'd tell them everything. Perhaps the less they knew, the less they could be hurt by press coverage.

Her uncle spoke up. "The mayor called me almost immediately, as soon as he heard the news. He said you were down at the station house and that you were cooperating in the investigation. We thought you were behaving in a very commendable way, but still, a lawyer should have been present. I was going myself..."

"A lawyer?"

"To protect your rights," he said with scarcely disguised impatience.

"Willy, I didn't even know who the victim was until—" Molly pulled up short.

"Until?" Serena queried. The milk began to simmer. She turned the flame down and went over to the cabinet to search for the chocolate.

"Until he was identified," Molly finished lamely.

"And then you knew who he was," her uncle said.

Molly objected, turning his remark into a joke. They were going down the wrong alley now. "No, I don't mean that, either."

"Don't nag her, Willy," Serena said. "Ah, here it is."

The judge slammed his cup against the wooden tabletop. "Dammit, Serena, she's been missing for hours, we've had the mayor and police chief on hold, and all you're interested in is stuffing her with hot chocolate."

Serena merely laughed in her calm way and continued puttering at the stove. "I doubt the mayor is awake at this time of night or the chief of police either, now that you mention it. Go on with your story, Molly."

She hadn't started a story yet, Molly thought.

"I'm glad you didn't come down to the station," she told her uncle.

"The mayor said you made it very clear why you were cooperating." He reached across the table and patted her hand.

"I told Willy to go anyway," Serena remarked. "I told him that you'd expect him."

Willy said, "I reminded Serena that the child was grown up and would want to handle it without the judge coming to her rescue."

Molly threw him a grateful smile and then quickly outlined the finding of Sergeant Klein's body, her interview at the police station and the unexpected visit of the assistant district attorney.

"We know you left the police station around nine," her aunt said. "It's the time intervening that made us frantic."

Molly felt her face grown warm. "As a matter of fact, we went for something to eat..."

"We?" her aunt interposed, handing her a mug of chocolate.

"The assistant district attorney." Molly took a long drink and then said, "Oh, we stopped back at my apartment for some clothes. And I discovered that my tapes for the past year are missing."

"Your tapes? Which tapes?"

"Not music. My work. A year's worth of interviews gone, just like that."

Serena put her hands on Molly's shoulders, then bent low and kissed her cheek. "Oh, Molly, pet, are you sure?"

"They were on my desk. They're not on my desk now, Serena."

"What about the police? Is it possible they took them as evidence?"

"They claim no. Anyway, evidence of what?"

Her uncle chimed in. "Obviously Sergeant Klein surprised a sneak thief at work in your apartment and got paid for his diligence."

"Of course." Molly let out a breath of relief. His was such a simple, intelligent explanation. Odd that Rick hadn't thought of it, nor she, for that matter. "It's the best explanation I've heard so far." She finished the last of the chocolate and got up. If she escaped their questions now, she might never have to admit she'd met Klein in the course of a search for her stolen tape recorder. Nor, for that matter, need she mention the mugging. "I'm safe, I'm sound, I'm bushed and I've an early class tomorrow," she said. "If you don't mind, I'm going to tuck down now."

But it was Serena who stopped her at the door with one remark. "Molly, you're an absolutely charming liar. I'd really like to know the whole truth."

Molly felt a small knot of fear pull tight in her stomach. She was aware of her uncle's deep blue, unswerving gaze. "What are you talking about?" she asked.

"This district attorney in whose company you've just spent the past several hours, which you've tried to telescope into nothing. What's his name? Why all the mystery?"

Molly was aware of a relief so great that it took her several moments before she could speak. "His name is Rick Boulter," she said at last, and even exaggerated her smile. "He's very nice."

"Good-looking?"

Molly shook her head, then said, surprising herself, "Yes, I suppose he is. More *interesting*, really."

"Lovely," Serena said.

Molly turned to her uncle. "Do you know him?"

"Richard Boulter," her uncle said. "We've met in the course of our business. An earnest young man who'll have Creedon's job if the D.A. doesn't watch out."

Serena stared thoughtfully at Molly and Molly caught the look. She was being measured for romance, one of Serena's favorite games.

"Good night, Serena, Willy." She kissed each in turn and hurried to the guest room, the room that had been hers through all those years of growing up.

RICK OPENED HIS EYES SLOWLY. Something was wrong. He glanced around the hotel room trying to figure out what it was. He'd been on the telephone with Creedon for five, six minutes, then, hearing the shower in Molly's room, had lain back on the bed. He must have dozed off.

That was it: the shower. He glanced at the clock. Easily a half hour had gone by and the shower was still running. He leaped off the bed and headed for Molly's room. Her bed was untouched, every vestige of her presence gone.

"Damn." He went over to the bathroom door, knocked briefly and pulled the door open. Clouds of steam escaped into the room. He rushed in and turned the taps off, cursing himself for a fool all the while.

Where the hell had she gone? More important, why? He picked up the phone and made a call to the lobby. Yes, he was told in a voice that held some mirth in it, the party in the room next to his had come down and checked out. Yes, she had called for a taxi and asked to be taken to Arlington.

Rick slammed the phone down and uttered another expletive. He could have sworn Molly planned to spend the night at the hotel. He looked back at the open door between their rooms, his brow furrowed. He had called Creedon, certain Molly was in the shower. But what if she had come out, heard his conversation and something in it had ticked her off?

Then his own words, so casually tossed out, came back to haunt him: *I have powers of persuasion I haven't even used yet.* Molly Ryder, with those big, innocent eyes, wasn't a pushover after all. She was with Judge Ryder now, being

handed some pretty crafty advice. From here on, she'd play
everything close to the chest, prompted by an eminent jurist busy checking his rear.

A simple remark, and Operation S.N.A.R.E. had been
put in jeopardy. The absolute irony of the day's events
struck him. The incriminating evidence on Molly's tape
could lead to the solving of Halloway's untimely disappearance. With the right people put away for murder and
extortion, S.N.A.R.E. would be snuffed anyway, just a little sooner than planned.

Finis to S.N.A.R.E., and he'd be back to the old grind of
shuffling papers and prosecuting your average, everyday
criminal. Molly Ryder could be perfectly right. He remembered her sarcasm earlier that evening. Headlines were always in the consciousness of the district attorney's office,
and the one about the judge's niece would be a honey.

Rick eyed the bed. He'd been looking forward to an interesting night with Molly Ryder in the next room, the door
open between them. Well, no use sticking around when he
had the Camaro downstairs and a change of clothes at
home. He wondered which he'd regret losing more: Molly
Ryder or his vested interest in S.N.A.R.E.

MOLLY LET HERSELF OUT OF THE APARTMENT into a crisp
New England morning. It was well before her aunt and
uncle were up, although coming awake hadn't been easy.
She had tossed and turned during the night, chased by a
dream at the center of which was a relentless Rick Boulter
with a knowing grin and a raised eyebrow. Rick hadn't
quite caught up with her and when he was closest, Molly
had sprung awake.

In the clear light, Molly at first felt safely removed from
the problems of the day before. That sense of well-being
changed when she picked up a newspaper. The headline,

she saw with heat reddening her face, was almost exactly as she had predicted: JUDGE'S NIECE QUESTIONED IN COP KILLING. She tucked the paper under her arm, vowing not to read further. If someone was out looking for her, there wasn't any doubt he'd catch up, and the notion, even under the benign blue sky, had her scurrying for the bus that would take her to the university.

She was hard at work alone in the tiny office she shared in the university's English department when the sounds of students arriving for class began to filter through to her. There was no way she could get through the pile of papers on her desk, and the day offered a crowded calendar. Along with her classes she had a staff meeting and then a meeting with the chairman of her dissertation committee. With all her tapes missing, she could never convince him that her paper would be in on schedule. She was back on square one, only this time it wasn't made of marble; it was made of quicksand.

THE ORDEAL WAS ALL OVER AT FOUR that afternoon. Molly had been held at bay for hours by too many questions, too many raised eyebrows, too many students who allowed themselves to be impressed with her sudden notoriety. Her colleagues expressed surprise more than once at her appearance. They expected her to be in jail, living on bread and water, or giving television interviews.

Fortunately the head of her dissertation committee was out with a spring cold. Molly was left with the chairman of her department, who told her the university didn't look kindly on such unexpected goings-on as murder. Molly nodded her apology, and then under the chairman's subtle prodding, regaled the woman with a detailed description of finding the body.

She also successfully discouraged a couple of tenacious reporters, who had followed her into the cafeteria at lunch, with a very determined "No comment."

When she returned to her office late that afternoon, there were a great number of messages waiting for Molly on her answering machine. She sat down and listened to them, taking notes and feeling grateful that the instructor who shared the cubbyhole with her had a schedule that scarcely ever clashed with hers. There was a flurry of calls from worried friends, from the media, one from an unknown T. Marin, asking Molly to call at four-thirty on the button, three from Jason Loring in his sonorous announcer's voice, one from her aunt, another from her uncle. Rick Boulter had called twice. She had no intention of calling him back and didn't even bother taking his number down.

It was the T. Marin who interested her. The name wasn't familiar, and for that reason she thought of it in connection with her tapes. She checked her watch. It was four o'clock. She spent the intervening time working on an accumulation of papers. When she looked at her watch next, it was near enough to four-thirty to make the call, although as she dialed she was tempted to hang up. Someone wanting to sell her a magazine or insurance, she was certain of it, but at least he wouldn't ask annoying questions about murder.

A deep, rather pleasant voice came on the line after three or four rings. "Who is it?"

"I'm looking for T. Marin. I'm returning his call."

"Who is this?"

"Well, it's Molly Ryder. I said I'm returning his call."

Someone was tapping lightly on her door—a student, no doubt. Her heart made a surprised little leap when the door opened and Rick Boulter peered in. What amazed Molly was the inexplicable yet intense feeling of pleasure that flooded through her upon seeing him. It wasn't at all what she had expected. She'd expected to be angry.

The voice at the other end of the line jarred her ear. "We want the tape and we..."

With a sharp intake of breath, she gestured to Rick with the receiver. In one stride he was at the phone, his head close to hers, listening.

"...any lengths to get it. We'll call again, anytime, anyplace, anywhere. Just have it ready to hand over." There was a click and the connection was broken.

She was shaking when Rick took the receiver out of her hand. "Did he call you?"

"Here, look." Molly shoved the paper at him, trying to gain control over her nerves. "This message came in on my answering machine. It said to call at four thirty. It's that now."

"I don't expect much, but let's try a trace on it." As Rick busied himself for the next few minutes, Molly went outside, paced the corridor and then came back, feeling no better for it. He was sitting in her chair but relinquished it as soon as he saw her. "Phone booth, probably, and the phone left dangling." He stared at the note. "T. Marin." A clever joke on somebody's part. The caller wasn't Tinky Marin, but could be one of the voices on the tape, although he wouldn't make book on it. "Do you know this name?"

"No."

"Then," he said coolly, "why did you call it?"

"I return my calls. Maybe I've won a contest, or maybe he was selling life insurance. At the rate things are going I might need insurance and plenty of it. And the last thing I need is you nagging me about phone calls. Rick, I'm scared. I don't want to have worry about who's on the other end every time I pick up the receiver. They want the tape and I don't have it."

"All you have to do is request police protection. If you can prove you're in danger, you've a right to it."

She thought of her aunt and uncle. If she asked for police protection, she could see the headlines: JUDGE'S NIECE REQUESTS PROTECTION. The judge's niece wanted to be left alone by everybody.

"Look," she said, in a desperate attempt to make sense out of her feelings, "the semester is over at the end of the week. Then I'll leave town until it all blows over. As for police protection, no. I'll have to watch my rear, that's all, and how I answer the phone. I just wish," she added thoughtfully, "I could trust you."

Rick came over and put his hands gently on her arms. "You eavesdropped on a talk I had with my chief, the D.A. That's what got your back up, isn't it?"

"Among other events, certainly. And how did I know you were talking to the D.A.?"

"I wasn't aware of having to announce my intentions."

She moved away from him. "I wasn't aware of your powers of persuasion, either. I thought, under the circumstances, that I ought to remove myself from the vicinity."

He laughed and picked up some papers from the only other chair in the office, the one belonging to her colleague, and sat down. "Molly, you can't run your life as if nothing had happened. You misunderstood what I said. You were a complete fool for running off like that last night."

"Put them on the radiator," she said, gesturing to the papers he was still holding. "You didn't come running after me last night, either," she added and then was sorry at once that she'd said it.

"You were angry, and the only way to get back at me was to go running to your uncle. What did you tell him?"

"Nothing." She almost shouted the word, deflected only by a knock at the door. One of her students immediately peered in at her.

"Hi, Miss Ryder, are you busy?"

She glanced at Rick, but his expression was unreadable. "See me tomorrow morning early, first thing before class, okay?"

A disappointed sigh drifted across the threshold. "Sure thing."

"I'll give you all the time you need then, I promise." She was rewarded by a relieved smile.

Molly turned to Rick once the door was closed. "I told my uncle nothing," she said simply.

"Why?"

She expelled a quick breath and reached out a hand for his. "Rick, I'm pretending to be cool, but I'm not, believe me."

He turned her hand over and rubbed his fingers across her palm. When he looked at her, his gaze was resolutely clear and without a hint of guile. "Molly, I'll expect you to tell me everything, to leave nothing out. I know you're worried about your uncle's reputation, if not about yourself."

"I've told you everything," she said.

He continued to gaze at her. "No, you haven't, although you've just given me a cry for help." He closed her fingers over her palm and then held her hand tightly in his. "You want me to dry your tears by magic, not the truth. What is it?" He asked the question softly, almost as if it were irrelevant. "What is it, Molly? Who is it?"

"No one. I said I was scared. Don't talk nonsense."

"If I have to dig into sensitive areas around the Ryder compound, I will."

She snatched her hand away. He was impossible, just a man doing his job, not caring who got stepped on in the process.

"You don't care who gets hurt, do you?" she said, giving her words an extra twist to hide the fact that she had wanted desperately to trust him. Foolish. She wasn't going to let him affect her. What troubled her was the way she was so totally aware of Rick Boulter, of everything about him, of the hard, muscled contours of his shoulders straining the material of his jacket, of his long legs stretched out before him.

There was something frighteningly masculine about him, something she couldn't deal with at the moment. The expression in his eyes revealed that he understood what was running through her mind. He leaped out of the chair and in an instant drew her up into his arms. His lips descended on hers in a long, drawn-out kiss. When he pulled back, his breath was warm on her mouth.

"Of course I care," he said. "More than I should."

Molly let out a breath she hadn't even known she was holding.

Chapter Five

"Don't look so shocked." Rick released her and waved at the work strewn all over the desk. "Come on, I came here on business. I want you to go over some mug shots, see if you can pick out the kid who took your tape recorder. We're leaving the back way. I saw a couple of reporters out front."

Molly assented, but her mind was on the kiss. She shouldn't have allowed it, and yet knew that somehow she had set the whole scene up. Resisting an impulse to put her fingers to her lips as though she might actually touch the warm imprint of his kiss, Molly silently gathered her work up. She stuffed papers into her briefcase without any order and then led the way briskly out of her office. Still on her desk were all those other, unanswered messages.

The Camaro was parked illegally in the faculty lot, but Molly merely smiled. She suspected that Rick would always test the limits of the law and she liked that reckless side of him. She slipped into her seat, reflecting on the inevitability of his kiss and of their being together with something between them that had little to do with a murder and a suspicious bit of tape.

Just before Rick engaged the engine, he said, "Molly, I . . ." Then he thought better of it and backed the car out.

He said no more until they were at police headquarters and Molly was seated at a table in a worn wooden chair, staring helplessly at a heap of books containing mug shots.

"I should've told you about the call to the D.A.," he said, bending over her and laying his hand momentarily on hers, "before I made it last night. I was checking in with him, that's all."

She made no attempt to take her hand away, but instead gazed up at him. "At midnight?"

His grin held a little embarrassment. "Was it that late?"

"Later, come to think of it."

"I woke him up, as a matter of fact."

"Nice to know I'm so important you had to wake the district attorney just to tell him you had me in your clutches and hadn't pulled out all the stops." They weren't alone in the large, square room. Molly, however, was hardly aware of phones ringing, people coming and going, even of someone across the table leafing slowly through a book of mug shots. "Am I supposed to be looking for the mugger or the two men who shot at me or both?"

"A youth in his late teens who grinned at you from the other side of a train door. We'll get to the other two later." He had carefully placed the book containing Tinky's photos on top of the heap. With her identification of Tinky Marin, they'd be able to pull him in again and this time find out just why he had grabbed that specific tape recorder and why he had decided to pawn it. *If* they could find pal Tinky.

Molly began to turn the pages. "If he's here, I'll recognize him," she said. To the end of her life she would remember this one and the unexpectedly thoughtful look in his eyes.

When she came across his mug shot, however, she gasped with surprise and then angrily blurted out his name: "Martin 'Tinky' Marin. T. Marin. He's the one all right. I told my friend Liz I'd see him through the justice system and have him incarcerated for life.''

Rick, who was hovering close by, talking to an officer, started at the sound of Tinky's name. He came quickly over.

Molly hesitated, then said, "Wait a minute, something's decidedly funny. He was speaking on the phone as if *I* had the tape."

"First things first," Rick said. "You're sure this is the fellow who grabbed your tape recorder?"

"This is he, Martin 'Tinky' Marin, every miserable inch of him. Five eight, brown hair, brown eyes. Nineteen years old. A petty sneak thief with a deep, cultured voice. Remarkable."

"Everybody goes to college these days," Rick said, knowing he wasn't going to deflect her. Then he added, "This is only the beginning, Ryder. With your kind of luck maybe you'll find the two who took a potshot at you."

"Amazing," she said, fixing him with a curious look. "Finding him just like that. What do you intend to do with him?"

"Pick him up. Put him in a lineup and have you identify him in the flesh." The job sounded easy, but Tinky had gone underground. The police had already put out an alert for him, although they suspected he'd left the Boston area a couple of hours after they had questioned him.

Rick set up a fresh collection of mug shots for Molly to go through, which contained photos of small-time hoods, mobsters and union officials pulled in for one infraction or another.

"Nothing," she said repeatedly as she plowed through the photographs. Then, finished with the last, she leaned back. "You'd think I'd have met up with a few of these characters in my peregrinations through the seedier sides of town, but no—no luck.''

''Any of these?'' Rick shoved a collection of loose photographs at her, including one of Gentry Perot he had borrowed from the newspaper morgue at *The Boston Globe.*

Molly went through them slowly, nonplussed because the photos were of men who appeared to be ordinary, honest citizens. The photographs were eight-by-tens, the men middle-aged and poised. Rick was getting at something, but she had no idea what. ''They don't look as if they'd know the firing end of a gun,'' she said.

Rick, gazing closely at her and, finding nothing in her remark but a mild reproof, said, ''Keep looking.'' He had questioned enough people in his time to know when someone was holding back.

She was walking a fine line, Molly decided. Obviously Rick wasn't going to tell her what was going on or what he expected from this charade, but she went doggedly through the photographs. These men weren't gunsels and they weren't familiar. Then suddenly there he was, Gentry Perot, who had been at Windward on the day of the taping. She clicked her tongue and smiled up at Rick, aware for the first time of how closely he'd been watching her. ''Gentry Perot. Friend of mayors, governors, and the powers that be. What's he doing in this lineup?'' But he didn't have to say a word in explanation, it was all there in his eyes. Rick knew a lot more than he was telling her, and it was time to ask a few questions herself.

''Come on,'' he said hurriedly. ''I owe you dinner.''

She got to her feet and picked up her bag, glad to get away. ''You owe me an explanation, that's all you owe me.''

THEY WERE SEATED, NOT FAR FROM police headquarters, in a Chinese restaurant that Rick insisted, in spite of its pedestrian atmosphere, was quite good.

Molly held her tongue until the order was placed and only when Rick poured their tea, did she speak. "You're following through on this Tinky Marin, aren't you?"

"With what they call in the trade an all-points bulletin. If he's still alive, we'll find him."

She stared at him openmouthed. "'Still alive'? What are you trying to tell me? 'He who steals my tape recorder loses his life'?"

Rick, his hand wrapped around the teacup, tried to assess the damage that could accrue from his telling her too much. Whatever he said would have to be carefully calibrated, as it would almost certainly get back to her uncle. He couldn't even caution her to keep silent about it, not yet at any rate. Maybe later, if he managed to gain her trust.

"You've figured some of this out, haven't you?" he said.

"I'm not stupid. I realize I might have taped something inadvertently and someone was pretty worried about it. That someone hired Tinky Marin to steal my tape recorder. Tinky did and now possibly may be dead because of his good deed. What that someone doesn't know is whether or not I heard the tape, and the easiest way to solve that particular problem is to kill me, too. Except it looks as if they'd given up trying."

"They don't have the tape, Molly."

"Right, because they came to my apartment looking for it." She paused, then looked Rick in the eyes. "Then who has it?"

The waitress interrupted them with a tureen of hot and sour soup filled with thick mushrooms and chunky vegetables. *Saved by the bell,* Rick thought, as the soup was ladled into their bowls, although he guessed that Molly wouldn't let the matter rest. For a while they ate seriously, concentrating on the subtle flavors of the food. Molly hadn't realized how hungry she was, and was glad of the respite. The soup was followed by lemon chicken and noodles. They ate quietly, talking of generalities, until the last plates were cleared away. Only when Molly felt her energy returning did she go to back to her question. "Rick, who has the tape?"

"A story's in order," Rick said.

"I knew it, knew you were holding back on me."

He told her quickly and succinctly about a sting operation mounted by the Boston police to catch purveyors of stolen goods and how her tape had ended up in the district attorney's office.

"Why didn't Sergeant Klein just come out with it and tell me the D.A. wanted to see me?" Molly asked.

"We told him not to scare anyone off, just to get the information and let us know. He was a bright guy, a self-starter, and he didn't listen. He also bent the law a bit by breaking and entering. We never sent him to your apartment," Rick assured her.

"But thanks to my carelessness in having my pocket picked in the first place, Sergeant Klein lost his life."

"He lost his life because of his zeal and because *he* was careless. We'll find his murderer, Molly."

"Will you?"

"With or without your help. Preferably with it."

"What was on the tape that turned it from a police matter to one the district attorney was interested in? Did you listen to it?" Then a new notion struck her and made her smile. "Well, at least something was saved from all the work I've done this year."

"There you are, then. You'll get it back in due course. Where was the beach party held?"

"You won't let up, will you, Rick?" As he shook his head, Molly decided she couldn't justify continued silence. Sergeant Klein was dead, the district attorney had the tape, and all Rick Boulter wanted was a simple answer to a simple question. "It was at Windward, my uncle's house in Marblehead Neck. What was on the tape, Rick?"

"At a party, is that right?" He decided to make a trip out to Marblehead Neck to set the house in his mind so that there would be no doubt it was there the recording was made.

"A Sunday-afternoon gathering. My aunt and uncle often have them. They're very sociable people and gracious hosts. Do you intend to answer my question? Perhaps if I got a lawyer?"

He signaled the waitress for the check, which she brought along with a plate of fortune cookies and oranges cut into wedges. Rick opened one of the cookies and pretended to read. "'Don't feint,' Molly, 'when you've got a blunted épée.'"

She laughed, feeling the tension break. "You're talking to a linguist, and that's the clumsiest aphorism I've ever heard." She reached for the slip of paper he was smiling at. "'Open mind and open heart will find an open invitation to love.' Deep. That épée business of yours could get you a job as a fortune-cookie writer." She took a cookie for herself and broke it open. Fortune cookies were all such nonsense, yet here she was, reading the message aloud as if there were meaning in it. "'Speak the truth and all your problems will be solved.'" She cocked an eyebrow at him. "You wouldn't happen to know the cook would you?"

"No, but I do believe in fortune cookies."

She wished fervently that they had met under other circumstances. But they wouldn't have, and this was it, this was all the Rick Boulter she had. "Let's go," she told him. "This is the last week of class and I've a ton of work to do."

Later, outside the apartment house on Arlington, Molly and Rick sat for a few minutes in his car. "There's something I want from you," Rick said. "A list of people who were at the party."

Molly gave him a surprised look. "I don't remember who was there."

"Ask you aunt."

She felt a sudden warning, the pain of it dragging right through her. Something on a tape that couldn't be told and a list of guests to be stolen from its owner. "Rick, if you want the names, telephone Serena and ask her for them."

"*You* get me the list."

"I see. You want me to sneak around after it." She wasn't playing; she couldn't. It was Willy, something he'd said or done that she had inadvertently recorded. The words *fraud* and *influence peddling* came unbidden into her mind, and she closed her eyes briefly, willing herself to forget them.

Rick's hands were on her arms. "Don't try to imagine anything, Molly. Just trust me."

"Trust? That wasn't in my fortune cookie."

"It's in the cards, however. Trust me and everything will turn out all right. I gather from the look in your eyes that your aunt keeps a physical list and that you won't have to ask her for it. All you have to do is lift it."

He was absolutely serious, and for a moment Molly wavered. The list Serena kept was merely the record of a very efficient woman who was careful about noting whom she invited to her parties, when, and what she fed them. "Gentry Perot," Molly offered up at last, noting the faintest smile of satisfaction at the corners of Rick's mouth. "I *think* he was there. And Jason Loring—you know, the television muckraker. He's doing a story on corruption in high places.''

Rick remembered the voice on the tape urging Molly to hurry. Jason Loring. The D.A. had granted Loring an interview a couple of months before. Sonorous tones, self-important, irritating, Sam Spade in tweeds. He found himself more annoyed than he should have been.

"Also," Molly went on, "Perot's wife. Some of my uncle's golf and cardplaying cronies, I guess. Maybe some business friends of my aunt's." She gave a small laugh. "You know, the usual suspects."

He traced a finger along her neck. "Names and addresses."

"And what do I get in return?"

There was a long, pregnant silence before he answered.

"My everlasting gratitude."

"I get that from my students every time I give them a passing grade."

He leaned across the seat and pressed his lips against hers in a brief kiss that was chaste and yet full of promise. "I'm not asking for nuclear secrets, just a list," he said, keeping his mouth close to hers. "Let's get it out of the way, so we can go on from there."

She shook her head and pulled away. "You're taking an awful lot for granted, Boulter. You lied to me about the tape when it was in your possession the whole time. You won't tell me what's on it, although you and the cops didn't mind grilling me over it. You expect my cooperation—"

"To save confrontation with the two people you love the most."

"And stop kissing me."

"I doubt I'll be able to do that."

Molly opened the car door. She doubted she wanted him to, either. And he was right, of course, about confrontation with her aunt and uncle. When she stepped out into the street she turned back and peered in at him. "I'll make a deal. The list for a listen to the tape."

He gave it some thought and then lied quite openly. "Deal."

Liar, she thought, walking briskly away from him. For a great kisser he was such a damn liar. He caught up with her at the entrance to the apartment house. "There's something else," he said. "That telephone call today."

"I haven't forgotten it." The doorman was smiling at them through the glass door. She returned the smile and then said to Rick. "I'll be careful. I'm safe up there," she added, looking upward as if she could see right through to the penthouse.

"If a call comes in . . ."

"Play it through and let you know at once. How do I know you'll be around?"

"Just call me. I'll get the message and come running. Don't go anywhere without telling me. Don't meet any mysterious men in back alleys."

Spontaneously she put her hand against his cheek. "I'm pretty tough," she said.

He gave her one last look before leaving her, wanting to gather her into his arms and resisting the temptation. "I'll come by tomorrow morning and drop you off at school."

"Right." She waited until he was in his car before stepping into the lobby.

It was almost ten when she let herself into the apartment. The lights were still on but subdued, which meant the housekeeper had gone to bed and her aunt and uncle had either retired for the night or weren't home. Molly went quietly through the wide entry hall and along the corridor that led to the bedrooms at the rear. The walls were ivory-colored, and paraded in wide mats and narrow gold frames was a series of etchings of old Boston.

The door to Serena and Willy's room was ajar, a single light was shining near the bed. They weren't home. Molly walked past, then stopped. The list Rick wanted would be in the library or in their room. She thought of Rick with a certain softness and longing. She thought of the phone call from T. Marin, who obviously wasn't her mugger. She thought of living on the edge, where *fraud* and *influence peddling* might become words she could never excise from her vocabulary. She thought of two people who had opened their arms to a sobbing orphan and had never let her go.

"Damn." The expletive escaped her lips. They were innocent and she'd prove it. She could check their room now, while they were out. She dropped her bag and briefcase on a hall table and went into the bedroom. The library would be a cinch for later; everyone knew it was her favorite place.

The bedroom had been recently redecorated and still held a pleasant fragrance of fresh paint mixed with an expensive perfume. She went across the thickly carpeted floor to the window and glanced at the street below. A car drove slowly by without stopping. Dark and light and the movement of a night breeze through the trees made an ominous mix. She couldn't tell substance from shadow.

At her aunt's small white desk, Molly pulled the single drawer open. It rolled smoothly out. Inside all was in meticulous order. Packets of lavender notepaper, pencils, pens, erasers, clips. A small, private work space for sending invitations and thank-yous. No list, not even in the housekeeping book Molly found, where expenses were duly noted in a small, precise hand.

Molly felt like a sneak thief rummaging through the night tables on either side of the bed, but they revealed nothing

other than neatly arranged medicines. Again no list, and
Molly was willing to believe none existed.

She was nearly through with her search when she heard
the sound of the lock in the entry door. She took in a flustered breath but managed to escape the room before her
aunt and uncle came into the apartment.

"Hey, there," she said, calling down the hall to them. "I
was wondering where you two were."

"Molly." Her aunt slipped out of her coat and gave her
niece a brilliant smile. "Come talk to us."

"I'm bushed," Molly said, wondering if she had disturbed something in the bedroom that would reveal she'd
been snooping around.

"Bushed at your age," her uncle scoffed, coming toward her.

Her aunt headed for the kitchen and in another moment
peered out at Molly. "No more troubles, I hope. Police
giving you any headaches? Did you see those impossible
headlines? What a day! I had a dozen phone calls to field
because of you, Miss."

The warmth rushed to Molly's face. This whole business
of subterfuge and dissembling would be worse before it got
better. "I was a fifteen-minute celebrity at school," she
said. "Students and teachers alike, including the head of
my department. They couldn't get enough gory details."

Her aunt laughed. "Willy talked about pulling a few
strings, I mean at the *Globe* and *Herald* as well as the net-
works, asking them to cool it, but I told him to stay back.
You'd hate that, for one, but more important, the media
would find out, and I don't think any of us could stand the
attendant brouhaha."

Molly reached her aunt in a few steps and hugged her.
"You're so clever. That's what makes you the best real-
estate agent in Boston, not to say the best of all possible

aunts.'' Then she remembered her aunt's telephone call earlier that day. ''Oh, I'm sorry, you called me and I never called you back. Or Willy, either.''

Her aunt smiled. ''Never mind. We just like to keep tabs on you.''

Later, in her room, Molly stood in the dark and stared out at the shadows, believing her heart would burst with unhappiness. These two dear, caring people meant everything in the world to her, and she had started on a trail of deceit that could destroy their relationship forever.

A SOFT TAP AT THE DOOR brought Molly awake the next morning. Serena called, ''Honey, there's someone here for you.''

Spring light, which had a special warmth and brightness, penetrated the narrow, slatted blinds at her window. Molly glanced sleepily at her bedside clock. Seven-thirty. ''Who is it?''

''Rick Boulter.''

She sat up quickly. ''Tell him to go away.''

Serena laughed. ''You tell him. I have to get ready for work. You uncle's already gone. Come on.'' She opened the door and smiled in at Molly. ''I wouldn't keep a man like that waiting. He said his car is double-parked.''

Molly threw her covers back. ''What makes you think he's *a man like that*?''

Still smiling, Serena shook her head and withdrew. *A man like that*. Molly grabbed her robe and headed for the shower. *The man who invented the word deceit*.

Later, while applying makeup, Molly examined herself carefully in the mirror, noting that she still appeared a little tired around the eyes. Small wonder after the past few days.

The sound of voices could be heard from the kitchen—Serena's low-pitched, naturally flirtatious one, and Rick's deeper rumble. When Molly came into the sunny room, she thought with a surprise that pleased rather than annoyed her that Rick Boulter was quite adept at making himself at home.

Serena was leaning against the sink with a coffee cup in her hand and her jacket thrown over her shoulders. The housekeeper was at the stove, preparing bacon and eggs. Molly threw Rick a friendly greeting, which she knew her aunt was waiting for, and then headed for the coffeepot.

"I have to run," Serena told them. She turned to Rick. "Come by again and we'll talk. Dinner soon, if Molly can manage it."

Molly scarcely heard the remark. She was staring at Serena's large brown leather shoulder bag. Creamy, roomy, and it cost enough to send a rocket to the moon. And of course, one of the suede pockets held the party list. She looked up to find her aunt smiling at her.

"How about it, Molly?"

"I don't know..." Molly began. How about *what*?

"I'll see to it," Rick put in.

Serena flashed a satisfied smile and solemnly shook hands with Rick, then gave Molly a hug. "You figure it out between you."

"You didn't waste any time," Molly began as soon as Serena was gone and the housekeeper had left the room.

"Getting here? No problem at all. I thought you'd be thrilled to see me."

She felt her face grow warm at his words, given with a sly smile that yet held something pleading in it. "We're not talking about me but about how you've wasted no time charming my aunt."

"She's a charming woman. Did you get the list?"

"No." She had awakened well past midnight and gone into the library. She had found a file of past parties in the desk, but none for the fateful day. "I can take a guess where it is." Molly glanced through the kitchen door and realized that the housekeeper was in the dining room clattering about.

"Go on."

"It's in her bag. She's planning a party for this coming Saturday. . ."

"And doesn't want to invite the same people," he finished for her. "It's a little late in the day to be issuing invitations for a party less than a week away."

"I think she's been planning this one for some time, but often delays making things official," Molly said. "She and Willy are never certain they'll be here or at Windward on the weekend. I have to leave," she added, scarcely giving him time to finish his breakfast. "I'm late."

"I'll pick you up at lunchtime and deliver you to your aunt's office," Rick said. "By hook or by crook, I want that list."

"You want me to ask her for it, is that it?"

"No, I want you to liberate it from her bag. We'll take it to the nearest photocopying machine, and then you'll put the list back where you got it posthaste."

"Thanks. Thanks a lot."

"Molly," he said, coming over to her and putting his hands gently on her arms. "Look at me."

She raised her eyes to his and for a long moment they regarded each other. Whatever there was in the air between them couldn't be said, not quite now, when there was so much to be discovered and understood.

When Rick spoke, his tone had softened. "I'm not asking you to turn on Willy and Serena. I just want a little simple help from you, the kind that's easiest all around. I know how you feel about them, and I know what I'm beginning to feel for you. I can't afford to let any of it color my judgment. You understand that, don't you?''

The housekeeper came back, skirting around them and casting a shy smile at Molly.

"Let's go," Rick said to Molly, releasing her. "You said something about being late for class.''

FRAN, CREEDON'S SECRETARY, wasn't at her desk when Rick came by later that morning. In fact she was at the water fountain in the corridor, smiling flirtatiously at a slim, nondescript individual with slicked-back hair and a sallow complexion.

When she caught sight of Rick she made a motion to join him, but he waved her away. "I'll let myself in.''

Busy little beaver, he thought, and then opened the door and walked right into Creedon's wrath.

"No telephone taps for the lady," the district attorney told him at once, as if reading his mind. "Let Molly Ryder get her phone call from T. Marin, tell him she has the tape and agree to meet him. We'll take it from there. She doesn't make a move without calling us. Simple. If you ask me, that message she got fits the MO so far. There won't be another call. There have been threatening moves in her direction, I agree, but she's walked away every time because they're not out to add Molly Ryder to the body count. They want to know two things. One, do you know what's on the tape? Two, do you know where it is? Now, why," he added, fixing Rick with a look that showed he expected an answer, "do you suppose that is?''

"Whoops, oh, hi, sorry, I didn't see you.''

"What the hell is that supposed to mean?''

"If you'll recall the tape, Molly saw someone going into the library, and he's the gentleman who's trying to make her lose her memory permanently."

Creedon moved impatiently in his chair and then said, "So far, they've shot pretty far off the mark."

Rick shrugged. "Okay, maybe they're trying to keep the body count low. A cop and the judge's niece, to say nothing of Halloway. Not nice news in Boston at this time of year."

"And I see your mind turning, Rick. No police protection for your lady friend, either. If there was a pattern to these acts, or if there was a real threat from a person we could identify, then we might be able to afford protection day and night. If she were the Prime Minister of Tombouctou, we might. But the niece of Judge William Ryder? Every harried spouse in Boston would be on the wire asking for protection. As for the bullet that missed by a mile," the district attorney added, "we've managed to keep the incident under wraps and the newspapers off our backs. The bullet was scare tactics, nothing more."

"She needs police protection," Rick said.

"Protect her on your own time."

"Precisely what I intend to do."

"And you're taking up *my* valuable time," Creedon pointed out. "I called you in to talk about Judge William Ryder and whether or not he's involved in influence peddling or fraud. If the judge has anything to do with the initial northeast sewer project and Daniel Halloway, then he's got something to worry about."

Rick said, "He can't ask his niece about the tape if she hasn't told him it was stolen. He can, however, enlist a little outside help in trying to locate that particular piece of property. Failing that, he can try, through this selfsame outside help, to scare her into telling him that the tape was stolen and that she knows what's on it—in effect, that she recorded two of his pals talking murder in his library.''

They were silent for a while. Rick was the first to speak. ''I've persuaded her to locate the list of people who were at Windward that day. So far she's come up blank.''

''Or told you that.''

Rick gave the district attorney his dark, determined look. ''She's telling the truth.'' He felt, rather than saw, the beginnings of a knowing smile on Creedon's face.

''Oh, brother.''

''She's going to liberate the list from her aunt's bag today, at her office, if possible. If she does, I want to go a step further,'' Rick said. ''I want to tell her about S.N.A.R.E.''

Creedon shook his head. ''Oh, brother.''

''The lady's life is in danger. She may be trying to protect her uncle, but I've convinced her the only way to help is to start at square one, with a proper list of who was at Windward. I want her to hear the tape, I want her to try to identify the voices, and failing that, I want the list. If she's in for a dime, she's in for a dollar.'' Rick got to his feet and stretched the kinks out. ''It's not negotiable, Alex,'' he added.

Creedon shook his head once again, but this time the gesture held a certain amount of agreement in it. ''One word, one word of this gets out, and your head rolls, Boulter. Remember.''

Rick nodded and quickly left his chief's presence. He'd remember.

''MR. BOULTER, PLEASE.'' Molly was cramped into the small telephone booth near her aunt's office building. She tapped her fingers impatiently while she intoned, ''Please, please pick up, Rick. Rick, pick, quick.''

''Boulter.''

She let out a breath of relief. "Don't ever ask me to do anything like that again. She doesn't have it."

"You failed in your duty."

"I walked into her office, invited her to lunch, suddenly began sniffing and went, like the little girl with a runny nose I used to be, right over to her bag and began rummaging through it for a tissue. She laughed, said I was still her favorite brat, picked up the telephone and paid absolutely no attention to me. Incidentally, her bag is extremely neat. I never realized that before. She has everything compartmentalized, but her famous book of lists isn't in it. We had lunch, and I'm on my way to class. I had to keep sniffling all through the meal, and she insisted I consume a huge bowl of chicken soup and endless cups of hot tea. And stop laughing."

"What time do I pick you up?"

"You don't. I'm working late and you're not running my life."

"How about four at your office?"

"That's the end of the dirty work I'm going to do for you, do you hear?"

"Four o'clock. Don't move without me." He disconnected before she had a chance to object.

JASON LORING WAS SITTING ON THE EDGE of Molly's desk, sifting through her mail, when she returned to her office. He was wearing his usual jeans, black turtleneck sweater and baggy tweed jacket, with a white scarf thrown around his neck for effect.

"Jason, get off my desk, blast you." She wasn't happy to see him. He was self-serving and ungrateful, a rather rough-looking individual with black hair and an impressive black mustache, who seemed to think that one day she'd marry him. The thought was the farthest thing from her mind. "And quit nosing around my private papers. How'd you get in, anyway?"

Loring grinned and nodded at the other small desk that crowded the office. "Your roommate. He was here when I came by. Friendly chap, although a linguist who stutters strikes me as an anomaly."

"He doesn't stutter. You probably impressed him. He impresses easily." She flicked on her answering device and then, realizing that Jason might hear a message from Tinky Marin, flipped it off immediately.

"Go on, it doesn't bother me if you get phone calls from other men."

Molly sat down at her desk and began to sift through her mail. "Can I help you, Jason? I'm really busy. I've got appointments lined up to here."

"I've been trying to get you at your apartment ever since that business with Sergeant Klein. Why didn't you call me? How do you think I make my living?"

"Why would I call you? So you could interview me for the six o'clock news?"

"I haven't seen you since last Sunday," he complained.

Then a notion hit her. He could be a lifesaver, after all. He'd remember who was at Windward. An opportunist like Jason Loring had the memory of a herd of very large elephants. "Speaking of Windward, I've been going crazy trying to figure out who that tall fellow was, remember?" she asked, keeping her voice casual. "The one who wore a baseball hat backward?" No one at Windward answered the description, but the question could start Jason's memory motor.

"Why, are you interested in him?"

"Not that way, Jason. He had a very unusual accent. Boston upper class but as if he'd been educated in England."

"Baseball cap?" Jason shook his head. "Gentry Perot? If he had a baseball cap on, someone put it there. I'm not sure about his accent."

"No," she said hastily. "I know Gent Perot."

"Elliott Lawrence? No."

Elliott Lawrence, the union official, one of her uncle's cardplaying friends. She remembered now.

"Thomas Beam. He's also with the construction union. No, not tall enough."

"Right," Molly said. "Not tall enough." She made a careful mental note. She had no idea who the man was.

Jason easily rattled off a bunch of other names and then decided the rest wouldn't fit the bill because the people were too elderly for the frivolity of baseball caps. "Listen," he said, tired of the game, while Molly was trying to commit the names to memory, "that's not why I'm here. I read the statement you gave the police. I know some other things, too. The theft of your tape recorder and some report about shots being fired at you on Monday. You've had a busy week, my girl. Want to talk about it?"

"Nothing to talk about." She sighed impatiently, wondering how to get rid of him so that she could call Rick.

"I've got news for you," he said, getting serious. He pulled the chair from behind her colleague's desk and sat down. "I've come up against some interesting information about your uncle. Some of his friends are beginning to look like a problem."

She drew back, feeling a coldness come over her. "What are you talking about, Jason?"

"Gentry Perot, Halloway Construction. The head of the company, Daniel Halloway, wins the contract to the northeast sewer project, puts up the necessary hefty bond, starts work and then leaves." He snapped his fingers. "You know, like disappears?"

"And what's that got to do with my uncle?"

Jason leaned back, giving her a satisfied smile. "Nothing. Perot steps in. Turns out he's a silent partner and says in reply to my ardent questioning that Halloway has packed it in for a while and that he's on an extended vacation. No, there's no way he'll let Halloway be hounded by the press. Do I want to talk about how the project is getting on? Gentry asks me. If not, get out, Gentry says. Needless to say, I took the hint and got out."

"I said, what has that got to do with my uncle?"

"Man runs a small, tight construction company known for doing a job, for never having cost overruns and for coming in on time. Man bids on a big job, namely the initial northeast sewer project, gets same and disappears into thin air. I'm doing a story on corruption in high places, Molly."

"What has that got to do with my uncle?" she repeated evenly.

"Okay, okay, don't get steamed. Thought maybe you could tell me something about Halloway or ask your uncle. He knows Perot, maybe he knows Halloway."

"Jason, keep my uncle out of your corruption-in-high-places story. He likes his privacy."

"Just letting you know." Jason stood and went over to the door. "Incidentally, I took some Polaroid pictures when I was at Windward and left them on a bookshelf in the library. I never did go back for them. Did you see them?"

"Polaroid pictures of what?"

"We went sailing, remember? When we returned to the house I snapped some of the guests. Maybe your friend with the baseball cap and the Oxford accent is among them. When are you going out to Windward? Could you pick them up for me?"

The answer, when she gave it, was calm, although she didn't feel calm. Photographs of her uncle's guests, announced just like that. She couldn't believe her luck. "Of course. I'll call you."

"How about coming out for a drink?" Jason asked.

"No, thanks. Don't forget what I said about my uncle. You've been a guest in his home and you might remember that when you do your story."

Jason went to the door, opened it and leveled a gaze at her that was dead serious. "Maybe it's about time the judge dropped some of his poker buddies and began going to the opera instead."

Chapter Six

Clicking steadily at the back of Molly's mind all afternoon was Jason Loring's bombshell: photographs that could tell the district attorney a lot were sitting on a bookshelf at Windward. She had to balance this new knowledge with student interviews, telephone calls and sundry problems that needed her immediate attention. In fact, the student traffic in her office hadn't eased up when Rick appeared.

"Ever try to balance your students' problems against everything that's going on in your own life?" she said, throwing down her pen and reaching for her cup of cold coffee. "Don't try it, Rick." She took a quick swallow and then thrust a scribbled list of names at him, smiling triumphantly.

"The list?" he asked, turning it over in his hands. "I thought it had ceased to exist."

"That's one I put together for you. Jason Loring stopped by this afternoon and was extremely obliging—meaning he came up with the names of some of the people who were at Windward." She waited for his look of surprise, which was unexpectedly slow in coming.

She hugged the news of Jason Loring's photographic bombshell to her chest. That was the pièce de résistance and she wanted to build up to it. But there was something else besides, a decision she had made, and that would be a bombshell, too. All she had to do was figure out the right moment for her announcement.

Rick checked the carefully documented names one by one, but there was something off-putting about the way Molly had handed the list to him. Maybe the reason was that he just didn't like Jason Loring coming around without his permission. Maybe he was beginning to put his feelings about Molly above his professional judgment.

"Well?" Molly said.

Rick stirred and went back to his reading. Gentry Perot, Elliott Lawrence, Thomas Beam, and five others whose names were unknown to him. Notations next to Lawrence and Beam indicated that they were union officials. "Not much of a list," he found himself saying in a distant tone, "considering the number of people at the party."

"Well, you *are* grateful," Molly said. "I'm *so* pleased that I risked life and limb to get it."

"I know of Elliott Lawrence, but who's Thomas Beam? Do you remember him?"

"Elliott Lawrence is a poker buddy of my uncle's. I don't know Beam or any of the other names. Anyway, we've got to race out to Windward, because, my dear Rick, there's a lovely bunch of photographs Jason Loring took, which he placed on a bookshelf in my uncle's library and forgot to retrieve. Being the unselfish sort, I promised to get them for him. I have the plan all worked out."

"I've got other plans for us," Rick said peremptorily, not certain why Molly's idea didn't appeal to him.

"Other plans?" she asked. "Dinner can wait."

"Dinner will wait, I guarantee it. Come on, we're going to my office. There's something I want you to hear. Incidentally, any phone calls?"

"No threatening phone calls, if that's what you mean."
But Molly wasn't about to be deflected from her plan.
"Listen, Rick, I've the whole thing worked out to perfection. We'll retrieve the photographs and show them to my
aunt. I'll explain that Jason was the photographer, that I
drove out to Windward as a favor to Jason and picked them
up. Then Aunt Serena and I will have a cozy little discussion about who's who in each and every photograph. A
very simple, very elegant plan."

"Very simple, very elegant," Rick said, pulling her
around and planting a kiss on her forehead. "You'll remember every name as your aunt rattles them off. Or do
you plan to write the list down in front of her, explaining
that your friend down at the D.A.'s office needs it?"

Molly stayed in the circle of his arms, raising her hands
and clasping them around his neck. "Rick, I do declare,
you're jealous because I worked it all out for you without
one bit of input from the great Boulter. I'll explain that
Jason asked me to identify every guest. Aunt Serena will
buy it without a question."

"She'll enjoy the publicity, is that what you're telling
me?"

"Well, she let Jason take the photographs, didn't she?
She hasn't anything to hide. Anyway, I can always use my
trusty tape recorder without her knowing it—for a little
while, anyway. I'll tell her all about it later."

"She has nothing to hide, did you say? She's managed
very well with her list."

"It's in her office, I guess," Molly said.

"It'll be easier to break into her office than to drive out
to Windward."

"Richard, that's the kind of remark I'd expect from one
of my students, not from you."

"Which shows how little you know me." Something he couldn't quite put his finger on made him waver between Molly's plan and his own. He had come with the intention of letting her listen to the tape, following it with a run-down on S.N.A.R.E. Now that he knew the list was in her aunt's office, he wanted to go after it that evening, with Molly in tow. "You're telling me your aunt allowed Jason Loring to photograph everyone at Windward that day?"

"I haven't discussed it with her," Molly said, a little annoyed by his remark. "Jason didn't tell me whether he photographed absolutely everyone. In fact, I think he said he had taken some pictures of some of the guests."

"Some of the guests. Okay, linguist, how about clarifying the word *some*?"

"An unspecified number," she said tiredly. "You win."

Rick gave in. It meant putting off his plan, maybe temporarily, maybe permanently. He wouldn't have to tell her about S.N.A.R.E. after all. The D.A.'s office would investigate the guests in the photographs and she'd be safe—maybe. "Let's get the photographs," he said brusquely. "Your aunt might volunteer any names that are missing."

Molly checked her watch. "I've a couple more students coming by."

"Use your out-to-lunch sign."

She quickly scribbled a note with a marker and tacked it to her door. "Sorry, emergency," it read. "Had to leave. Come by early tomorrow morning." She shook her head. "I'm going to be in hot water with everyone around here."

Molly was at her office door with her bag and briefcase in hand when she turned to Rick and tossed him the second bombshell she had held back, the one for which the time was now exactly right. "Incidentally, Rick, there's one thing more."

"Name it, sleuth."

"I want to know what's going on and I'm willing to make a deal," Molly said.

"A deal?" He looked at her in surprise. "I doubt you're in a position to make a deal, Molly, but go ahead, say your piece."

"You can have the photographs and the list of names in exchange for telling me what the devil's going on. I want to listen to that bit of supposedly incriminating conversation I inadvertently taped, and I want to know why it's incriminating, whether to my uncle or to one of his friends."

Rick exploded. "That's extortion, Molly, and I'm not buying. We can subpoena the list and get a search warrant for the photographs."

"In Marblehead? It's out of your jurisdiction in more ways than one. I grew up with the daughter of the police chief, not to mention the close relationship between the powers that be and my uncle."

Rick shook his head admiringly over her logic and then, flipping off the office light, pushed her gently into the corridor. "Molly, I'm a past master at picking a lock. I don't have to succumb to blackmail."

"I have to protect the people I love," she said simply.

"I know you do." He took her arm. "I'm not giving in to extortion. I'd planned to let you hear the tape anyway. You just put a whole new complexion on things when you offered up the photos. Let's move."

"MY TAPE RECORDER!"

In the confines of Rick's small office, Molly let out a shout of glee. Then as she turned the wished-for instrument over in her hands, she felt a tug of apprehension at her heart.

"The original tape is at the lab," Rick said. "I've a couple of copies under lock and key." He opened his desk drawer and drew out a manila envelope, from which he retrieved a copy of the original cassette. "Here's the culprit."

"I suppose the incriminating stuff is at the very end, just before the tape ran out," she remarked, knowing she hadn't been exactly forthcoming over the events at Windward.

"You held out on me concerning what happened that day," Rick said. "We're even in the truth department. Go ahead, turn it on, tell me who owns the voices."

She hesitated, knowing that up to this moment all she had was a belief in her uncle's innate decency and sense of fairness. Still, she had moved out of the apartment on Arlington in her second year at college and was now only a visitor in the lives of her uncle and aunt. She saw them on weekends, at dinner on occasion, and spoke with them on the telephone, but the time for deep intimacies was well past. What did she truly know about Judge William Ryder?

"Go ahead," Rick urged.

She clicked the tape into place. Then she pressed the on and fast-forward buttons, waiting until two thirds of the tape had gone through before pressing the sound button and exchanging a long look with Rick. The tape ran on silently.

"Damn," she said, "the recorder's broken." She fiddled with the sound button. Nothing emerged.

"Wait a minute." Rick came to her rescue, but it became clear after a moment that nothing was wrong with the recorder. The tape was blank.

"What the hell—" Rick began to open desk drawers and slam them shut, a look of intense concentration on his face. "Nothing."

"What's happening?" Molly asked, frowning.

"Beats me. Wait here." Without a word, Rick dashed out of his office and came back hurriedly with another manila envelope. "Locked in the D.A.'s office. Had to bribe the secretary with a smile to get her to fetch it for me." There was no humor in his voice, however.

"Just a smile?"

"Never mind what else." He wasn't worried, not quite yet. They were dealing with machines so far, not human beings. It was possible that somewhere along the line he had pushed the wrong button and cleared the tape. Anything could happen in this extraordinary case. "Go ahead, click this one into place."

"No use winding it through without checking first," Molly said. They waited as the tape ran silently on. "Nothing," she said at last.

"Run it to the end." His words were tight now. It looked as if things were going to come crashing down around them. He picked up the phone and called the laboratory to which the original had been sent for voiceprint analysis.

When he put the receiver down a few minutes later, Rick dropped into his chair. "They were wondering why the package never arrived at the lab. Damn it." He slammed his fist against the desk. "They were wondering why and never bothered calling. Someone," he added, his voice deadly calm, "has a very long reach right into this office."

"You mean the original is gone and all the copies?" In her vast relief over finding the tape empty of incriminating talk that could involve her uncle, Molly almost overlooked the fact that her interviews were destroyed, as well.

"If it's any consolation," Rick remarked, almost to himself, "a typed transcript fortunately rests in my brief-case, and that's still in the car."

He picked up the manila envelope and stared at it. "I can go through the motions, have the place picked apart, but this is the envelope and that's the tape I sealed in it. Damn it, I thought we were on top of things here. We're playing it so close to the chest . . ."

"Playing what, Rick?"

He picked up the telephone to let the district attorney in on the bad news. While waiting for the call to go through, he said, "If it was only speculation before, it isn't now. Someone in this office knows a little too much. The trouble is, we can't call the cops."

The district attorney came on at the other end. Rick held his finger to his lips. Molly would learn about S.N.A.R.E. soon enough. Meanwhile he had Creedon to deal with, and the result wasn't going to be pretty.

MOLLY READ THE TYPED TRANSCRIPT in Rick's car. Two men discussing the probable murder of another sent chills down her spine. She might have been reading the words in *The Boston Globe* and not the transcript of a conversation taped in her uncle's study. "I've never heard of Halloway Construction," she said at last.

"Its trucks have plied the city for the past five years."

"I don't go reading trucks."

"Nobody's off the hook yet, Molly."

"I am," she stated quietly.

He looked quizzically at her.

"Obviously, whoever called and threatened me has a copy or has destroyed the tape for good and all. I'm safe."

"I'd like to think so. Did you know that Gent Perot is the president of Halloway Construction?" he added.

She shrugged. "Why would I? I've met him a couple of times, always on social occasions, and I've hardly said two words to him outside of 'How's your tennis game?'"

"You greeted someone on your way out of the library. Who was it, Molly? You must have bumped into him."

"Jason Loring?"

"You said, 'Hi, sorry, I didn't see you.' "

She shook her head in disgust, checking through the transcript and finding the words. "You really expect me to remember every remark I made on a day fraught with incident?"

"It was your voice." He remembered his first intrigued reaction to her sultry tone on the tape.

"I don't remember the remark. I was hungry, talking to Jason and hurrying after him all at the same time."

"It wasn't your uncle, then, whom you bumped into, and you didn't say to him, 'Hi, sorry I didn't see you'?"

"No." She responded rather sharply, then flushed and repeated in a quieter tone, "No."

"Gent Perot?"

"I know Gent Perot. No."

"Elliott Lawrence?"

Molly sighed. "Rick, if I knew whom I bumped into, I'd tell you. If, incidentally, it was a he."

It was time, Rick decided, to open up entirely, to tell Molly about Operation S.N.A.R.E. and to pay an illegal visit to Serena Ryder's office for the complete list. Molly didn't have the key to her aunt's office; she had made that much clear already. He was convinced that a midnight ride to Marblehead for an indefinite number of photographs could be a waste of energy and time. Serena Ryder's real-estate office won in a walk. Rick had energy to waste, but not time.

"YOU'RE WRONG, YOU KNOW THAT." They sat in the Camaro, parked opposite Serena's office building. The time on the car clock said a little after six. Learning about Operation S.N.A.R.E. had made Molly privy to a lot more information about corruption both in and out of government than she wanted to have.

"What am I wrong about?"

Rick's voice held a certain kind of tenderness that she hadn't heard before. The knowledge that he was worried suddenly made her weak with indecision. "About Uncle Willy," she said at last.

"I hope I am."

"You're so far off the mark," Molly said, "that I'm willing to prove it by sneaking into my aunt's office to retrieve that list. I've made my mind up about one thing, though," she added.

"You've used up your bargaining power."

"Rick, if I get caught I can talk my way out of it. If you get caught, it's goodbye career."

"You worry about that slip of paper, I'll worry about my career. We go on as planned. Your aunt closes up shop about six-fifteen. The building doesn't lock up until seven. Once we see your aunt and company leave, we'll saunter into the lobby like we own the place."

Molly pointed out a dark gray Cadillac waiting in front of the building, along with several other limousines. "That's hers, and that's their chauffeur in the front seat. They'll pick up the judge, and off Serena and Willy will go, perhaps to dinner with friends or to dinner and the theater or home, where there'll be a small and very intimate dinner party. Then to bed with mounds of paperwork and reading matter."

"Remarkably well-regulated life."

"They're busy, organized and enjoy every minute of it."

"But it's not for you."

"No," she said after a while. "It's not for me. I'm tuned in to another station."

"Great. Maybe they'll be playing our tune."

"Our tune?" Molly was spying on her aunt and it was no joking matter. Rick instinctively understood. He took her hand in his and held it tight, but she didn't relax, and neither did he.

The wait was long, quiet and tense. It was six-eighteen when Serena came down with her secretary, waved goodbye and stepped into the limousine. Molly dug deeper into her seat, turning away from her aunt and gazing at Rick with imploring eyes. "Do we have to?"

"You know we do. Or do you want me to handle it myself?"

Molly didn't answer.

The limousine moved off.

"Come on," Rick said. "Let's go."

The day had been unnaturally warm even for the time of year, and in the warmth there was a faint portent of much-needed rain. Still, Molly drew her raincoat tightly around her as they made their way across the busy thoroughfare; she was apprehensive that Serena might have forgotten something and would come back.

There was an early-evening sense of movement and purpose in the office workers surging through the revolving doors of the modern, glass-fronted building. Inside, the crowds flowed around a large, square bronze sculpture balanced on end. Molly and Rick had to buck the human tide to get to the elevators, but that was to their benefit. When they walked past the elevator captain, he smiled absentmindedly at them. They smiled back and stepped quickly into an elevator just as the doors slid shut. They were alone. Molly let out an audible sigh.

"Just what I figured," Rick said, pushing the button for the eighth floor. "All you have to do is act as if you own the place."

"I ought to report the captain for dereliction of duty," Molly said, and a small laugh erupted to break the tension, if only for a moment. "My aunt's office is on the tenth floor, Rick."

"I know."

The elevator slid to a smooth stop at the eighth floor and the doors opened. A man standing there peered in, looking confused. "Going up," Rick said. The man smiled and stepped back. The doors closed. "Just a little precaution in case someone's checking on us from below." He reached over and hit the button for the tenth floor, and when the elevator stopped, he said, "Your last chance to turn back."

"I'm going to watch you every minute of the way." They were saying unnecessary things to each other because if they had stopped to examine what they were doing, they might have seen the folly of it.

"Going down," Rick said, as the doors opened on a waiting woman. He bundled Molly out of the elevator. The woman stepped in and the doors closed.

"Think she'll remember us?" Molly asked.

"You can always say you came looking for your aunt."

Ryder Real Estate was around a bend in the corridor. The mahogany office door was closed and presented a blank front. There was a buzzer on the left-hand side and Rick pushed it. "No one home," he said, trying the buzzer again to make certain.

"What do we do now, kick the door down? Does it occur to you that we haven't planned very intelligently for this?"

"Stand aside," Rick said. "I've covered every contingency. You're about to see an expert at work." He extracted a small file from his wallet and with a precision that surprised Molly, proceeded to pick the sophisticated lock.

"I'm not sure about a burglar alarm," Molly said dubiously. "What happens if—"

"Why would she have an alarm, unless she has a helluva lot to hide?"

"She doesn't." The words rang out along the empty corridor.

The lock gave, and Rick quickly ushered her into the office. "You'd be surprised what I've learned in my trade," he said. The reception area was windowless, but the fading light from outside shone through the glass partition of a secretary's office. Rick shut the door and locked it behind them.

Molly smelled her aunt's perfume and even the warmth of bodies that had only recently vacated the place. "Well, let's get it over with," she said.

"Which is your aunt's office?"

"She doesn't have any files in it."

"We'll check her desk, anyway."

"The files are in the secretary's office," Molly insisted.

"Where's Serena's office?"

Molly gave him a long, perplexed look. His face was set, and if she hadn't known before, she knew now: Rick Boulter meant business. It didn't matter what happened to her or Aunt Serena or Uncle Willy. All that mattered was his career and S.N.A.R.E, and the notion was doubly chilling.

"I asked a question," he said.

"It's a corner office. Left."

The door was locked, but Rick opened it deftly and without a word. He whistled at the elegant, traditional decor and the view out of huge windows that took in downtown Boston and the harbor. "Nice money in the real-estate business."

Molly frowned but said nothing. She didn't want him admiring the decor or talking about her aunt's business.

Rick found the desk drawers locked and, giving Molly an apologetic smile, picked the central one that released the others.

"You could give Tinky Marin lessons," Molly said.

"I'm not trying to catch your aunt at anything," Rick said impatiently. "My mind's a blank but for a list in her handwriting pertaining to a certain party."

"Well, thank you very much."

"Nothing," he said, moving quickly and without disturbing any dust through the contents of each drawer. "Why keep nothing under lock and key?" He paused, read a scribbled memo or two, but they weren't easy to decipher and seemed to refer to leases and contracts.

"It's a reflex action," Molly said. "After all, the price of real estate is nobody's business, including yours."

"Let's check out those secretary's files." He followed Molly out of the office, making certain he locked up behind them.

"How do you suppose her secretary files the list?" Molly asked, unable to keep annoyance out of her voice. "Under Parties? It's ridiculous. There is no list, not this time around. I made a mistake, so let's go."

"Humor me," Rick said. "I can always have her files subpoenaed."

"The whole thing's a mistake, Rick. Let's get out of here."

Rick took her arm between tight fingers. "We're wasting time, Molly. I want to see those files."

She gazed defiantly at him. "You tricked me. Why? What has Serena got to do with S.N.A.R.E.?"

"What are you afraid of?" he asked, still holding her arm in a tight grip.

"You, everything." She pulled herself away and marched through the secretary's office to a black steel file cabinet. It wasn't locked, and in pulling the top drawer open, she knocked an ashtray to the floor. "Damn, it's all your fault." It seemed to Molly that the crack was the loudest she'd ever heard.

Rick touched his fingers to her lips and pointed to the door. From the corridor they heard the sound of footsteps, which came to a stop outside the door. There were a few moments of silence, as if someone were standing there listening. Then they heard a buzzer sound and a voice call out, "Mrs. Ryder, you all right?"

Chapter Seven

"The guard," Molly whispered. "That ashtray sounded like a gunshot."

"Always there when you don't need them," Rick said. They waited breathlessly while the guard rattled the doorknob. Rick put his arm around Molly and drew her into a crouch behind the desk.

"That you, Mrs. Ryder? It's me, Tim."

There was a clicking of keys, and Rick clasped a hand over her mouth, as though he felt the scream that Molly was trying to stifle. The door was pulled open and a footstep shuffled into the reception room.

"Mrs. Ryder?" Then a pause. A tentative step forward. Molly stared at the fallen ashtray. It was made of marble and wasn't broken, but it could be seen quite clearly from the door. "Right, everything hunky-dory." The guard muttered a few more words to himself and then backed out and locked the door behind him.

As the guard's footsteps clattered down the hallway, Molly said, "This is crazy. You have only your job to lose and five years in the pen. I'll have a lifetime of my aunt and uncle never talking to me again."

Rick pulled Molly to her feet. "He won't be back. He probably thinks his hearing aid blew a battery." He held her tightly, his breath soft against her cheek. "You're still shaking. I was stupid to bring you into this."

"It's a little late now to worry about that, Rick. I'm not afraid of you; I don't know what got into me. All you want is a lousy little list of names."

"That's not at all what I want," he said. Then his lips came down hard on hers and they stood there locked in an embrace, their senses heightened by the danger they knew they were in. The kiss deepened and his body moved against hers, Molly uneasily responding to the thrilling madness of the moment.

Rick pulled away. Taking her face between his hands, he said, "Story to be continued as soon as we get the hell out of here." He kissed her nose and then her lips. "But right now, let's take a peek at those files."

"You do it," Molly said. "Pretend I'm not even here."

Rick began opening drawers, reading off information. "Leases," he said after a while. "A to L. Allen, Carter, et cetera, et cetera." He was about to close the drawer when he stopped, a perplexed expression on his face. "Well, I'll be..." He lifted out a file.

"Found it?" Molly asked anxiously.

"Not quite. It's a brand-new lease. Care to have a look?"

Molly came over and gazed down at the file. There, on the lease for offices in a building her aunt managed on Tremont, was the name Georgia Boston Construction, Inc., the front for Operation S.N.A.R.E.

Molly shut the file away, resisting the temptation to slam the drawer as an act of finality. "It doesn't mean a thing," she said to Rick. "It's a huge building, and I happen to know it. The ASL has its offices there, too."

"What's the ASL?"

"The American Society of Linguists. As a matter of fact, Serena rented the society some space at a real bargain price as a favor to me. I'm rather active in the organization."

Rick said, "From the rent she's charging GBC, I'd say she's making it up in the construction business."

"We're looking for a party list and not the way my aunt conducts business. Come on, that list isn't here and I feel like the worst sort of thief rooting around in her files."

She went over to the door, but Rick was beside her, an arresting hand on her arm. "Molly, take it easy. You have guilt and fear written all over your face, although why you should beats me."

"So my aunt has a client for one of the buildings she manages and it happens to be Georgia Boston Construction. What does it mean? She runs a top real-estate and management agency and it's coincidence, that's all."

"Hey, I said cool it. Nobody's accusing your aunt of anything but being a very social creature and a good businesswoman."

"Which is why GBC used her to find the proper location for its offices."

"Precisely. Finding a copy of the lease in her files took me by surprise, that's all. GBC is a legitimate company that came north from Georgia to compete against companies like Halloway. We didn't ask the company where it intended to set up offices; we wouldn't have any reason to. We needed discretion and help, and GBC agreed to join the operation. GBC will come in as lowest bidder for the northeast sewer extension, then S.N.A.R.E. steps in. Georgia Boston is in business to make money. They're bidding on anything that comes their way, just like Halloway, just like everybody else. They have a telephone, a mailing address, and office personnel, also just like everybody else."

"Fine," said Molly. "Then let's get out of here."

Rick agreed with her. He glanced around the office. Either the list existed or, like the purloined letter, was residing in the most obvious place of all—wherever that was.

"I'll never forgive myself for snooping around my aunt's effects," Molly said when they hit the street. "How am I going to face her?"

"With a big smile. Your aunt runs a tight, successful ship, and if I were you I'd quit the linguistics business and hire on with her."

"That's just what she'd like me to do," Molly said.

"And?"

"And I could use a good, strong cup of coffee right now. I've got to get my act together concerning the first smile I'm going to give the dear woman when I walk into her apartment."

Rick suggested that they go to a café on Boylston near the Common. It was only when Molly was seated at one of the small marble tables at the rear of the café, her hands wrapped around a cup of steaming cappuccino, that she relaxed.

"Rick, I've been thinking of moving back to my apartment," she stated. "I'm making arrangements first thing in the morning to have the rug taken out and a cleaning lady in to give the place a good going-over."

"Because of what happened tonight?" he asked. "The fact that your aunt holds the lease for Georgia Boston? Going back to your apartment isn't a good idea, Molly."

"The tape is a big zero. I'm safe. I can come out of hiding now."

"You were never in hiding," he pointed out. "I'd say our pals know to the minute where you are and what you're doing."

"Including raiding my aunt's office?"

He gave her a sheepish grin. "Maybe even that."

"They no longer need me for the tape, Rick."

"Molly," he said patiently, "they're not certain what you know. You're still in danger."

"Then why haven't they killed me? They know how to kill, don't they?"

Rick winced. "It would be very easy for me to have your apartment declared off-limits, still the scene of a crime."

"I know nothing and I'm no longer at risk," she insisted, wondering if he was being stubborn because he was leading up to something.

"You stepped out of the library, bumped into someone going in, said hello and then left. He knows who you are and you don't remember who he is."

"I remember charging after Jason, and I remember being hungry. It was one of those mindless days filled with activity. I don't remember half of what went on. Look, maybe I don't want to go back to my apartment. Maybe I am nervous, but I can't stay with my aunt and uncle and work behind their backs as if they were guilty of heaven knows what. They're not. Would you like to know what I'm really distressed about?"

"Shoot."

"The fact that my uncle, even in his innocence, could have invited those two men to Marblehead. They certainly made themselves at home in his library."

"Nobody's accusing the judge of anything, except maybe poor taste in the kind of company he's been keeping."

Rick's agreeing with her about her uncle only served to get Molly's back up. "You know, all I've seen is a typed transcript and your word that it came off a tape I've made."

After a brief silence, Rick shook his head in wonder. "Are you accusing me of concocting a scheme as wild as that?"

"You mean besides S.N.A.R.E.?"

He laughed. "Point made. Do you trust me or don't you?"

"Does it matter whether I do or don't? *You* hold all the cards, not I."

"Molly, I'd hate to think I did a foolish thing in telling you about S.N.A.R.E."

"I didn't ask to be told, and now here I am, burdened with it."

"I think your life is in danger, that's why you had to know. We're trying to clean the city of corruption, your city—"

"Even if it means taking my uncle down with it. And you expect my unbiased cooperation."

"Cooperation. I don't care how biased it is," he said in a softened manner. "I expect you to help us, and that includes not going back to your apartment."

"Don't tell me what I can do and can't do, Rick. You're moving in on my life, and I don't like it one bit." She bit her lip, knowing she hadn't told all the truth; she wanted him with her but not on the terms he was laying down.

"Molly, if I'm right, and I'm certain I am, a man is dead at the bottom of the sea because he defied an extortion attempt. He's not on the French Riviera playing the crap tables; the dice in fact were loaded against him a long time ago. With GBC's help I hope we'll not only find out who killed him, but also put an end to racketeering in city construction jobs. Maybe when a ton of cement is poured, it'll be of the right quality and guaranteed to last forever. We need your silence, your safety and your unqualified cooperation."

"Something's rotten in your own office," Molly reminded him. "You said you had my tape and now you haven't."

"We're on it," he told her grimly. No, he hadn't forgotten that for one minute.

Molly expelled a sigh. "I'm moving back to my apartment." She saw his fist tighten around the cup handle. "Look," she added, "I'll compromise with you. I'll not talk to Aunt Serena and Uncle Willy for the moment."

"And find me the list," he said.

She could see that he relaxed visibly and once again the notion struck her that S.N.A.R.E. meant everything to him, but whether for personal reasons or because he wanted to clean up the world, she couldn't tell. "And find you the list," she amended. "Meanwhile, there's my other life, you know, my pedagogical one. I've papers to correct, classes to give, students to advise, meetings to attend. You and S.N.A.R.E . . . My life is turning out to be very untidy, indeed. Shall we go?"

He gave her an amused smile, although she could read the depths of seriousness in his eyes. "That chin of yours," he said. "Determination, stubbornness, it's all there."

She smiled back. "Love me, love my chin."

They walked along Boylston holding hands and wishing there was nothing to think about but each other. When they reached the Arlington Arms, they were relieved to find no reporters hanging around the front entrance. The story was still front-page news, but it focused more on the efforts of the police department to track down the killer and less on Molly as the niece of Judge Ryder. The momentum was slowing, for which she was grateful. Molly said, "Sorry it's been a fruitless day."

"As a matter of fact, it hasn't." Rick pulled her past the front entrance and into the shadows.

She felt a sudden, inexplicable breathlessness but went willingly along, knowing that the evening hadn't ended quite yet and that there was more to be said. "What is it now?" she asked with mock impatience. "Haven't we been over everything twice, and then some?"

"Not this, and this is the one thing that's been on my mind ever since our little adventure in your aunt's office." His arms were around her and his lips descended lingeringly on hers. Then, before she had a chance to react, he released her and with a firm grip on her arm, escorted her back to the front door. "I'll come for you tomorrow morning early."

"Oh, Rick," she murmured, then turned and glanced up at the building. She left him, dragging her steps, reluctant to go in. What she was doing to her aunt and uncle was untenable, and Molly didn't know how much longer she could live with it.

THE NEXT DAY, AFTER CLASS, Molly had turned on her answering machine and was sifting through her mail when she heard "urgent," underlined in Jason Loring's deep voice.

Of course, Jason always put an urgent face on things; nevertheless she picked up her telephone and called him at the studio.

"What's up, Jason?"

"A photo, old love, for your eyes only. I was checking through the archives at the station on a completely unrelated matter and voilà, a very revealing photo you might be interested in seeing. Meet me at Faneuil Hall and I'll show it to you."

"Whose photo, Jason?"

"Meet me at Faneuil, front entrance."

Molly hated his penchant for drama, the way he invested every event with a cloak and a dagger. "Jason, get to the point."

"Let's see, it's four o'clock, make it five-twenty, and better make it Donovan's Bar."

"Jason." But he had already hung up. So that was it, a ruse to get her out to dinner. She considered calling him back but decided against it. He'd have to produce a photograph or risk her everlasting enmity.

She tried to get Rick on the telephone, but he was in court. Molly left a message, calling once again when she arrived at Faneuil Hall, but he still hadn't picked up his messages. So much for his instant accessibility.

The huge edifice was already crowded with after-business-hours customers: people picking up exotic cheeses and gourmet foods in boil-a-bags to take home, others drinking a little early or meeting friends for a preshow dinner. Molly liked the place and its cheery commerciality, its scent of food and pickles and coffee and candles, its Victoriana and Edwardiana, its crafts and fashions and chocolate-chip cookies—all the good things of life associated with success and an open wallet. It made nice statements about mixing past and present pleasures, attachment to the old while preserving it along with the new.

She expected Jason to be late, as he usually was, and so she wandered around for a while, arriving at Donovan's five minutes after the appointed time. Of course he wasn't there, but Molly ran into a couple of friends and had a beer with them, so she wasn't aware of how late it was until an hour had rolled by.

"Well, that takes the cake," she told her companions. "Being in television doesn't give anyone an automatic license to be rude." She left when they did, a scant fifteen minutes later.

RICK, WHO HAD BEEN IN COURT ALL DAY, arrived back at his office at six o'clock to find that both Molly and the district attorney had called. Creedon asked him to stop by his office. Although Rick was expected on the double, he picked up the telephone first and dialed Molly at the Arlington Street apartment. She wasn't in, the housekeeper told him. "Left for the university in the morning and hasn't been back." No, she added when pressed, Molly hadn't said any special time. On a whim Rick tried Molly at her own apartment but met with no success.

The district attorney had just come back from a meeting with the mayor when Rick dropped by. Creedon's secretary was sitting there, her pad on her lap. She gave Rick the welcoming smile with its twinkle of invitation, which she usually reserved for him. He smiled back.

"News conference," Creedon said at once and with a sour look on his face. "News conference with all the wrong questions. That over, I'm told the police union issued a statement splitting the pawnshop scam wide open. An expensive operation gone down the tubes. The only fish they netted after all their work was Tinky Marin, and he apparently has skipped town. An unfortunate finish all around to an expensive police-department scam." The telephone rang at that point. Creedon turned to his secretary and regarded her for a moment. "Take it outside, Fran, and hold all my calls until I tell you otherwise."

Both he and Rick were silent until she had closed the door behind her. "What we've got to do is watch our tails or S.N.A.R.E. will go the same route as the P.D. scam."

"How's the investigation of the staff going?" Rick asked. He had his eye on the closed door. The rose scent Creedon's secretary wore still hung in the air.

"You talking about her?" Creedon remarked.

"I'm talking about everybody."

"She doesn't know about S.N.A.R.E.," Creedon said.

"She typed the transcript."

"She typed *a* transcript. It doesn't connect Windward, Judge Ryder and Halloway. Anyway," Creedon went on, "she's been with me a dozen years. I'm more worried about people like the janitor, the cleaning lady, the elevator operator—somebody who has no stake in what goes on here and can use a couple of bucks. We're on it. We're looking under the rugs, in the water cooler, you name it."

"Check on Fran, anyway," Rick said.

"I'm checking on you, too, my friend."

Rick laughed. "Be my guest. My life is an open comic book."

Creedon forced a smile. "What I called you about is no laughing matter. I've got something I want you to look at, a very interesting conversation between Gent Perot and an unidentified man." He slid a couple of typewritten sheets across the desk. "We had a helluva time justifying a tap on Perot's phone, but it looks as if we hit pay dirt."

Rick picked up the transcript and read it through. If Perot's cool matched his words, the incriminating conversation on Molly's missing tape was news to him.

Perot: "Let me get this straight. You know about a tape made in the library at Judge Ryder's place at Marblehead a couple of weeks ago. The D.A.'s office is interested in it. You figure on releasing the news to the press, is that it?"

Unknown voice: "That's it. It would be interesting to watch all the politicians coming out of the woodwork trying to cover their rears."

Perot: "What has that got to do with the construction business and the price of bananas?"

Unknown voice: "Everything. From what I've learned, the tape has to do with Halloway Construction."

Perot: "And you're telling me the D.A. has it but isn't about to release the information to the press?"

Unknown voice: "I'm thinking of doing the public a favor and releasing it for him."

Perot: "I don't know what you're talking about, but if it concerns Halloway, you'd better think twice. Excuse me, I have another call to make."

Rick finished reading the transcript and handed it back to Creedon. "What tape does the D.A.'s office have?" His tone was sarcastic and admitted defeat.

"Don't rub it in. This whole Molly Ryder thing is about to come out, and we'll be left with egg on our faces. Jog her memory, Rick. Show her the faces of every politician in town, every union official, every owner of every construction company in the city."

Rick smiled in admiration. "Might not be a bad idea."

"We picked up the telephone conversation right at its beginning. Perot made the call in answer to a message he'd received. He didn't identify the caller or himself."

"The receiver was in a telephone booth, I bet."

"You're right first time out. Any idea who the unidentified voice could be—without hearing it, that is?"

Rick said, on a hunch, "It's my guess that it belongs to Jason Loring. He has so many connections in this town that the telephone company could use him for a switching station. It sounds like he was hoping to goad Perot into cooperating with him on Halloway's disappearance. Didn't work, did it?"

Creedon agreed. "Well, we can find out if it's Loring's voice easily enough. Meanwhile, I want to make this clear, Rick: if Molly Ryder doesn't produce the needed information about that business at Windward, I'm going to talk to Judge Ryder and his wife and level with them."

"It's not a good idea," Rick said in an even tone.

"Maybe not, but unless you come up with a better one, it's what I'll have to do."

Chapter Eight

Molly took a cab to the apartment on Arlington and was relieved to learn that both Serena and Willy were out. She was tired and not hungry but raided the refrigerator, nonetheless. The housekeeper had prepared an impressive cold strawberry soup. Molly spooned some into a dish, but realized after a couple of minutes that she was forcing herself to eat.

There was the spooky business of finding the GBC lease. Mere coincidence, that was all. But Rick had promised he would check on why GBC had selected that building for its offices. She took up the kitchen phone and dialed Rick's office, to no avail. Then she tried Jason Loring at the television station and at home, and got a harried, uncommunicative receptionist at one and his telephone-answering machine at the other. She didn't bother leaving her name with either.

There were those photographs at Windward, but Marblehead was fifteen miles away, and the idea of driving out in early-evening traffic didn't appeal to Molly. Besides, she had a ton of work to do.

When Molly went into the den, she had every intention of extracting a batch of student papers from her briefcase. Switching on television news was almost automatic. Maybe

Jason had been corralled into covering some unexpected news event, in which case she'd excuse him. He was often used by the station for the human-interest side of stories ranging from fires to the Red Sox winning a pennant. Her mind slid back to his telephone call. His voice had seemed a little insinuating, as if she wouldn't be pleased with the photograph he had to show her. Jason was a muckraker all right. Interesting, if you weren't part of the muck. She listened with half an ear as she made herself comfortable on the couch with the papers on her lap.

"Here's a late-breaking story."

Molly glanced up at the screen. The announcer, a sincere-looking young man with a square jaw and eyes of a remarkable blue, held a sheet of paper in his hand but did not read from it. Instead, he seemed to stare straight at Molly, words issuing from lips that scarcely moved.

"Jason Loring, reporter for Channel Five, died tonight at his home in Brookline. The police suspect suicide by asphyxiation."

She failed to hear the rest. The location on-screen was shifted to Jason's red-brick town house in Brookline with its attached garage. Molly's blood pounded in her ears, and she saw the yawning mouth of the open garage, and the police cars and the barricades. She passed a hand over her forehead and realized it was covered with beads of sweat. She went quickly over to the phone and tried Rick's office.

"I'm afraid he came in and ran out," an anonymous voice told her.

"You wouldn't know where he went."

"I'm afraid not."

He could be at the murder scene. She toyed with the idea of going out to Brookline, but gave up the idea almost at once. Judge Ryder's niece was in enough trouble without making an appearance at the scene of Jason Loring's death.

Maybe the mysterious photograph was already in Rick's possession.

She collapsed onto the couch and held her face in her hands. Jason gone, just like that. His last words rang in her ears: *Better make it Donovan's Bar,* where they'd hung out and where they'd had a few laughs. She knew Jason had been self-serving and entirely too centered on himself, but he had cared about her and had talked about marriage more than once. He had been fun as long as she hadn't taken him seriously, and they had had some good times together.

Yet the sense of loss she should have felt was crowded out by something even more urgent. Jason was onto something, she was certain, and it could lead directly into the Ryder household.

She couldn't sit around speculating. She needed action. Then a thought came to her: the photographs at Windward. She had to see them. There was a commercial on the screen; Jason was dead, followed by a commercial. She switched off the television set and grabbed her bag. If there was any possibility that his photographs showed who had attended the party at Windward, Molly meant to have them. She could explain to Rick later.

OUTSIDE LYNN, MOLLY GLANCED at the illuminated dial on her car clock: 8:00 p.m. Five more miles, and she'd be at Windward.

She was still shaken by the news of Jason's death. Twice she had pulled over to the side of the road to sit quietly and collect herself. A bundle of what ifs racked her brain. If she had arrived right on time at Donovan's, maybe he would have been there. If she hadn't left the restaurant without calling Jason at home, maybe she would have found him in time. If she had made him tell her over the phone who was in the photograph... If, if, *if*. She couldn't get rid of the notion that what the police called suicide by asphyxiation was murder and that the mysterious photograph had something to do with it.

She read the road signs overhead, taking solace from the names of towns: Swampscott and Marblehead to the right, Salem to the left, farther north to Gloucester and Rockport and little Pigeon Cove on Cape Ann. But the litany of names didn't change anything. It was dark, she hadn't been able to get hold of Rick and she was headed for Windward without having told anyone where she was going. Traffic was heavy; more and more people were making the daily commute from the littoral above Boston, even from as far away as Cape Ann. There were always two or three cars trailing her, as she trailed others onto the Marblehead peninsula, which poked into the Atlantic.

Windward was located on Marblehead Neck, a projection from the larger peninsula, reached by a causeway. She drove along the wide, well-kept road, and the cars trailing her dropped back one by one. There was only a small sport model ahead of her, which at last disappeared around the curve as she pulled into the Windward driveway. The house, which was large, old and of weathered gray shingles, sat on a bluff overlooking the harbor and a clog of moored sailboats in the bay.

The key to the house was set into a specially built well above the terrace door at the rear. Once inside, she planned to call the local precinct to let the police know she was in the house. The Neck was patrolled assiduously, and the last thing Molly needed was a surprise attack by the local gendarmes. It wouldn't sit too well with her aunt and uncle.

The terrace door led into a comfortable, chintzy den that was decorated in the English style and scented with potpourri. Molly slid the glass door closed and was very careful about locking it behind her. She put the lights on immediately and dialed the station house.

Molly knew the policeman who answered, and he in turn recognized her voice. They had a quick, satisfactory conversation about why she was there and how long she would stay, which wouldn't get back to Serena or Willy.

She put the receiver down and was about to head into the library when she heard the scrape of a shoe on the terrace outside. She drew in a breath and stood stock-still. She hadn't heard a car drive up, so possibly a neighbor had come to see why the back light was on. She let out her breath, but something held her in check. There was another scraping sound and then some shuffling, as if someone were creeping instead of walking toward the door.

Her heart began a heavy drumming, and she could feel a line of sweat break out on her forehead. She was the biggest damn fool in the world, coming out to the house without telling anyone where she was going. Even if she called the police back, they wouldn't get there in time. Time for what? Someone had followed her all the way from Boston, she was certain. Her breath came in uneven gasps as she muttered a thin prayer and wondered what she might use as a weapon.

She was facing a large, square mirror that reflected the terrace through floor-to-ceiling glass doors. It took her a moment to focus on the figure standing just outside the doors. In spite of the mind-stopping fear that gripped her, Molly still registered the stranger with utter clarity. He was of medium height. He wore a well-tailored double-breasted suit with the collar pulled up, a hat that skimmed his eyebrows, and round, rimless eyeglasses. He bent his head as if gazing quizzically at her. Molly didn't dare turn and face him. Through the medium of the mirror, she saw and was mesmerized by the gun he held in his hand.

No answer, just a damned machine. Rick left a message for Molly that he'd called, and tried her apartment once again. Another machine. She was unable to come to the phone, please leave a message. He left a message.

On his desk was the late report of Jason Loring's death: no sign of a struggle. According to Loring's secretary, a photograph he had with him when he left his office to meet Molly Ryder was missing.

Murder, Rick told himself, although the report wasn't yet complete. Loring wasn't the kind to commit suicide in the middle of the most important story of his life. Suicide made no sense at all.

Loring, a bachelor who'd been divorced for a decade, had made enough enemies with his abrasive, hard-hitting reportorial style. It wasn't Loring's past, however, that had made him a target but the current investigation of corruption in high places. He'd been onto Halloway Construction and had passed some of the information to Molly. That put Molly in jeopardy, too. As far as Rick was concerned, the voice in that phone conversation with Perot was Loring's.

Rick picked up the telephone receiver and called Loring's secretary at home. The police had questioned her, but he wanted confirmation of the reporter's very last moments. He learned nothing new. The secretary had no idea whether her boss had caught up with Molly. He was running late at the time, she confirmed. And no, she had no idea what or who was in the photograph.

So Jason Loring had wanted to show Molly a photograph. The photograph was missing. Molly might have it, in which case she was marked, just like Loring. If she hadn't met Loring, however, once she learned he was dead, she'd head for Windward and a collection of photographs he'd left behind.

It took him twenty-five minutes to negotiate Boston streets and the artery that led north to Marblehead. Once he was through the Callahan Tunnel and on the other side of Boston Harbor, the gridlock eased up, although there was a stream of lights in both directions. He did some illegal weaving and managed to hit sixty and seventy for part of the trip, and it was a little after nine when he reached Marblehead Neck.

Rick was grateful that earlier that week he had driven out to Windward and fixed its location in his mind. To the left of the house was a small, thick copse of low-lying trees, planted either for privacy or to soften the landscape. Molly could be in danger, and he couldn't have afforded to waste time looking for the place.

Windward was set well back from the road, but it was still visible against a black sky. The half-moon had not fully risen above the copse, and through the trees it cast an eccentric pattern of white and black along the grass. The house itself was dark. Parked down the road was a sports car, probably a Jaguar. There was no one abroad, on foot or in cars. He knew the police made the rounds of the Neck every hour or so. In fact Rick had hoped to meet up with a patrol car as he came over the causeway, but was out of luck.

He parked the Camaro several houses back. A dog barked fitfully but gave up after a moment or two. A light went on briefly at someone's front door; a curtain was pulled aside and then dropped. The light was turned off. Rick picked up his wide-beam flashlight and hiked up the rise to the house at an angle. He kept far to the left of the path. No use announcing himself. His urge was to rush to the house and grab Molly, yet some intuition sensed trouble and he held back.

Molly's car was in the driveway. Until the time of her arrival, then, she hadn't been particularly worried. He touched the hood; the engine was still warm.

The front door was ajar. No sound came from within. He remained in the dark, listening. An overpowering sense of dread infused every nerve in his body. His heart beat erratically. If he was too late, if they had reached Molly.... He couldn't finish the thought. Distant noises took on specific meanings. A car honked somewhere. A boat engine started up, then fizzled to silence. Laughter floated up from the harbor along with the plop, which sounded uncannily close, of something in the water. A dog yipped and stopped. He forced himself to concentrate. Molly was nearby—every fiber of his being told him that—but something else also; an unseen danger so close that he could almost touch it.

Rick stepped through the doorway and sensed at once that the house was empty. He made a quick, silent tour of the rooms, using his flashlight in spurts. Nothing and no one, merely the car in the driveway and the open door to show that Molly had come to Windward. Back outside, he circled the house and found the terrace door locked. There was a smell of fear in the air—real, palpable fear. Dammit, where the devil was she?

Then he heard a sound coming from the copse, a scuffling of dried leaves underfoot. The thicket fronted a broad open space, which he'd have to traverse.

Rick's mind had never been clearer. There was too much at stake. He knew something now with a certainty: Molly Ryder meant more to him than he had been willing to admit. Anger rode in on the edge of fear, a fury aimed at whoever was putting her in danger.

He stood listening, and again the sounds of the world intruded. Rick wound his way around the house and back to the street. There was a house across the road from Windward, perhaps a hundred yards away, with a light shining in the window. Had Molly gone running there? The silence was too complete, however.

Rick could have summoned the police, if he had wanted to waste precious time. He opted for wading right in and went quickly, silently, along the road until he was opposite the copse. Then he climbed up the grass, treading with all the stealth he could manage. An acre of forest had never looked more menacing.

Just as he moved inside the fringe of trees, something hard poked his back and a hand was clamped over his mouth. Damn, was he born yesterday? He'd done everything wrong and by his stupidity had put Molly in the most mortal danger. He felt the blood racing through his veins and knew that he had to make the next few seconds count. For a moment he stood rigid, trying to determine what moves he had left.

Molly's perfume, a friendly floral scent, sent relief pouring over him.

"Rick, please don't say anything." Her voice was uncannily soft and clear. He felt his heart leap. He turned and gathered her in his arms, but she put her finger to her lips and held up the rock she had prodded him with. "There he is," she whispered, pointing to a figure backlit by the moon and advancing rapidly into the trees.

"Stay here," Rick said, unceremoniously pushing her to the safety of a thick-limbed maple. "Don't move."

"No way."

Rick crouched low, aware of Molly close at his heels. He gripped the flashlight but kept it off, using the light cast by the moon to make his way. He caught the outline of his quarry against a tree trunk and motioned Molly to stop. When the intruder was directly opposite and Rick was certain he could catch him off guard, he turned on the flash. Caught in a yellow circle of light was a man disguised by a hat tipped low over his eyes and a jacket collar pulled up to his chin. Yet something about the man, the way he stood or moved, or maybe the rimless glasses, struck Rick as oddly familiar, although he couldn't say why. The thought was lost almost at once as the stranger's hand came up, gripping a .38 pointed straight at Rick.

"I've a gun in my hand tells you to drop it," Rick said.

The stranger's laugh was abrupt and had a rough, nasty edge to it. "I'll call you on that one, Mac."

"I said, drop it."

Molly gave Rick a warning touch, then hefted the rock she was holding and lobbed it straight at the gun. It fell short. Rick quickly switched off the flashlight, diving to the ground and pulling Molly with him. "Not too clever," he told her as the gun went off. The bullet flashed wide of its mark, but the sound ricocheted off the trees and brought every dog in the neighborhood awake. They lay listening to the sound of footsteps tearing through the underbrush, then a clatter along the road and at last a car door slamming as lights went on all around them and voices called out.

"Not so clever," Molly remarked, "but expedient." She took his face between her hands and kissed his mouth ardently.

With Molly in his arms, Rick decided reaming her out could wait a while, but when a dog came loping up the lawn, barking, he pulled her to her feet. "Come on, that Doberman looks hungry."

"Her name is Lady and she's a noisy pussycat."

It was only when they were back in the house that Rick allowed himself to express his real anger. "So far you've done everything you could to get a bullet through your head. What happened?"

"Just now? Or before you arrived?" She led the way into the library and began checking the bookshelves for the photographs.

"I know about *just now*. Begin at the beginning."

"I suppose you know that Jason's dead."

"I know about him. I know he had a date with you. Did you meet him?"

"No. He never showed up. That's why I figured on coming out here—" She stopped. "I called you, Rick. If you want me to keep in touch with you, you'd better leave a forwarding number."

"Loring's secretary said he had a photograph he was going to show to you."

"When I heard he was dead, I came running out here to pick up the ones he left in the library." Molly turned to Rick and shrugged. "Not here. Now, what do you suppose?"

"What about our friend with the .38?"

"He was outside the terrace door. He scared the hell out of me. I bolted out of the den, through the front door and into the grape arbor at the side of the house. The trouble was, I couldn't get to my car without being seen."

"Never thought of your neighbors?"

"He was holding a gun, Rick. I expected the police to come by on their rounds momentarily. I figured all I'd have to do was run out into the street and hail them the minute I saw them. That make sense?"

"No. Who was he, Molly?"

"I don't know." She turned back to her search. "I don't know if he's the one who fired at me on Monday. Come on, I can't afford to speculate. Let's find the photographs." But a quick inspection of the library, including her uncle's desk, yielded nothing.

"We can search the whole house," Molly said.

" 'Search the whole house'?" The voice that spoke to them from the open door to the library was the warm, deep one belonging to her uncle. Behind him was a stocky, smiling man whose name Molly felt she should know but couldn't recall. One thing was certain—he had been at Windward on the day of the taping. And one thing more— she drew in a quick breath—he was one of the people who had participated in the game of football with her tape recorder. He knew the machine had been on in the library— like her uncle, like Serena, Jason Loring, the others Jason had named.

"Search the whole house for what?" her uncle asked once again.

"We were just leaving," she told him hastily to cover her confusion. "Then I thought I heard a noise, but thank goodness it was you."

Her uncle relaxed visibly. She could see he was trying to work out why she and Rick were at Windward, but with his usual discretion, wouldn't ask. He'd figure it out soon enough, at least to his own satisfaction. Implicit in her being there with Rick was that they had come to Windward to be alone. She could almost hear her uncle laughing with Serena over how he had burst in upon them.

"I admit I was a little put off when I saw the lights from the road," her uncle said. He looked briefly around the library. "But then, of course, I found your car in the driveway." He advanced into the room, his eye on Rick although his words were for his companion.

"Elliott, you know my niece," he remarked in an offhand manner, while the color rising to his face revealed something far different. Disapproval.

Elliott Lawrence grasped Molly's hand in a warm manner. "Good to see you again," he said affably. "The last time we were together, your tape recorder was being tossed around the terrace like a football.''

"I know," Molly said, glancing quickly at Rick, surprised that he was frowning. "I was really upset. Oh," she added, "my uncle, Judge Ryder, and Mr. Lawrence. This is Rick Boulter."

"Judge," Rick said, extending a hand, "we've met, although I'm afraid you won't remember."

"Oh, I remember all right," her uncle said. He then referred to a case that had come up before him in the state supreme court. It had covered the indictment of city officials, he reminded Rick, who had been one of the prosecutors.

Elliott Lawrence, after shaking Rick's hand, busied himself at the bookshelf, examining some of her uncle's law books.

Molly, standing to one side, saw that her uncle, with a simple remark, had won part of the battle for himself. Rick was caught off guard by the charming Judge Ryder. She smiled but only for the briefest moment. Her uncle was examining Rick with piercing, intelligent eyes. There was no doubt Molly's words had struck him as odd. *We can search the whole house.* She tried frantically to work up an excuse for being at Windward in the first place, during the week and at this time of night. She came up with a complete blank. She was aware of an unexpected and awkward silence in the room.

It wasn't like her uncle to string anyone up as he was treating Rick, who didn't help by at last making an inane comment about Marblehead Neck and the view. Not a half hour before, Molly had escaped being trapped by a stranger carrying a .38, and now they were equally trapped, but this time by her uncle.

"I've been telling Rick about Windward," she said, "and we were out at the shore having lobster and on a whim we decided to drive up."

Elliott Lawrence pulled down a book and began leafing through it.

"Well," her uncle said in his practical voice, "anyone want a drink? It's chilled up a bit outside. A glass of sherry all around?"

Rick, for his part, seemed to give no thought to the judge's offer. He was regarding Elliott Lawrence with a thoughtful air. "Construction workers," he said. "Mr. Lawrence, now I know where I've seen your name."

Lawrence looked up from the book, slapped it shut and then gave Rick a broad smile. "You got it."

Her uncle turned to Lawrence and said, "El, where did you say you left your briefcase?"

"Living-room chair?" Lawrence's response was more a question than a statement. He stepped across the hall into the darkened living room.

"Elliott and I drove down tonight to look over the Marches property. He's thinking of buying it," the judge said offhandedly. "We dropped by so I could make a phone call or two."

"Is it for sale?" Molly asked. "The Marches property? I didn't even know." Her mind was working on another level, however. Could he have seen the photographs and taken them? She had no way of knowing and no way of asking.

Lawrence came back into the room, waving his brief-case. "Right where I left it."

The strain in the air was all but visible. Whatever happened, she'd have to play her part to the hilt; she had come to Windward to be alone with Rick and now, discovered by her uncle, had to turn around and go back to Boston. She kissed her uncle on the cheek. "It's getting late. See you later."

Molly hoped the judge hadn't discovered that she and Rick had arrived in separate cars. Rick agreed to make a show of their leaving together in Molly's car, and they were about to drive away when her uncle came to the front door and called out to her.

"Molly, about the batch of photographs in the library."

She exchanged a quick glance with Rick. "Yes," she called back, "what about them?"

"Do you want them here or in the city?"

"I'm glad you reminded me. I'll take them back."

"Well, never mind," the judge said. "I've already got them in my jacket pocket. I'll bring them home."

Molly exchanged another look at Rick. He shrugged. "Okay," she called, "see you back in Boston." She sank back in her seat, laughing. "Well, that's the first funny thing that's happened all day."

Rick drove her car to his, which was parked four houses down the road, but when he was about to get out, Molly said, "Rick, I know what you're thinking, and I don't mean about the photographs."

"You don't know what I'm thinking."

"About the company my uncle keeps."

"Perfectly respectable union chief, Elliott Lawrence," he said, not deigning to hide the sarcasm in his voice. "Men make good pay, have good benefits and come in under budget."

"He was on the terrace when I announced that my tape had run out," Molly said. "Whether his was the voice on the tape or not, however, I can't say."

"I can," Rick said quietly. "It was, and I'd stake my life on that."

Chapter Nine

The man squinted, rubbing a hand over his chin, as he examined his face in the mirror. He didn't pay attention to his face very often. Plastic mirror, plastic furniture and a broad who gave him a headache every time he looked at her. There was something about being here, where he didn't want to be, that forced him to look at himself. He picked up his cigarette and took in a searing drag.

An ordinary face with a thin, determined mouth, brown hair that had once been red, gray, myopic eyes he supposed they'd call small. Not close together, just small, an inheritance from his mother's side, like the once-red hair. He stared at his reflection for a few seconds longer. His was a face that melted into the crowd.

He heard the woman in the other room moan softly and call his name. Damn her, he couldn't wait to be rid of her. She was just foolish enough to get him into trouble. Unfortunately, he still needed her.

"Just a minute," he called, trying to hide his irritation. He'd have to be careful and not rouse her suspicions. She was the one who insisted on out-of-the-way hotels, meetings in strange places, as if she were living a romantic fantasy.

Well, he promised himself, her turn would come soon, too, just like the others who got in his way—the cop poking around where he wasn't supposed to be, Loring with a photograph that shouldn't have been in his possession.

Molly Ryder, she would come next. He didn't trust her, not like the others did. Lay off, they'd told him; she knew nothing. If she knew anything, the D.A. would know it, too. Like hell she knew nothing. Molly Ryder could still identify him. She'd bumped into him outside her uncle's library. Maybe she knew who he was, maybe she didn't. It certainly didn't pay to ask.

He was through waiting for the ax to fall. She'd heard the tape, he was certain of it. It nagged at him that Molly Ryder had heard the tape. With her ear for voices, she could probably identify him on a whisper. It was no skin off his nose if she died, and the ways of handling the job could be almost poetic. Caution was necessary this time around, however, to catch her when she least expected it.

The woman called his name again, drawing it out slowly. Might as well get his money's worth. The room was paid for until eleven. He went to the bedroom door and gazed over at her. She had the covers drawn up and tucked around her breasts. She gave him her sexy, wide-eyed stare, inviting, promising.

"I heard you," he said in his raspy wheeze. He came slowly over to the bed. He hated owing favors, hated debts accumulating. When he put his hands on her shoulders, he had to fight hard not to place them around her throat. Well, he'd make her work for it this time. He reached over and turned off the light. In the dark she wouldn't notice his anger. In the dark he could imagine she was Molly Ryder and that he had her in his grip and could do anything he wanted to.

"Oh, you great big, wonderful man," she said in that baby voice she affected. "You're so strong. I'm really afraid of you."

He grabbed her then and pinned her to the bed.

HAD THE SEMESTER REALLY ENDED, just like that, not with a bang but a whisper?

Molly put her suitcase down and stood squarely in the middle of her living room, surveying all that had once been so familiar and was now alien. The apartment was scrubbed clean and the offending rug removed. But that wasn't nearly enough. She would have to come to terms with what had happened and her part in it if she ever wanted to call the apartment home again.

Then, too, Molly had an uneasy feeling of having run out on her career, of gifted students not having been given the last-minute succor they needed to get them through the summer, of everything suddenly gone, with no advance warning.

Even the photographs she had risked her life for were of no use at all. She had gone over them with Serena and Willy. Jason had photographed Molly a dozen times that day, on the boat, on the beach, and mingling with the Ryder guests at lunch on the terrace. The focus was on Molly, the others blurred or out of range. She had not imagined Jason could be so sentimental.

While she was standing there, uncertain about what she wanted to do, the telephone suddenly rang. Molly jumped. Only her aunt and uncle and Rick knew she had come back. Molly let the phone ring two more times before going over to her desk and reaching for the receiver. Her imagination was working overtime. It took an act of faith to remember that she was safe. The tape no longer existed. She knew nothing.

"Molly." It was Rick. A feeling of relief swept through her at the sound of his voice. "You all right?"

"Of course I'm all right."

"I tried to get you earlier."

"I had a pile of work to do and then the head of my department threw a small, spontaneous bash in her office. Obliged to attend and all that, but I sneaked out. I felt too many questions about my dissertation coming on. Rick, my life is in a shambles. What am I going to do? No leads on the murderer, no leads on my…lost…cassettes—" She stopped, swallowed and stared unbelieving at her desk, at the dozen familiar cassettes set neatly between her Art Deco bookends.

She heard Rick's urgent voice. "Molly, what's going on? Don't hang up."

Gingerly she picked up a cassette. "Just a minute, my tapes…" The label was still affixed and referred in her own handwriting to a recording she'd made that past August at a Red Sox game. Had it been erased? Had they all been erased?

"Look," she said to Rick, as she touched each cassette, one after the other, "I think they're all here. Let me call you back. I'd better play them. I can't think for the moment."

"Molly, are you talking about the cassettes that were lifted from your apartment?"

"Yes. They're all here. I can't believe it," she crowed. "I can't believe it."

"Molly, listen to me, don't touch them, don't play them. I'll be over as soon as I get hold of the police."

But she wasn't listening. "They're all here. Fantastic! Don't worry about a thing." She put down the receiver and with a cassette in her hand went over to her tape deck. Surely they hadn't been erased. No one could be that cruel. It was only when she was slipping the first cassette into the deck that Molly stopped, suddenly frozen to the spot. There was no need to check them, no need at all. Her dissertation material was perfectly safe, and she knew exactly why.

When the intercom rang, Molly was sitting on the couch, legs tucked under her, an untouched glass of white wine on the cocktail table before her. Letting Rick in, she said dully, "It's all right, I haven't tried them."

"You know what this means, don't you?"

"Yes." The word came out in the form of a deep, torn breath.

"Very foolish of him," Rick said.

"Go ahead, dust them for fingerprints." She was angry with the world, with Rick, with her uncle for caring so deeply about her that he'd risk everything to see that she finished her doctoral dissertation.

"As a matter of fact, we're going to have to," Rick told her. He checked the door lock, but it showed no signs of having been jimmied. "How did you get in?"

"It was double locked. I didn't even stop to think . . ."

"You just opened the door and walked in. Nothing strange about the place?"

"I'm minus a rug and there was a smell of disinfectant and ammonia. I wasn't looking for forced entry."

Rick went past Molly to the terrace door. "If they came in this way, you wouldn't know it." He checked the apartment windows, all duly locked. "Who has a key to the place?"

"Someone picked the door lock," Molly said, unable to believe the sound of her own words, "and was very careful about letting himself in and out."

"I've called the police and told them to send a search team, Molly."

"Another sign across my door telling the world this is the scene of a crime?"

Rick pulled a key chain out of his pocket. "Here, the keys to my domain. You know I don't want you here alone." He pressed the keys into her hand. "Don't say no, Molly."

"I won't say anything, Rick—not yes, not no. The crime is being reversed," she said, trying desperately to find a funny side. "Next I'll come in and there will be Sergeant Klein waiting to talk to me. Or I'll wake up soon and discover it's all been a bad movie I fell asleep over."

"It isn't a movie, Molly."

"It qualifies as a meganightmare, I'm afraid."

"Listen," he said, putting his arm around her and placing his cheek against her hair, "even I don't want you jumping the gun about who's innocent and who's guilty. Ten to one your landlady took the cassettes from some little kid paid to deliver them and arranged them on your desk for you."

"I'll go ask her."

"Let's leave the detecting to the detectives."

"Are you telling that to me, after the way we took my aunt's office apart?" Molly shook her head. "Okay, okay, it was the best way to handle it. I wouldn't have wanted the police swarming all over her property. The end of the semester came today," Molly added, as if that explained her mood. "Sort of snuck up on me. I keep thinking I shortchanged a couple of my brightest students. I'm going to have to make a few phone calls and talk to them somewhere along the line. The trouble is, I feel so played out. Rick, this doesn't necessarily lead to my uncle's door, does it?"

He gazed at her for a long moment. "You tell me."

The intercom rang and Molly let in the search team from headquarters. "You're not going to take the tapes, are you?" Molly asked them anxiously.

Rick managed a laugh. "They won't, but at the rate things are going, your dissertation material would be safer at police headquarters than here. Come on, we could use something to drink." He took her arm and drew her firmly into her tiny kitchen. "Your neighbors will have to be asked a few questions, too," Rick said. "If they heard anything, noticed anyone."

Molly groaned. "I'm going to be persona non grata around here if this happens one more time."

"You have the cassettes back. Count your blessings."

"I'm counting them. My blessings come in at minus one." From the kitchen door she could see the search team setting up equipment. "I suppose my tapes could have been returned as soon as the apartment was released from being the scene of a crime," Molly said. "That was on Wednesday, wasn't it?"

"Wednesday."

"Which meant Wednesday night, Thursday, or some time today."

"We'll find out."

"Actually I'd bet on my landlady handing a package to my cleaning lady, who couldn't resist opening it. She found the tapes and put them in place. That sounds absolutely right. My uncle needn't have had anything to do with it."

"Someone wanted you to have them back. Incidentally, we've heard from the French police," Rick told her. "So far no one answering to Daniel Halloway's description has been spotted anywhere in the south of France."

"He could have changed his mind and gone somewhere else. South America is big enough to get lost in."

"Once I'd heard from France, I called up Gent Perot's office and asked for an appointment. He has plenty to answer for concerning his erstwhile partner. Mr. Perot, I was informed, is out of town."

"My aunt reminded me about the party she's giving tomorrow night. Gent should be there with his wife. If you come with me, you can talk to him."

"You couldn't keep me away."

"You can engage Perot in party conversation," Molly said with unexpected enthusiasm, "and add a couple of *incidentally*'s, such as 'Incidentally, I went to school with Dan Halloway, and I've been trying to get in touch with him.'"

"Smooth," he told her. "You should join the D.A.'s office. Halloway is about twenty years older than I am."

"You'll think of something. And speaking of incidentally, incidentally I expect you to behave yourself. No marching my uncle off in handcuffs."

"I always behave myself."

They could hear voices from the living room, so Molly resisted the temptation to put her arms around him and hold him close. "Sometimes," she said, slowly, her eyes locked with his, "I wish you wouldn't—behave yourself, that is."

Later, when the search team had gone, Rick opened the doors to the patio and went outside. The garden beyond was a tiny attractive square bordered by evergreen bushes and centering on a dolphin-topped fountain. To the left were clay pots that held ivy, and a couple of wrought-iron chairs set at a small glass-topped table. It was surrounded by the fenced-in gardens of other town houses, and the friendly quiet of lives going on behind lighted windows. Rick understood why, even with all she had gone through, Molly couldn't resist returning. His own apartment, a sublet, was merely a pad he dropped into and escaped as soon as he could.

The sky was cloudy, the moon showing through an occasional rent in the clouds. "Rain tonight," he said to Molly when she came out and joined him.

"We could use some."

He put his arm around her and for a while they stood there silently, side by side, taking in the sounds of the city and the living that was going on around them.

He kissed her then, as if every care in the world would be washed away by the expected rain. And this time there was no hesitancy on her part. Her arms went about him, pressing him close, and her breath was sweet against his mouth. He parted her lips, wanting, with a desperation that surprised him, to have her surrender totally, to give in to what they both knew would happen inevitably.

Rick had heard of other men in his position becoming involved with the woman in a case but had avoided that pitfall. And now, in spite of the cool resolve that had always been his guiding principle, he found himself drowning in those brown eyes. His blood was running so high, he could barely contain himself. He wanted never to give up tasting her mouth and marveling at the touch of her skin. Desire for her invaded every nerve and muscle in his body. He'd have one hell of a time explaining it to himself one day.

He pulled her greedily closer, excising every doubt from his mind. He could feel the tension in her body, but the only thought in his mind was to tear down her resistance, to convince her that the only reality was his body and hers. He put his hand on her breast, cradling it as his lips found the soft flesh of her throat. He heard her soft, purring gasp and an intake of breath.

But then with a great effort she pulled back and, holding him at arm's length, searched his face. "It's time for you to go, Rick.'' There was a catch in her voice. "I can't handle anything else right now."

"Molly," he began softly, but when he saw the seriousness of her expression, he relinquished her. "You're right. I'd better leave." When he reached the front door, he said without looking back, "Lock up after me and don't open the door for anyone." He turned. She was standing just inside the terrace door. "You'll hear from me more often than you want."

"I'm not afraid of staying here alone."

"Molly, I have to call you. Do you understand?"

She nodded and Rick felt a sudden unfamiliar yet oddly recognizable rush of emotion, which he knew she read in his eyes.

THE NEXT MORNING RICK FOUND Molly at her office on campus and dragged her out to his Camaro. "School's over," he informed her and insisted that Saturday belonged to him.

To Molly it felt good to be taken in hand, although she wondered idly when the subject of her aunt and uncle would come up again and that dreaded list of names. It was only a matter of time, she supposed.

"I can hear the wheels grinding," Rick said. "And I'm not talking about the car. We're putting the pressure you're feeling on hold, Molly. It's Saturday, time for a little fun."

"Do you think the man who's following us will enjoy himself?"

"What?" Rick swerved the car into the curb and applied the brakes so quickly that they drew rubber. He cut the engine and with a swift movement closed his fingers tightly around her arms. "Try not to do that again, Molly."

"I'm sorry, figure of speech, Counselor. I can't imagine he's given up, that's all. I feel that whoever he is, he's hovering on the edges, someone who's been close but who manages to disguise himself as Everyman. A voice on a tape I haven't even heard, a hand out of a window holding a .38, a man calling himself T. Marin. I don't know who he is: I can't identify him, yet he's worried about me and I know he's lingering just out of sight. My dark companion. He's there. I can sense the gravitational pull, but there are so many other objects in the way, I can't make him out.''

Rick released her and leaned back against his seat. "What the hell are you keeping from me?"

"Nothing, just a feeling I woke up with that it won't be over until it's over. Stupid, I know.'' Molly pasted on a smile that she didn't feel, yet she was surprised and deeply touched by his reaction. It couldn't be easy for Rick to worry about her on a personal level, knowing that the success of S.N.A.R.E. might be built on the ashes of her uncle. "Rick, I'm sorry," she said softly, placing her hand on his arm. "It's nothing." They shared a long look and then Rick turned away and started up, easing into traffic, his profile set and determined.

"Hey, lighten up," she said. "I hate it when the law is nervous, too.''

He laughed. "You're right, the law is worried about your health.''

"Maybe you're in the wrong business. You're supposed to be dispassionate, aren't you?''

"I think the word reads passionate.''

"Really? I suppose that was your favorite course—Passionate 101. Did you always want to be assistant D.A.?''

"No, I fell into it.''

"Like into a vat of melted butter?'' The moment of tension was over, although nothing was really settled.

"No, took a little time to make up my mind about going into the good-guys/bad-guys business. After getting my law degree, I bummed around for a year, trying to delay being serious," he went on. "Some time-out for skiing in Colorado, and then I made my way to California with a rock group, in charge of lighting."

"In charge of lighting?" Molly burst in. "What's that?"

"Just what I said. Actually I was in charge of lighting and amplification. The group split up in San Francisco, and I made my way down to Los Angeles. I was tending bar in a little joint off Cucamonga when a fellow poked a very big rod under my nose, which reminded me when I came to my senses minus the day's receipts that I had taken my law degree with the idea of working in the justice system. Came back to Boston, and the rest is history."

"How come you weren't enticed by one of the big law firms?"

"Not exciting enough, Molly. I wanted the Sturm und Drang of criminal prosecution. Of course I was young and innocent then. The idea of being a prosecutor seemed—" he paused and said, smiling "—romantic."

"Is it?"

He turned his attention to the road. "Right now, I'd say yes."

Molly laughed, and with a sudden desire to know him better sat seriously studying his profile. The sun, streaming in through the car window, highlighted the planes of his face and picked out golden threads in his hair. Some tiny spark she'd been nurturing since she met him darted around, refusing to disappear. She liked what she saw in Rick Boulter. He was casual on the surface, but with an easy, self-confident power not at all disguised by the cut of his tweed jacket and dark turtleneck sweater. She wondered if this was his "Trust me, I'm your friend" attire, a contrast to the usual buttoned-down look of the D.A.'s office, meant to send shivers down the spines of suspects.

"If I might draw your attention away from examining me," he said, "I'd like to point out the sight on our left. What we have here," he went on in a nasal voice, "is Boston Common, the oldest park in the contiguous forty-eight, not to mention Alaska and Hawaii. It's also the most famous common of them all, at least on this side of the Atlantic."

"Charming spiel. Well done," Molly said, applauding the information that had been fed to her as a child along with her morning cereal. "You don't miss a thing, do you?"

"I wouldn't be much good in front of a jury, if I did. The fact is, I had a job on a tour bus one summer. This is where we get out." He pulled into a No Parking zone and turned down the visor, carefully straightening his identification card with an exaggerated gesture.

"I hope they tow your car away," Molly said, once they were out and the doors locked. "It's people like you who make the whole parking business a sham."

"Somehow I fail to be moved by your tears." He came around and looped his arm through hers.

It seemed as if everyone in Boston was on the Common, either wandering along its paths or sitting on the lawn. Through the trees just bearing the first hints of pale green the sun zigzagged a patchwork of light.

"Tell me," Rick said, draping his arm across her shoulders, "apropos of everything, how come a lady like you is running around free?"

"Mind sending that through again?" she asked, although she understood exactly what he meant and was hoping he didn't mean it.

"With your looks, smarts and connections, you should've been lassoed a long time ago."

"'Lassoed.' What a male chauvinist remark," she declared hotly. "It's okay for you to be single and in your thirties, but for me to be fancy about being free is a puzzlement."

"And one I'm grateful for," Rick said. "Call me anything you like, but I still can't figure out why all the men in Boston aren't beating a path to your front door."

"Maybe they are. Following me in the black of night, too, and also showing up dead on my living-room carpet. Not to mention the nasty phone call from someone calling himself T. Marin. Oh, and the gunshot just to get my attention. Really, Rick, the truth of the matter is I'm the most popular female in Boston and heartily tired of it."

He drew her off the path and offered her a patch of grass spotlighted by the sun. "Have a seat and try not to get hot under the collar. I'm searching for a compliment that'll suit you."

"Oh, damn, I'm sorry," she said, "I'm talking about things that aren't funny." She sat on the grass, drawing her legs up and hugging her knees. It had rained the night before, but because of the prolonged dry spell the rain had soaked through leaving the ground dry. Rick joined her, sitting opposite, so that the tips of his shoes touched the tips of hers.

"It's reasonably easy to meet men in the sort of work I do," Molly said, "but frankly, I haven't the time or the temperament for casual relationships." She gave up when she found him grinning at her. "Oh, great, I walked right into your little trap."

"I got the answer I wanted."

"Called leading the witness, isn't it?"

He looked at her seriously and then reached out and drew his finger down her cheek. "Leading the witness. Now, why do you suppose I did that?"

She grasped his wrist, resting her face for a moment against his open palm. "I've been singularly unforthcoming about what makes me tick."

"And singularly dense about how interested in you I am. I just wanted to make certain you weren't taken."

She felt the heat rise to her face. "Rick," she began, "this is a vulnerable time for me. It's not..." She stopped and let out a breath. What in the world were they going on about? They'd known each other for less than a week, and her practical nature had kept her clear of sudden moves, sudden attractions. She couldn't afford to change the way she was—not now when her life might be turned upside down forever.

"Molly, look, I only needed to know one thing and now I know it. There's one other: I'm separating you from your family; I want that understood between us."

She turned her head away and scanned the crowd, picking out a lone figure near a huge beech tree, wondering if that were he, the stranger who held her life in his hands. But then he waved at a woman and went toward her with his arms outstretched. She turned to Rick, knowing he had watched her all the while. "I'm not certain I can live with your way of seeing things," she declared firmly. She realized that she was still holding on to his wrist and drew her hand away, staring down at her open palm.

"Molly," he said, "I'm beginning to feel things for you."

"No." Her response was sharp, telling him that the discussion was closed.

"All right. I understand." He sprang to his feet and then pulled her up. "Come on, I'm buying you lunch, and something tells Poppa that you're a cranky little girl when you're hungry." He put his arm around her and drew her close. She was aware of the crowds around them on the grass, aware of being watched curiously but in good fun. It was possible that one of her students was there or a member of the college faculty. Rick's mouth was close to hers, and all of sudden she threw caution to the winds and placed her lips hard against his.

"No, no, no," she murmured, not taking her lips away. "You stay on your side of the fence, Mr. Assistant D.A., and I'll stay on mine." She put her arms around his neck and heard a whistle, long, sexy and low, from several feet away.

"Attagirl," someone called. "That's telling him."

"Kiss, kiss. Love, love," someone else shouted.

She allowed the kiss to linger, feeling a faint shudder race through him that quickly sent a spark through her. She pulled away and took Rick's hand and drew him along to delighted laughter and scattered applause.

"I like your openers," he said when they reached the path. "I was going to suggest lunch at Quincy Market, but I know a spot in Beacon Hill where we can finish what you started."

"Quincy Market," she said firmly, wondering what in the world had gotten into her, but not at all sorry.

AT THE QUINCY MARKET COMPLEX near the harbor, Rick suggested they have lunch in an airy, pleasant restaurant that specialized in northern Italian cuisine.

They found a table near a window with a view of the interior arcade below. The day was a particularly warm one. There was a general air of celebration in the crowds sauntering among stalls retailing everything from candy to candles. Of course, Molly told herself, it was a time for celebration, a time for timpani and trumpets: school was out. And she was on the edge of falling in love.

"How about a glass of wine?" Rick asked. "And I recommend the pasta *primavera*. It'll take them an hour to prepare, but it's worth the wait."

"Spring pasta, wonderful." She smiled, with a heartfelt sigh intermixed, wondering whether the weight she carried around with her would ever be lifted so that she could enjoy herself totally, without guilt or reservation.

"What are you thinking about, Molly? I'd call that smile wistful, not wholehearted. What's up?"

"I was supposed to meet Jason Loring over at Donovan's," she said, nodding in the direction of Faneuil Hall, "the day he was killed, remember?"

Rick laid his hand over hers. "You don't think you had anything to do with his death, do you?"

She shrugged. "He wanted to show me a photograph. The photograph wasn't found with him when he died."

"He was working on a tough story about corruption in high places. He might have touched the wrong button, Molly. Nothing to do with you."

"He liked mystery too much. If only he'd told me the name of the person in the photograph. He said he'd discovered it in the station files."

"Forget it," Rick said. "The station archives contain a ton of photos of every celebrity in town and some not so celebrated. How well did you know Loring?"

"We saw enough of each other. I met him when he came to the apartment to interview my uncle for one of his programs. That was maybe a year ago."

"You hung around together?"

"We saw each other from time to time," she said. "He was one of those people who carry around a sense of duty twenty-four hours a day. There was no way you could take Jason Loring in large doses."

The waiter came by, and while Rick ordered lunch for them, Molly stared idly down at the crowd winding in and out of the arcade stalls. She had all but forgotten her fears, but suddenly she drew in a sharp breath.

Rick caught it at once. "What's up?"

"That man down there, the one with the cap pulled across his forehead near the candy stall."

"What about him?"

"I caught him looking up here."

Rick took her hand. "Hey, don't go getting paranoid on me."

"It's not paranoia. I caught him watching me and he quickly pulled his hat over his eyes and turned away."

"He can't be difficult to tail, if that's what you want."

"No, he's leaving." In a moment the stranger had stepped below the balcony overhang and was out of sight. "But I'm not paranoid," Molly repeated. "Why did he turn away when he caught me looking at him? Rick, did you see his face?"

"No, only his back. Molly, has it occurred to you that you're uncommonly pretty and that he was admiring you? Did he look familiar?"

"I don't know. There was something about him and the way he gazed up at me, as if he'd just caught me and was about to stick me to a piece of velvet with a very large hat-pin. There was just… Oh, I don't know." She stopped and looked helplessly at Rick. "Maybe it was the way he moved. Forget it."

Their wine arrived and a basket of crisp, freshly baked bread. "I'm afraid we're going to have to," Rick said. "Forget it, I mean. Whoever he is, he knows you saw him." He handed Molly her glass and then raised his own. "Not planning on leaving these shores for the summer, are you?"

"Not with a dissertation breathing down my neck."

"Then here's to a lot more lunches, Molly." He smiled and touched his glass to hers.

But something had intruded, and after lunch, when they went down to the arcade, Molly found herself searching the crowd for the man in the cap. He was nowhere in sight, but she was still uneasy, as if he were just beyond them, watching and waiting.

"Do you see him?" Rick asked as they went through the exit to the square.

Molly shook her head. "No," she said, "and maybe that's what worries me most of all."

Chapter Ten

"Look again," Rick said.

"He changed his cap. He took the cap off. He's wearing a wig or a mustache. I don't know, I just feel extraordinarily uneasy," Molly told him. "Rick, you haven't even nagged me about that famous list. How come?"

Rick took her arm and directed her out into the sunlit square. "It's Saturday. Crime is taking a holiday. Where did I leave that car?"

On the road, Rick began moving northwest.

"Where to?" Molly asked.

"Beacon Hill."

"A tour of old Boston?"

"Better. A tour of my apartment," Rick said.

"Your apartment? Are we talking Beacon Hill?"

"Why do I have the feeling you're surprised?"

"Well," Molly said, flustered, "you never told me. I mean," she added after a moment, "I thought you lived in one of those reconverted Wharf condos overlooking the harbor, something like that."

"You mean, how does an assistant D.A. rate an apartment in Beacon Hill? I can see the lights flashing, Molly. 'Payoff,' they say so clearly that I can see them a mile away. I'm on a sublease. Sorry to disappoint you."

"Payoff? Farthest thing from my mind. I just realized how close you were to the Back Bay and Arlington Street all that time I stayed with Serena and Willy."

"I knew," he said quietly. "And that was enough."

Molly was silent for a moment. Is that what the day had been leading to all along, his taking her to his apartment? She realized she hadn't the slightest desire to challenge him. More than that, the thought of seeing how Rick Boulter lived was enticing.

The street he drew up in was old and cobblestoned, with a mixture of nineteenth-century buildings shaded by trees in fresh leaf. A brass plaque on the front of the red-brick building read 1825. "Third floor," he told her. "Mine for the next six months. After that I'm on my own again."

When he opened the door to his apartment, Rick was glad Saturday morning was the maid's time. The truth was, he wasn't home enough to rough the place up and his life would have been on the line if he had.

In fact, he hardly entertained there, and the last time he'd had a woman to the apartment had been weeks before. He couldn't even remember her name. Ushering Molly in, he reflected that the place wore an air of eat-and-run. He hadn't noticed it until now. Someday soon he'd have to get his life in order.

A wide foyer led to a spacious white living room. There were no curtains on the window, which drew in the changing colors of the sky and the stately buildings across the way. Beyond was a partially obstructed view of the Charles River.

Several museum posters hung on the walls; the couch was linen-covered and comfortable; the oak floor was highly polished, with a small flokati rug in the center. The only signs of human habitation were contained in some papers on the coffee table, which Rick had been working on the night before.

"Nice," Molly said warmly, as he helped her off with her jacket.

"Thanks. The papers are mine and some of the books. Outside of that, you can send your congratulations to the owner in Mexico." Rick was seeing the apartment through the eyes of someone he cared about and now had to face the fact that he'd have to clear out when the owner returned and that he wouldn't be happy about it.

Molly went over to the bookcase and ran her fingers along the spines. "Law books." Then she picked up a small Mayan statue and turned it over in her hands. "Not yours, am I right? You live out of a suitcase."

"I live out of a suitcase."

"And you keep putting off reality, like admitting you're in Boston for good and you might as well settle down. Woman or man, your landlord? I mean the one in Mexico."

"A woman. Something to drink?"

"If that means seeing the domestic you in action on your own semiturf, certainly. Older or younger? The woman in Mexico, I mean."

"About your age."

Molly put the statue down carefully. "Were you living with her before she left?"

He raised his eyebrows in surprise. "Does it matter?"

"Yes," she said softly.

"I'll move out tomorrow if it makes a difference."

She smiled and came toward him. "I don't think I want anything to drink right now."

He hadn't realized how ready he was for her when she came into his arms. His hand moved to her face. He traced its outline with a feathery touch. "Everything you think or feel is in your eyes," he said. "Do you know that?"

She shook her head and he took her lips in a gentle kiss. When she didn't pull back, his touch became insistent, more assured.

Molly closed her eyes tightly, feeling like an innocent who believed in magic and miracles. There was nothing wrong that couldn't be righted. She stopped thinking or wondering. The hard, strong feel of his body against hers crowded in.

"I was a stranger who came into your life ready to disrupt it," he said, whispering against her lips. "It isn't true anymore, Molly. No matter what happens, I want you."

Her voice, when she spoke, was ragged and breathless. "What about tomorrow? It will come, you know, and maybe with nasty little headlines that could ruin your career."

"The hell with that. We'll work it out." His mouth came down on hers, sealing his words with their shared sigh. "I can't promise you it's going to end happily for anyone else," he said. "I can't destroy evidence, I can't look the other way, I can't even give you any guarantees about what the future will bring."

"I know you can't, Rick."

"I had to say the words." For a long moment they held each other's gaze. Molly sensed the tension in the air and in a way felt she was facing the same danger as when they had first met. Only this time it had nothing to do with her uncle or with S.N.A.R.E. It had to do solely with the two of them and with what Rick might do to her heart if she ever gave it to him. She was trapped, mesmerized by forces she didn't even try to understand.

Rick must have seen the hesitancy in her eyes, and his mouth came down on hers with a desperate hunger that startled and thrilled her. It was like nothing she had ever experienced before. His tongue surged between her teeth, lightly seeking the moist warmth beyond, and she called his name with an ache she couldn't control.

His voice was rough, urgent. "Nothing else, Molly. Nothing. Just you and me." He caught her face in his hands and rained a scorching line of kisses down her throat. His hand at the small of her back urged her hips against the hard tension in his, while his other hand encircled the soft flesh of her breast.

Even as she uttered a barely audible "No," she moved eagerly and naturally against him. She was full of him—the scent, feel, taste of him—as every rational, reasonable thought was washed away.

"No?" he asked. "Do you mean it?"

"No, I don't, I don't mean it," she said against his mouth. He gave a low growl and swept her up into his arms, his lips still pressed against hers, and Molly knew she would remember every moment with a clarity that would defy time: the covers of his bed being turned down, their clothes falling to the floor, his hands gently caressing every part of her. She would remember his torn breath and that sudden surge of passion as his fingers found her warmth. And there was her own insistent urging, "Yes, yes."

His body on hers, his warm breath whispering words of love, his hands caressing her hurriedly, tenderly—everything was so new and yet so right. He raised his head and gazed down at her with a wild desire that released the most sensual feelings she had ever known. She gripped him then hard, sealing forever what she felt for him, letting him know that she wanted him, needed him.

He claimed her with a fever that matched her own, bathing her in a warmth that turned swiftly to a pounding, surging joy that speared her heart and took her breath away.

It was over more quickly than they wanted and in its wake was the reality of their having crossed a chasm. Yet there were still questions that neither of them could ask.

Hours later, when the room was lit only by the faint light of the moon, Molly opened her eyes. Their bodies were entwined and only the memory of their heated breath remained.

Molly felt a new kind of peace, as if she had been desperately running from something and then found the whole thing had been a mistake. The lingering remnants of a dream, she supposed. There was no mistake. It had happened and it was good. She drew her fingers through his hair, the smooth texture like silk. He stirred, murmuring her name, and then reached for her, moving his body over hers with a now familiar pressure. This time there was no rush to completion. There was time to explore the wild thing that had begun between them. When it was over, they lay curled in each other's arms, each reluctant to speak for fear words would shatter the fragile threads that bound them.

AT NINE O'CLOCK THAT EVENING they presented themselves at the Ryder apartment on Arlington.

They found Serena in the entry hall, greeting some guests who had arrived just ahead of them. She wore a low-cut blue gown with a diamond brooch at the neck. When she saw them, her smiled brightened. "Wonderful, you've come."

She knows, Molly thought, flushing faintly and grabbing Rick's hand for support; she knows we've been together and it's written all over my face.

"Thanks for having me," Rick said, spontaneously bending forward and planting a friendly kiss upon Serena's cheek.

Serena clapped her hands together. "Well, you two." Then she added, her approving eyes taking in every inch of Molly and the simple black dress she wore, "You look quite beautiful, my dear."

Molly offered her a kiss and then escaped quickly into the living room with Rick. "Don't say it," she warned him.

"Say what? I'm an innocent babe in the woods when it comes to eye contact between nieces and their aunts."

The living room was crowded, and through the sound of chatter Rick could hear the strains of Gershwin's "Rhapsody in Blue" played enthusiastically on a piano in the far corner. A mirrored wall opposite the fireplace echoed the gathering, making the party seem larger than it was and the room more spacious. The scent of good cigar smoke and perfume intermingled like the guests themselves.

"I'm impressed," he said to Molly.

"Typical of Ryder parties," Molly said. "An eclectic mix of shakers and makers."

"The cream of Boston's crop," Rick mused. "Over in the corner, staring straight into his companion's décolletage, we have the head of the city council. Over on the far right, the lieutenant governor. And then I recognize assorted judges, local politicos and our friend of the tape, Mr. Elliott Lawrence, talking to His Honor, the mayor. That's pretty heady stuff, Molly."

"You're a smug, self-righteous, arrogant snob," Molly told him. "And I hope everyone here can read my lips. What would you like to drink?"

"How many of the crowd do you know?"

"Ask me how many I'll notice and how many I'll forget. There's Willy. Come on, let's say hello."

Her uncle was standing near the fireplace, talking to a small, heavyset woman with a rather judicial air about her. When he saw Molly and Rick approaching, he excused himself and came over to them.

He bestowed a cheerful kiss on Molly's forehead and said, "The apartment okay? No problems? I wish you'd stay with us for the time being."

"Guess what? I found my missing tapes and I'm going to pretend this past week never happened."

He gave her a surprised smile. "Found your missing tapes?" Then without waiting for an answer, he said, "No, don't go into details now. We'll talk later."

Rick had caught sight of Gent Perot across the room, his head thrown back in laughter. He was with a silky blonde who Rick instinctively knew wasn't his wife. "Excuse me," he said to Molly and her uncle. "There's someone over there I want to say hello to."

When Molly saw where Rick was headed, she drew her uncle in the opposite direction.

Rick moved through the crowd, nodding to a familiar face here, shaking a hand there. He couldn't afford to get caught up in a conversation when his quarry was in sight. There was something to be said about large crowds. You could get lost in them.

He waited a moment, and when the blonde touched Perot's arm and excused herself, Rick moved in.

"Mr. Perot," he began in a voice that held something of the excessive politeness used in a courtroom. Perot turned to him with a frown, which was quickly erased. Rick allowed himself the luxury of disliking the man at once. "I'm Rick Boulter from the district attorney's office," he said, offering his hand.

Perot accepted it with a strong, quick grip, and then said, his eyes searching the room for a moment, "The district attorney's office. I'm a friend of Alex Creedon's."

Was this the voice on the tape? Rick doubted it. Certainly no catarrh, no wheeze, just an upper-class Boston accent that Molly could dissect a lot better than he could. "I've been wanting to talk to you," he remarked to Perot. "Is there somewhere we can have a few words?"

Perot hesitated. Once again his eyes searched the room. "Can't it wait? This is hardly the place."

"It won't take long, just a few minutes," Rick told him, smiling but letting Perot know that he wasn't about to back away. "Then I won't have to bother you again."

Perot gave him an easy smile. "Sure, why not? How about the terrace?"

"Suits me."

Perot moved quickly through the crowd with Rick at his heels. He bent to kiss the cheek of a woman who stopped him to whisper something in his ear. Perot roared with laughter. Rick waited for the show to end and then, with an exaggerated wave of his hand, bowed Perot onto the terrace.

Once there, Perot reached into his jacket pocket and extracted a gold cigarette case. Rick eyed it, noting raised initials set with small diamonds. He rejected Perot's offer of a cigarette and, leaning back against the low terrace wall, waited for the man to light his cigarette and replace the case. It was clear Perot was marking time and was worried because he had no idea what Rick wanted.

The terrace was wrapped around the northeast corner of the building and was lit by tall, freestanding torches. Planters filled with trees and fat bushes gave plenty of privacy to anyone wanting to be alone.

"I saw you come in with Molly," Perot said at last, after taking a deep drag at the cigarette. "Didn't imagine you were with the D.A.'s office. Bodyguard?"

Rick shook his head. "Does she need one?"

Perot shrugged. "The lady's a walking disaster area, isn't she? Maybe it's the city of Boston that needs protecting. First there's a body in her apartment, then Jason Loring dead a couple of days later. There has to be some connection." He gazed at his cigarette as if it were distasteful to him.

"I wanted to ask you something about Daniel Halloway."

Perot gave him a surprised look. "What's Halloway got to do with anything?"

"His family asked us to find him."

"Really? I thought he was estranged from his family." Perot pulled over a wrought-iron chair and then changed his mind about sitting. Instead, he joined Rick at the terrace wall, leaning his hands on top and letting the ash on his cigarette grow long. The view was of the Charles and the buildings of Cambridge, which sent up a soft glow like the flecks moonlight makes on a rippling lake.

"Look, Halloway doesn't want to be found," Perot said. "If he did, he'd have left a forwarding address."

"He just walked away from a million-dollar business without leaving a forwarding address?"

"He has a Swiss bank account, for all I know. I've got his money waiting for him. If he needs something, all he has to do is pick up the phone and whistle."

"You're telling me he never even said goodbye?" Rick laughed and shook his head. "Some businessman. What about new business? He letting you handle all that?"

Perot flicked the cigarette over the terrace wall and watched it float down to the dark below. "The man was sick, that's why I came on board in the first place. He needed cash because of some bids he'd made that really strapped him. I was in the market for the type of operation he ran. I heard about Halloway and bought in. I've been in the construction business all my life. The trouble was, the son of a bitch ran the company like a fiefdom. He wanted my money but no input." Perot warmed to his subject. "I know my way through the labyrinth of city construction jobs—who does what, who wants what, who needs what."

"You're not talking payoff, are you?"

Perot was silent for a moment. When he spoke, however, his voice held a certain amount of good humor. "And if it did, would I admit to handing out bribes? No, we clashed over the best way to get the job done. Anyway, he had a new lady friend and he was in over his head, the damn fool. Halloway was small potatoes. He came in with a ridiculously low bid on the sewer job and when he's strapped for cash he starts crying. Only he didn't want advice, he wanted money. End of story. I won that particular battle because I knew what I was about, and Halloway decided to take a vacation." Perot turned to Rick. "Halloway doesn't want to be found, especially by his long-lost relatives."

Rick looked at him hard. Perot didn't seem to be in the least disturbed by his questions. He needn't have answered, either. He was certainly within his rights. Score one for Gent Perot. "If you hear from Halloway, give me a ring," Rick said. "I'd like his family to know we keep on our toes here in Boston."

"Ah, there you are." Serena came sweeping toward them, her skirt swinging prettily about her ankles. She looped her arms through theirs. "The best-looking men at the party and you're out here on the terrace. Come on, time you spread a little of that charm about."

Perot smiled and gave her a peck on the cheek. "I was asking Rick about Molly and what's happening."

Serena stopped just inside the terrace door and cast Rick an anxious look. "Is Molly safe or isn't she? I'm beside myself with worry. She's being an absolute fool about not asking for police protection."

"There aren't enough police to go around protecting every citizen who feels threatened, Mrs. Ryder."

"Feels threatened? Is that all it is, just a feeling?" The questions were sharply put, and Rick suddenly understood just how much backbone Serena Ryder had and how much she cared for her niece. "I know, I know," she sighed apologetically. "Someone's using scare tactics, is that it?" When Rick didn't answer, she went on, "The right word to the right person would get that protection for her." She waved vaguely in the direction of the living room and her chatting guests. "We're not without friends."

"Mrs. Ryder," Rick said, "if your parties are this thick with influence, I'd say all you have to do is whisper the thought and Molly can take her pick of bodyguards."

She laughed. "Oh, I'm afraid we've been putting on the Ritz today. Usually we entertain a little lower on the ladder."

"So you can let your hair down."

"The city's for hair up," Perot whimsically put in. "Their place on the north shore is for hair down. Mrs. Perot, however, and I have managed to bridge the gap, haven't we, Serena?"

Serena gave him a smile Rick thought of as fond. "Some do, most don't. You'll have to come to Windward, Rick."

"I'm flattered. Mrs. Ryder—" Rick began, but she interrupted him.

"Oh, for heaven's sake, call me Serena."

"Serena it is, then. To get back to Molly for a minute, I'd like nothing better than to have her under constant protection."

"I was hoping you'd take up the cudgels," Serena said. "She hates our using undue influence."

"I'll try, but your niece has a stubborn streak. I was wondering if you'd consider a private service."

"Hey, gloom and doom," Perot said, breaking in. "I need another drink. How about it, Boulter?"

Rick still didn't like Perot and was hard-pressed to say why. Maybe it was just the way he burst in and changed the subject, maybe it was something else. On the surface the man was charming enough, but underneath was arrogance and a coating of forged steel.

"I've had this party in the works for a long time, otherwise I don't think I could've gone through with it," Serena murmured. She tucked her arm tightly through Rick's and led him across the room. One thing was certain. Serena wanted police protection for Molly, but understood that to use her contacts in government to get it would go against her grain as well as Molly's. Rick had already made up his mind to pursue the idea of a private bodyguard when Serena spoke up again. "That trio is wonderful, don't you think?"

The moment was gone. She had slipped back into being a brittle, busy hostess. "So it is." For the first time Rick saw a trio at the back of the living room. The air was hushed as the pianist, a young man with dyed blond hair, crooned an old Rogers and Hart ballad.

"If you'll excuse me," Rick said to Serena and Perot when he saw Molly across the room in deep conversation with a woman.

"Boulter." Perot drew him back for a moment. "Don't give Halloway another thought. He's doing what you and I might do if we had an ounce of good sense."

"Halloway?" Serena asked.

"Daniel, my partner," Perot told her. "Everybody wants to find the man and he wants to stay hidden. I hate talking shop on a night like this." He bowed to Serena. "Care to dance?"

"Delighted."

"Listen, Serena," Perot went on, putting his arm around her and leading her to the center of the living room, "I've been thinking about doubling my office space." Their voices faded away.

"Been looking for you," Rick began when he caught up with Molly.

"Been looking for you, too." Molly's companion waved goodbye and wandered off before Molly could introduce them. "That was Mrs. Perot," Molly said. "She was at Windward. I tried to discuss who was there and who wasn't, but all she remembered besides her husband was Jason Loring. Very impressed with knowing a television celebrity and absolutely devastated that he died before she'd had much of a chance to brag about him."

"I've just had a chat with Mr. Perot, who knows no evil, sees no evil and isn't about to tell the assistant D.A. any evil whatsoever."

"He doesn't know a thing about Halloway's disappearance?"

"According to Perot, Halloway ran away with his girl and doesn't want to be found. How are you doing in the recognition department?"

Molly raised her hands to indicate that she had come up almost empty. "I don't know, Rick. I see so many people all the time I think I'm face-happy. Everyone and no one looks familiar, if you can figure that one out."

"Your aunt tells me that this is a puttin'-on-the-Ritz kind of party, not like the easygoing ones at Windward."

"I'll have a big gabfest later with Serena. She always likes me to show an interest in her guests." Molly made a face. "I know, I know, and get that list. Rick," she told him earnestly, "I've got to square everything with Serena. All this pussyfooting is getting us nowhere, and I can trust my aunt. She'll want to protect Willy, and the best way she can do that is to produce the list."

"Be my guest. She's a very pretty lady, your aunt, and inordinately fond of you, although the reason why beats me." He took her arm and directed her toward the terrace. "Right now I've an uncommon urge to kiss you and I believe in indulging my urges."

"Here, in the middle of all these power brokers? Don't count on it, Rick." Still, she let him lead her out to the terrace, glad of the breath of air coming in from the river.

"Around the corner here," he said, "where it's dark, private and waiting for us."

From the terrace they could hear music and voices but softly, almost sedately. "They give very elegant parties. No kissing allowed unless it's a gentle peck on the cheek."

Rick smiled. "Saw plenty of that tonight."

"Indulged yourself, too, I noted. My aunt was bought with your kiss on the cheek, lock, stock, and definitely the whole barrel."

"Good. One down and one to go. How do I win your uncle over?"

"You don't. You're the man he found in his library with his beloved niece. I doubt he was able to take that in very calmly. This mean you no longer consider him a suspect?"

Rick put his hands on her shoulders, pulling her close. His mouth hovered over hers for a second before closing in for a long kiss. Molly felt the heat rise in her body. "How about cutting out of here?" he whispered against her hair.

"Just leave without saying goodbye?"

"I hate goodbyes when I have something important to do."

"We can leave through the library," she said, indicating the door opposite.

"Fair enough. Come on."

"My bag," Molly said, suddenly remembering. "We're out of luck. I left it on the fireplace mantel."

"Stay put," Rick told her. "I don't want you wandering off with anyone else."

"But—"

"Stay put."

"Rick, you don't even know what my bag looks like!"

"Molly, old girl," he said, hugging her, "I know everything about you."

He left her looking out over the river. She had no desire to go back in and be detained by empty conversation. She didn't even want to make thin excuses to Serena and Willy about why she wanted to leave. She wanted to escape with Rick and be with Rick and blot out everything but his touch and what he could do to her.

After a while the realization came to her that the music had stopped and except for a laugh or two the party seemed to have ground to an unexpected halt. Somewhere far away a fire truck screeched. There was the steady grumble of an airplane heading west from Logan. Perhaps because of those distant sounds, the air seemed especially charged and ominous. Molly shivered and was about to head for the library when she was aware of a faint rustling noise close by that she couldn't quite identify. She turned, but there was no one there. The music started up again, distantly, floating out to the terrace from the living room and curving around to where she stood at the terrace wall.

The first sickening feeling came over her of being trapped. From where she stood she could see right through the glass door to the darkened library and to people moving around in the hall beyond. She caught sight of the blue of her aunt's gown, which flashed by and disappeared. She went quickly over to the library door and groped for the knob with shaking fingers. The knob slipped under her touch. Her palm was wet with inexplicable fear. An odd sound reached her from somewhere in the shadows as of a breath unsuccessfully suppressed. She rapped her knuckles against the glass door as the panic overtook her, but no one inside heard her.

In the distance she heard Rick call her name, but when she turned, it was into a sudden, blinding blackness.

Chapter Eleven

"Molly, stop squirming. The best medicine is a fat, sloppy kiss to make it well."

"That's your solution to everything," Molly said, but let Rick kiss her anyway. There was a slight bruise over her left eye, as if she had been swatted with somebody's fist. "Where were you when I needed you?"

They were back in Molly's apartment, having escaped the Ryder flat before anyone noticed what had happened on the terrace. Rick had unwittingly scared the intruder off by appearing suddenly and calling her name. He was balancing two dishes of a fragrant pasticcio and almost dropped them when he stumbled over Molly's prone body. When she came to in Rick's arms, Molly declared she had no idea who had attacked her. Not wanting to involve Serena and Willy, she insisted upon going through with their original plan of slipping out of the apartment through the library. Fortunately, all of the Ryder guests were in the dining room, lining up at the buffet for pasticcio.

Now Molly was safely ensconced on the bed in her own Back Bay bedroom. Rick, his tie loosened and his shirt open at the collar, sat down on the bed beside her. "Ready for a little chicken soup?"

"Will you stop cosseting me? I'm okay," Molly said.

She let Rick gather her into his arms and lay his cheek against hers.

"Dammit, why didn't you come back inside when you heard someone come at you?"

"I couldn't get the library door opened. I panicked when I heard him breathing the way heavy cigarette smokers do. You know, when they talk you have the feeling they're going to cough up the entire constellation Andromeda."

"That fits," Rick admitted. "We caught some wheezing on the tape."

"Half of Boston wheezes. This is the season for it."

"Fine, that cuts our work in half."

"Where were you, anyway?" Molly asked. "You took your time getting back."

"Your aunt grabbed me and headed me toward the dining room for some pasticcio. How could I refuse such an offer? The result is two plates sitting on the terrace wall waiting for someone to find them."

"Oh," Molly groaned, "Serena will love that."

"She'll know why we snuck out and why we didn't have any appetite. And why we're going to spend Sunday together cloistered in this apartment."

Molly smiled. "Is that what you think she'll think?"

"Better safe than sorry." Rick reached out for her once again and pulled her close, the familiar longing filling them and blotting out everything else.

WHEN MOLLY OPENED HER EYES, the early-morning sun lay strips of light across the room. Rick was beside her, breathing evenly, his arm thrown across her chest. She wanted him awake, talking to her. She needed the contact only he could give. With careful fingers she drew a line down his forehead and to his lips, and then she bent to kiss him. Almost at once she felt his response. His arms wound around her, pressing her body along the length of his. Wordlessly he began to caress her. Within moments, she was beneath him, reveling in the welcoming heat of his body, urging him to continue, knowing she would never get enough of him. When she felt his hand brush against the wound on her forehead, reality and the grim future invaded but were thrust aside at once as his lips crushed hers.

THE SMELL OF COFFEE MINGLED with something else: bacon, crisp, wonderful bacon. She could hear the clang of pots on the stove and Rick in the kitchen humming off-key. Molly stretched awake. It wasn't a dream; what had happened was real.

When Rick came into the room, carrying breakfast on a tray, she was still in bed, the covers pulled around her. He had fashioned a flower out of a napkin and stuck it in a juice glass. There were two plates of scrambled eggs topped by bacon, and a pot of steaming coffee.

"Did I ever tell you what my favorite kind of Sunday is?" He placed the tray across her legs and carefully moved in next to her.

"No, but I'm sure you will." She picked up a piece of bacon with her fingers.

"First you make a gargantuan breakfast. Second you get all the Sunday papers and spread them out on the bed. Then you disconnect the telephone and draw the blinds." He gazed at her quizzically. "I think I left something out."

"What could that possibly be?" She wondered what in the world she had done with her Sundays before she met him.

"Oh, yes," he said, bending carefully over the tray to kiss her. "None of the above applies unless you have exactly the right woman to share it with."

"And how often does that happen?"

"As a matter of fact, it's never happened before."

She laughed, and he kissed her again. "Let's see about your wound." He picked the plaster off.

"It's there," she said.

"No reddening," he told her. "Hurt?"

"Only when you don't kiss it."

"Fine. This calls for all-day therapy."

"Rick, why do I have the feeling you're keeping me locked in today for other reasons?"

"We'll get to that," he said with a grin, "after I build my strength up."

They didn't disconnect the telephone, and Molly received several calls from friends who hadn't found her in before. Serena called late in the day, admonishing Molly for leaving the party without saying goodbye, but since Rick had answered the phone, her words were tempered with good humor.

The day was languid, and yet both Molly and Rick knew they had captured something fragile and unique that could be shattered in the space of a breath. They stayed together through the night. The next morning Rick left Molly reluctantly and made his way to work. There was no way he could take time off to be with her. Monday was to be an auspicious day: the mayor was going to announce the winning bid for the sewer project. Operation S.N.A.R.E. was on the road.

"ALL YOU'LL GET IS A HAZY PICTURE," the district attorney's secretary said, "so don't waste your time. The antenna broke." She closed the door to Creedon's office behind her.

Rick slapped his hand against the set, and the fuzzy picture began to sort itself out.

"The usual circus," he said to his boss, who, not paying any attention to him, was punching in a phone number. "First we'll see His Honor being honored for being His Honor, followed by a long-winded speech about how much he's done for the city. By the time he gets around to announcing the winning bid, we'll all be asleep."

The mayor's visage materialized, and Creedon replaced the receiver without completing his call. "I know the script better than you do, Rick. I've been listening to various mayors since you were in short pants."

"I was never in short pants. I was the only kid on the block with ankle-length diapers."

The picture came clear, and Rick turned the sound down. They watched in silence as the mayor mounted the podium, his glasses pushed low on his nose, his expression serious.

"He doesn't like it," Rick said.

"Being part of Operation S.N.A.R.E.? When it works, he'll be all smiles with reelection stars in his eyes."

Fran opened the door and tiptoed into the office carrying two Styrofoam containers.

"Come on, come on," Rick said, coaching the figure on the screen. "Get it over with. I've got work to do."

"What's he up to?" Fran asked. "They found the murderer? Oh, right, the sewer contract. Right."

Creedon threw her a frown, and with a sheepish smile she backed out of the office. "Okay, here it comes, Rick," the district attorney said. "Turn up the sound."

"The bids are in for the extension of the current northeast sewer project," the mayor began. He then followed with a long statement about the success of his administration in obtaining funds for public works. Creedon impatiently tapped his pen on his desk and was about to make another telephone call when the mayor at last got to the point: "The low bid came in from Georgia Boston Construction," the mayor said, as though he wanted the whole ceremony over, "and Georgia Boston Construction wins the contract for the northeast sewer extension."

Rick lowered the sound, although he kept the picture on. "I'd like to see Gent Perot's expression right now," he said, "in color. Apoplectic. That's purple, I believe."

"A lot of people in town are going to cry foul," Creedon said. "A lot of people are going to say, Who's this upstart GBC? Where do these people come from, invading the Boston scene and bidding so low a body can't take a decent payoff?"

"Son of a gun," Rick said, staring at the picture on the television screen. "Speaking of the gentleman with the purple face, there he is: Gent Perot."

"What the hell." They stared. A scowling Gent Perot faced the camera, and a half-dozen microphones were shoved at him.

Rick turned the sound up. The voice of an off-screen reporter was heard. "Mr. Perot, the other day you seemed pretty sure that Halloway Construction would make the low bid on this construction job. Any comment?"

"You bet I have," Perot said. "As a matter of fact, I'm going to ask the mayor to look into the bidding process. Six months ago Georgia Boston set up business in this town. It looks to me as if they plan to take over the construction industry in Boston whether there's a profit in it or not. Nobody can compete with Halloway Construction when it comes to paring costs. And you'd better believe that the city will be soaked later if not sooner by cost overruns. I think the city owes the taxpayers a full report on what GBC's projections are."

"Are you accusing anyone in particular?" the reporter asked.

"I'm not saying anything else," Perot shouted, scarcely able to contain his impatience. With that he turned on his heel, and the camera followed him until he reached his limousine.

Reporters scurried after Perot, and just before he stepped into the car, someone called out, "Excuse me, sir, but we understand that Halloway Construction is claiming a delay and cost overruns on your contract in the *initial* northeast sewer project. Would you care to comment?"

"There's absolutely nothing to it," Perot said. He pulled the door shut and leaned back to be swallowed up in the dark interior of the limousine.

The reporter came on camera and began a summation, but Rick turned the set off.

"Beautiful, beautiful," Creedon said, washing his hands with air.

Rick excused himself. He had an uncommon urge to gloat over the scene with Molly.

"OH, MY GOODNESS, WHAT ARE YOU doing here? Why didn't you let me know you were coming to my office?" Serena jumped out of her chair and came around her desk to greet Molly with a warm hug. "I thought Rick had put you under house arrest." She nodded a dismissal across the room to her secretary, who was hovering in the doorway.

"He did. I got bored, Serena. I ordered up a cab, which is the safest way not to be sorry and figured you'd take me out for a drink and maybe dinner. How's that for calculation?"

"Not clever at all, Niece." Serena glanced at her watch. "I've a cocktail date at six, which gives me little enough time. It's five now. Why didn't you call?"

"Because I had to talk to you, Serena. I promise I'll make it quick and give you a rain check on dinner."

Serena switched off the television set, which had been on without the sound. "Georgia Boston Construction won the sewer extension bid," she said. "They're renting space from me, and I expect they'll be growing by leaps and bounds now. I don't want to lose them."

"You won't," Molly said, offering what she hoped was a disinterested smile, "you super saleslady."

Serena perched on the edge of her desk and motioned Molly to a chair. "I lose every now and then and I take it as a personal insult. Any special reason you wanted to see me, or are you just slumming? Or hungry?"

Molly waited a moment or two before answering. There was no delicate way to lead up to the matter of the missing list. She had to spill it out and do what she should have done the moment the recorder was stolen: come clean with Serena and then face Willy with the truth. "Not hungry," she said at last. "I need a favor..."

"Something to do with Rick?" Her aunt's brow furrowed, and Molly, for the first time, realized that she was very much on her relatives' minds. With their usual tact, they had been waiting for her to come to them. How foolish she had been to think she could run her life without them.

"It's a long story," Molly said. "And maybe not at all boring. It begins with a mugging a week ago when my tape recorder was stolen out of my bag, the recorder that Jason Loring used for a football out at Windward. Remember?"

"I remember," her aunt said patiently. "But why didn't you—"

Molly cut her off. "Tell you before? Well, it's pretty clear that the mugger wasn't an ordinary thief. He was told what to steal and then he did a very foolish thing: he pawned the recorder with its cassette, and by a circuitous route both eventually landed in the district attorney's office." Molly leaned forward in her chair and put her hand on Serena's arm. "Do you remember when I came bouncing out to the patio at Windward, talking about how I had left the tape running in the library?"

Her aunt nodded.

"Actually the red light was broken," Molly continued, thinking how easy the telling was now that she had made up her mind. "I had had no idea the recorder was on when I left the library. It's voice activated, as you know. A couple of men—guests—came into the library and began a rather odd conversation, which was captured on the tape."

"An odd conversation?" Once again Serena's brow was knit, as if so far the sense of what Molly was getting at eluded her. "Did you hear it?"

"No, as a matter of fact. The tape was in the hands of the police, but it was erased. I did, however, read a typed transcript."

"About what, for heaven's sake? Get to the point, Molly."

"About Halloway Construction—Daniel Halloway, to be exact. Look, Serena, it's very incriminating."

Serena got up, went behind her desk and sat down. "What's incriminating? An erased tape?"

"There *is* a typed transcription. I read it."

"And who are the two gentleman? Our guests, is that what you're saying?" Serena hesitated and then said, "All right, I understand. You don't even have to go into details. Who were they?"

"That's the point, Serena. No one knows." She wasn't telling the truth, exactly; Rick was certain one was Elliott Lawrence.

"What's the favor, Molly?"

"The D.A. thought I would be able to remember who attended the party, but of course I can't. I was out sailing

for most of the day. After that business on the patio with
my tape recorder, Jason and I went out to dinner with some
friends. I've really no idea who was at your party. The up-
shot is, I told the D.A. I could get a list of your guests from
you." Molly stood and, leaning across her aunt's desk, cast
an imploring glance at her. "You will give me the list, won't
you, Serena?"

Her aunt looked at her long and hard without turning
away. "Why hasn't the district attorney called me himself?"

"I expect he will, if you won't help me."

"Why the delay?"

Molly backed away and after a moment sat down. Why
the delay, indeed? Because they suspected her uncle and
believed Serena would protect him at all costs. Because the
tape had been erased and they were back, if not at square
one, then pretty close to it. Because Operation S.N.A.R.E.
was about to be put into motion, and if they didn't catch
the killers of Halloway one way, they'd catch them another.

"Your uncle Willy," Serena said. "Of course. A man is
judged by the company he keeps. Molly, our friends are
important and successful people. An incriminating tape?
Your uncle is above reproach and so are our friends." She
stopped and then said as an afterthought, "You haven't
talked to Willy about this, have you?"

"Serena, that's the idea, I haven't. I'm trying to protect
him. His heart, I know. But we can't bury our heads in the
sand. A policeman was killed in my apartment the same day
the tape was stolen. Then Jason Loring, when I was supposed to meet him." She stopped. There was no use in
trying to lead Serena through the peculiar maze that had
developed over the past week.

"The police don't think you have anything to do with Jason's death."

"The trouble is, Serena, you are burying your head in the sand. When Jason died, every paper in town mentioned the fact that the judge's niece was a friend of his—you know, that niece who chanced upon a murdered cop whose death is as yet unsolved. Just a mention, nothing conclusive. Tarred by the same brush, that's all."

"I know all about it," Serena said evenly, "but I took it for granted the police didn't believe you were tied in with his death."

"Jason called me. He wanted me to see a photograph of someone. Said he thought I'd be interested."

"Mind telling me why?"

Molly realized they were going far afield from her original purpose, but didn't know quite how to wind her way back. "About your party," she began, choosing her words carefully. "I asked him who was there, who he remembered."

"Really? Go on."

"I think he had a photograph of someone, who'd been there, which he wanted me to see."

"Anyone else you discussed the list with?"

"Oh, Serena, I'm sorry. I just wanted to protect you and Willy from all this nonsense you have nothing to do with."

Serena gave a deep sigh. "If someone were out to ruin your uncle's career..."

"I read the transcript. It was a conversation between two people about Daniel Halloway and what happened to him."

Her aunt pulled out a desk drawer and began rummaging through some papers.

Not there, Molly wanted to say, *you're wasting time.*

"What happened to Daniel Halloway?" Serena asked.

"They indicated he was dead."

Serena got quickly to her feet. "Dead? You mean murdered?"

Molly nodded.

"All right, I understand now. I thought the list was in my desk, but now that I remember, I gave a whole bunch of things to my secretary to file. Rick staying with you?" Serena left the door open between them and began looking through some papers on her secretary's desk.

"Nosy, nosy."

Serena came back in to the room triumphantly and held a piece of paper aloft. "Say hello to him for me."

"Dammit, Molly," Rick shouted into the phone, "I thought I told you to stay put. I've been trying to reach you for an hour. Don't you listen?"

"Stop blowing off steam," Molly said from a telephone booth at the back of a coffee shop near Rick's office. "I've just used up my one and only coin to dial you. I have Serena's little list. I'm at Sandy's, about two blocks away. Can you meet me here?"

"Don't move. Can I trust you to stay in one place until I get there?"

"In a booth at the rear."

When Rick arrived, Molly had summarily ordered grilled cheese sandwiches for them both and was ready to ask for more coffee. "You wanted the list," she reminded him, before he had a chance to read her the riot act.

He bent to kiss her cheek. "A simple call to my office would've done the trick, Molly." He slid in beside her. "You know, like, 'Hey, Counselor, I'm bored and I've decided to tempt fate by going off to visit my aunt.'"

"Were you hysterical?"

He put his arm around her and kissed her cheek once again. "Upholders of law and order don't get hysterical.

We experience a sense of dread and deep panic, however, and if you ever run out on me again, I'll have your badge.''

"Grilled Swiss on rye," the waitress said, balancing two identical dishes, as if trying to decide who ordered what.

As soon as she was gone, Rick put out his hand. "The list. How did Serena take the news?"

"She's worried about Willy. She feels most of her friends are aboveboard, but still, Serena's pretty sophisticated. She knows that some people in high places abuse their power and that friends of hers could be among them. I had the impression that if what the tapes say is bad for Willy and me, it's bad; but otherwise it's not that bad. In other words, Serena gave me the list. Incidentally, she likes you. Seems of the opinion we're living together."

"I suppose you both pulled me apart, microbe by microbe."

"Don't you wish, but forget it." Molly traced her finger down his profile. "There are some things I never tell Serena about. Those microbes stay put." She turned to her sandwich and bit into the crisp bread and melted cheese. "Eat first and the list after. By the way, my aunt mentioned the GBC winning bid without my bringing it up. She figures they're going to need more space. I felt like a beast all the time she was talking."

"I hope you didn't tell her to save her breath. GBC isn't moving for a long time. We've got it wired for sound and video recording, and we've got a telephone tap. Somebody comes nosing around, we'll be there." He picked up his sandwich and took a hungry bite. "Where's the list? Have you read it?"

"No. I figured we'd go over it together."

They finished their sandwiches and had their coffee cups refilled. Then Molly produced the list from her bag. She

spread it out on the table between them. In another moment she had folded it carefully and put it back in her bag.

"What the devil are you doing that for?" Rick asked.

"Why shouldn't I?" she said. "It's the wrong list."

Chapter Twelve

There was no bite at GBC until three days later, and even then it wasn't much of one. It occurred when the manager of Georgia Boston Construction played host to five visitors: Elliott Lawrence and Thomas Beam of the construction workers' union and three of GBC's own workers, including their union representative. The whole meeting was taken down by a discreetly situated video camera for later viewing by the district attorney's office.

Lawrence, a stocky, well-dressed man with an exceedingly winning smile and a strong handshake, did most of the talking. "Thought we'd stop by and introduce ourselves," he began at once. "Do a little preliminary planning so we can avoid trouble later on."

GBC's manager was all affability. "Well, we won the contract. We're going to be hiring pretty heavily once we get moving, and you can count on my cooperation as far as union labor problems are concerned."

"Not thinking of bringing personnel from out of state, are you? According to the way the newspapers read it, your bid came in so low, you're going to have to haul in people from the jungles of Brazil if you intend to make a profit."

Laughter and more affability on the part of the company manager. "Now, Mr. Lawrence, you know that's no

way for a construction outfit to settle down in new terri-
tory. We're already operating in Boston on a few small
contracts. We do everything by the book. We hire by the
book and we pay by the book.''

"That's the way we like it, by the book." Lawrence
turned to his associate and offered him a chance to agree.
Beam, a taciturn man with a small, pinched mouth, off
whose round glasses a mote of sunlight danced, merely
shook his head, whether in dissent or agreement, no one
could tell. As for the others, they deferred completely to
Lawrence, nodding but keeping their mouths shut.

There followed a long, complicated discussion of sala-
ries, overtime pay and working conditions. When they were
finished, Elliott Lawrence said, "Well, sir, you might work
miracles on the northeast sewer extension, after all.''

GBC's manager smiled, almost as if for the benefit of the
hidden camera. "We intend to, Mr. Lawrence. We run a
small, tight ship, and if you think we cut a little extra sand
into our cement, forget it. We don't want lawsuits five, ten
years down the road. We're in business to make a profit,
and we believe our personnel should get paid for their
work. Tight ship, that's how we do it.''

Lawrence also smiled, stood and offered a firm handshake once again. "Well," he said, "I think we're going to
see a lot more of one another.''

"I hope so, Mr. Lawrence. I hope so.''

Within the hour the film was viewed in the district
attorney's office by Alex Creedon and Rick Boulter.

"Lousy reproduction," Creedon commented, referring
to the quality of the black-and-white film. "You can't tell
what Beam looks like, the way his glasses reflect the sun.''

"Stop the action right there," Rick said, focusing on
Beam. "The cop at Windward that night I trailed Molly out
there... Had his hat turned down and coat collar turned

up.... I remember that I thought he looked vaguely familiar." He stirred in his chair. "The voice. I didn't connect it then to the one on the tape. The action moved a little too quickly at the time." No, he thought, it was something else that made the man seem familiar. Funny, but he'd had the same feeling out there at Windward, a fleeting sense of having seen him before.

Creedon was waiting. "Well?"

Rick shook his head. "Just a feeling. Nothing to go on. I'll have Molly in to take a look at the film in case she can identify him. Beam's a singularly shy man when it comes to having his picture taken. So far we've come up with nothing, which makes me think he's spent a lot of time plying his trade outside Boston."

"Well, this is it, I guess," Creedon said. "A chap with a pair of glasses flat enough to reflect light. If he's the same one you met with that night, we can pick him up."

"Looks your average, mild executive, the kind even his own shadow wouldn't recognize."

Rick pushed the rewind button and focused again on Thomas Beam and Elliott Lawrence. "Lawrence was the voice on the tape. The other character had a wheeze or a catarrh."

"Maybe he got over it."

"Listen." Rick turned the sound up, but all they heard was a crackling noise made by one of the construction workers nervously twisting a newspaper in his hands.

"Something tells me S.N.A.R.E.'s hit a snag," Creedon said. "Suddenly everybody's turning honest. Too much publicity coming down the pike. They're afraid to move."

"With all that tempting money at stake in the contract," Rick said, unwilling to admit his disappointment, "bet on it, they'll move as soon as the time is ripe. Lawrence was merely taking the measure of the man. They don't want to rock any boats until they're sure who's rowing. There's gold in those construction jobs and you don't let it slip through your fingers, no sirree. Give them time to regroup, they'll be around."

Creedon was silent for a while. Then he said, "What say we put your lady friend right in GBC's office?"

"Are you talking about Molly Ryder?" Rick jumped on him at once. The idea was crazy. "Mind sending that by me again?"

Creedon said patiently, "Put her in GBC's office. Let her see Lawrence, Beam, Perot, her uncle, whoever he is, in the pink flesh."

Rick gave him a pointed stare. "I hope you're kidding, Alex."

The stall in Operation S.N.A.R.E. seemed to have begun with Serena Ryder's supplying the wrong list three days before. Her action might or might not have been a clever holding action to protect her husband. When Molly had confronted her the next day, Serena Ryder had smiled and said with no apologies that the list had simply disappeared. She then had willingly given Molly a verbal list of names as she remembered them, and Willy, who had by then been apprised of the situation, had added a missing name or two. Thomas Beam's was included, but the district attorney's office had no way of knowing if the list was a complete one.

"What have we got, Rick?" Creedon answered the question himself. "We've got a setup waiting to be blown and we've got a Judge William Ryder in complete possession of the facts about Daniel Halloway's disappearance."

"Hold it," Rick said. "The conversation took place in his library. It doesn't mean he's a party to Halloway's murder."

"He counts a few deleterious characters among his pals. You were telling me that the American Society of Linguists has office space in the same building as GBC and that Molly Ryder is a member. I want her in GBC's office, starting this week. Incidentally, the heat's only partially off his niece, since the judge now knows that the tape was erased without her ever having heard the voices on it. What he can't be sure of is, does she recognize the 'Whoops, I didn't see you' character?"

"I'm not setting her up," Rick said.

"It's no setup," Creedon insisted. "She goes into the building, takes the elevator to the floor on which the American Society of Linguists has its offices, gets out, puts in an appearance and a little while later makes her way to the GBC office, unseen. At GBC we put in a one-way mirror to the reception room. Molly is behind it, waiting, safe as houses. When the Wheeze comes in, let her point a finger, and we'll take it from there."

"I still don't like it."

Creedon fixed him with a hard eye. "You're not much good when you begin to admire the lady in the case, Rick. You're letting the operation get away from you."

"I'm going to advise Molly against it strongly."

"Go ahead. She'll see it my way. After all, according to her, her uncle is innocent of racketeering, extortion and influence peddling, not to mention the possibility of misusing his office. She wants to prove her uncle's innocence. If she can help by sitting in GBC's office for however long it takes, mark my words, she'll jump at the chance."

Rick had trouble containing his temper. "Not if I have anything to do with it."

THE OFFICE WAS SMALL and not at all well lit. It had apparently been used as a storeroom and had then been fitted out to accommodate Molly. Ledgers lay open on the steel desk. There was a fancy, rather intimidating calculator and a computer with a word-processing program on it. She had come in under a false name, having been hired on, the staff had been told, as a computer programmer. She might look busy with GBC business, but Molly was discreetly working on her doctoral dissertation.

The computer was the reward she had won from Creedon for spending what might be the next month or two at GBC's offices. Opposite her desk was a large one-way mirror, giving her a clear view of the reception room.

It had taken Molly some time to get used to the idea of the mirror, and she had ducked spontaneously on a couple of occasions when someone had come into the reception room, only to giggle with embarrassment. There was a speaker, so she could listen in as well. She had been there for two days and had determined pretty quickly that the construction industry wasn't for her.

When the telephone rang at four o'clock on a fruitless Friday afternoon, Molly picked it up at once, glad of the diversion. It was Rick's voice at the other end. Her heart added an extra, welcome little beat.

"Anything?" Just one word, but she liked the sound of his voice in her ear and wanted to keep him talking. Molly hadn't given much thought to what would happen when the case was all over, when the sun might shine once again on an unclouded personal world.

She glanced through the one-way mirror. The reception room was empty except for the receptionist, who was pecking slowly away at a typewriter. "Nothing. Nobody with hands the size of sides of beef, no one who looks in the least surly, no one about to kick my door down." She glanced at her watch. "Four o'clock. Elliott Lawrence is scheduled to arrive. Where are you?"

"In court. I don't know when I'll get out of here. Molly, I still don't like the setup. They're a bunch of very nervous gents. For all I know, they could be watching the building."

"It's a skyscraper. Watching for what?"

"It might not happen overnight, Molly. It could take a month or two before they make a move."

"Then I'll ask GBC to improve the lighting system. This is a nice quiet place to work, except for certain phone calls that seem to come in with great regularity." Molly looked at the one-way mirror. "Oh, oh," she said into the phone and instinctively drew back.

"What's up?"

"Elliott Lawrence has just come into the reception room." With him were a couple of men in sport jackets and creased chinos, their hair peremptorily slicked down.

"Is he alone or with Beam?"

"My luck, no Beam. Just a couple of guys, maybe hard hats."

Lawrence smiled at the receptionist. His voice came through the speaker to Molly's office. "I'm Elliott Lawrence."

"Yes, you're expected, Mr. Lawrence. I'll take you back." The receptionist came out from behind her desk and led the visitors down the corridor to the manager's office.

The intercom sounded, and when Molly picked it up, the manager said, "Elliott Lawrence again with a couple of my foremen."

"I know Lawrence, not the other two. What we want is a man with a distinct catarrh, which lets out Elliott Lawrence. Besides, he's not the one I bumped into."

Molly disconnected and said to Rick, who was still hanging on, "Except for Lawrence, no one I know, at least not yet."

"Molly, don't go putting your nose where it doesn't belong. Call up the D.A.'s office when you're ready to leave, and they'll send a car and driver for you. I'll stop off at my place when I'm through here, pick up my car and come over to your apartment. Remember, you go straight home from GBC. Jury's back in," he said hurriedly and hung up.

Molly shook her head and went back to work. A half hour later she glanced at her watch. She had been told that Elliott Lawrence had the last appointment for the day. She could leave GBC, get an early start on traffic and present a gourmet dinner when Rick showed up at her door. The plan sounded good to her.

She checked over her work, decided she had no more to say and hit the save button, which consigned her copy permanently to the disk. Elliott Lawrence was still at the meeting. As an added precaution, Molly dialed the manager's office and said that if it was all right with him, she'd like to leave.

"No problem," he told her. That was signal enough to tell Molly that she wouldn't run into Lawrence on the way out. A glance through the one-way mirror into the reception room told her only the receptionist was there. Molly packed up and locked her office carefully behind her.

"Early days." The receptionist smiled enviously as Molly came through the reception room. "You programmers have the life."

Molly smiled back. "The brain works overtime." A moment later the elevator door opened and a man walked briskly out. Molly threw him a glance and was about to dismiss him when she realized he was staring at her with a surprised expression. For one blurred moment, she fought an overwhelming nausea. The library at Windward. This was the man. Thomas Beam, according to a rather fuzzy video film she'd viewed. Before she had a chance to react,

he turned and raced for the door at the end of the corridor
and the stairway that led down to the street.

She thought of telephoning Rick at the courthouse and
then of Creedon, but in the process she would lose Beam.
She punched the elevator button, glancing back at the receptionist. Asking her to call Creedon or the police would
do no good. Besides, Molly was afraid that Elliott Lawrence would make a sudden reappearance. The crowded
elevator stopped and she got on. For a terrible moment she
thought of screaming out what she knew. Beam had six
stories to race down.

When the doors opened onto the lobby, Molly kept well
within the people moving out. The fire door leading to the
stairs was closed. Either Beam was in the lobby waiting for
her, or she had the advantage and would find him first.

The lobby was bright, modern and busy. Beam was nowhere in sight, and Molly went hurriedly over to a bank of
telephone booths near a magazine kiosk. She stepped inside the only booth still available, closed the door and
waited.

She could hear snippets of telephone conversation on
either side; the woman to her left talking nonstop about a
deal that had apparently failed to materialize, and the man
to her right, whose deeper voice was cajoling someone into
having dinner with him.

Molly almost missed Beam. In his business suit of medium gray, he was a man who blended in easily. He came
past the line of elevators, then stopped, letting the crowd
flow around him. He took his time lighting a cigarette, letting his eyes wander casually around the lobby. Perhaps
because of the way he stood or the way he held his head, she
was certain that he was the man outside the terrace door at
Windward the night Jason had died.

As his attention wandered toward the telephone booths, Molly felt her heart miss a beat or two. She grabbed the telephone receiver, pretending to talk, bunching her shoulders and turning away from him. For a moment time ground to a halt and fear took its place. She had to stay hidden, but at the same time she couldn't let him get away, not now. Keeping her hand up and letting the receiver block her face, she managed to take in the entire lobby with a quick glance. For a moment she thought she had lost Beam, but then found him at the newspaper stand just a few feet away. He picked up a magazine, which he held open while checking the lobby in a surreptitious way.

Molly understood at once what had happened. He believed he had beat her down to the lobby and was waiting for her to come out of the elevator.

"Your loss, my gain."

The words floated through from the booth to her right. Her neighbor slammed down his receiver and stepped angrily out of the booth. She was horrified to find Beam coming toward her and once again she turned quickly, punching in Rick's telephone number and keeping her face well hidden.

Beam, however, came into the vacated phone booth and began to stab in a number himself.

Then Rick's secretary came on the phone. "Mr. Boulter's wire." Molly didn't dare respond and disconnected immediately.

"I'd like to speak to Elliott Lawrence."

Molly heard Beam's words quite clearly through the glass that separated the booths. His voice was gravelly, the voice of a man who smoked too much. It struck Molly that he might have been waiting not for her but for Lawrence. A minute or two ticked by. Beam spent the time checking the lobby, turning slowly but inexorably in her direction. Molly grabbed a notebook from her bag and held it to her face. Beam was distracted suddenly and began talking into the receiver. "Elliott, fold up your tents and get out of there." There was a pause, then he said, "It's a setup. Don't ask how, don't ask why. I've got something to do now. I'll get back to you."

Molly knew she had to make her exit before Beam spotted her. She stealthily opened the booth door while he was still talking and went rapidly through the lobby to the street.

It was surprisingly warm outside, but Molly shivered nonetheless. Tremont was crowded with cars and pedestrians. Molly turned left and then darted into the stationery store next door, where she planted herself at an angle to the window. In another moment Beam came out, looked around and then went to the curb. He unceremoniously shoved past a woman who had hailed a cab and waved at the driver to get a move on.

As the cab pulled away, Molly rushed out to the curb. "Well, I never," the woman said to Molly, who, without stopping for an apology, hailed the next cab to roll up.

"That's my cab," the woman cried.

"Really, I'm sorry, but it's a matter of life and death." Molly barely gave the emerging passenger a chance to pay the driver. "The cab that just pulled away from the curb," she said to the driver, "two cars down. That's my boyfriend in the back seat. We missed each other by seconds. If you'll follow him, I'll catch up to him when we get there."

"Get where?"

"Where he's going. Please don't lose him."

"Don't you know where he's headed?"

"No," said Molly, using the right amount of indignation in her voice.

"Ah, I get it," the driver said. "At the same time, it could be you don't like where he's going."

His accent wasn't native to Boston, and she listened to him with half an ear, sitting on the edge of her seat. Traffic was slow, with cars jam-packed, all trying, it seemed, to edge into their lane. "Don't give them any quarter," she said.

"Relax, it's my job."

"Chicago," she said. "You're from Chicago."

"You a magician?"

"Just about." She could have followed Beam to his destination on foot the way things were going.

Beam's cab moved south on Tremont and then cut into Charles. "He's going through the park," she announced unnecessarily. As the cab turned onto Charles, a panel truck broke in ahead of it, blocking Molly's view entirely. "Damn," she said.

"Stay cool, lady, he doesn't have much choice here. He's headed maybe to Beacon Hill, maybe along Arlington."

"Arlington." She leaned back, suddenly depleted. What would he want with Willy?

"Hey, don't knock Arlington. I can think of a lot worse places."

Traffic stalled. "Is he still there?" she asked anxiously, as if the driver could see through the van ahead.

The driver opened his door and stepped out of the cab to check. "He's still there," he said in a tired voice.

"Thanks." Molly moved into the corner of the cab. She was silent as traffic crawled along Charles and headed through the Common toward Beacon Hill. The whole thing was getting out of hand. She had no idea if she had acted like a fool by running in hot pursuit of Thomas Beam, considering that now she had identified him, the D.A.'s office could pick him up. Looking out the window, she could see life going on quite calmly, as though in that stop-and-start along Charles nothing at all dramatic were happening. People were strolling along the Common on her right or the Public Garden on her left, without a care in the world.

"Lost your boyfriend." The cabdriver spoke up suddenly, bringing her back to reality.

"What? What do you mean?"

"It's not the same cab. There's a woman in the back seat."

They were through the park and the panel truck had pulled right on Beacon, exposing the cab ahead. "When did you lose him?" Molly was uncertain whether to be relieved or not.

"Lady, I've no idea. What do you want to do now?"

She glanced at her watch. It was nearly five. She could backtrack to her apartment or wait for Rick at his. He said he'd stop home after court, and since he had given her the key, she decided to go there and wait for him.

"Hey," the cabdriver said suddenly, "he's behind you, your boyfriend. I swear it's the same guy."

Molly turned around and was sorry at once that she had done so. A cab had come from nowhere and she could see Beam quite clearly in the back seat, staring straight at her.

"Take the next right," she said when they hit Pinckney.

"I can't. It's one-way, the wrong way. I thought you wanted to find him."

"I don't care what I said. Take it anyway. I'll give you an extra twenty."

"You got it, lady." He made a sharp right turn and went tearing down the cobblestone street.

"Now left."

He took the left turn on two wheels and then skittered around a garbage truck that was taking up most of the road.

"Stop here," Molly said, realizing that they were coming up to a narrow lane that led to the block on which Rick's building stood.

"This it?"

"This is it." She dug into her bag for her wallet and thrust some bills at him. "Thanks, you've been a brick." She scrambled out of the cab almost before it had screeched to a halt in front of the truck, the driver of which promptly sat on his horn and rained curses on them.

The lane was guarded by a wrought-iron gate closing it to foot traffic. Molly carefully undid the latch and slipped through. She left the gate unlatched, flattening herself against the brick wall for a moment, breathing a deep sigh of relief. Then she peered out. The coast was clear. Beam hadn't followed her to Pinckney after all. Molly was about to turn down the lane when she heard footsteps behind her. She could feel her bones chill as she turned slowly around.

Beam was there, grinning at her, no more than three feet away. She understood now. He knew where Rick lived, knew she was headed there and had come for her.

"I've run out of patience," he said. She heard his characteristic wheeze and saw the slight, peculiar bend of his head that confirmed he was the man who had followed her out to Windward, the same man who had attacked her on her aunt's terrace.

She edged away from him and came up against an empty plastic garbage can. "What do you want? Why are you following me?"

He didn't answer, but moved steadily toward her. His right hand was in his jacket pocket, and his eyes, which were cold and empty, never left her face.

Without thinking, Molly turned to run.

"I wouldn't do that if I were you."

In a deft movement, she picked up the garbage can and heaved it at him. It was lighter than she expected and it bounced against his foot, throwing him off balance. Molly ran back into the street. The garbage truck had lumbered up the block. She raced toward it and called breathlessly up at the driver, "Listen, I'm lost. I wonder if you could help me?"

"You again? The lady that bolted out of the cab?"

She smiled ingratiatingly at him, still trying to catch her breath. "Sorry, I'm late for a party. I'm looking for—for Phillips."

"You're way off. You had some dummy for a cab-driver."

Keep him talking, she told herself. If Beam followed her, she'd ask the driver for help. "I know, that's the way of the world. He's from Chicago, and if you're not Boston born and bred, you can never make your way around town. He's just in the wrong business. If you're not in a hurry, if you don't even want to get there on time, if you want to come late, then traffic's running smoother than the Charles in summer."

"Hey, you're a poet." The driver grinned appreciatively at her.

Molly checked the street. If Beam knew where she was, he was keeping well out of sight. "Phillips," she said.

"Okay," the truck driver said. "Turn back in the direction you came."

She narrowed her eyes, taking in an impatient breath. She would have to keep in the driver's line of sight, which meant walking ahead of him, not turning back to that dangerous passage between two buildings. "Right," she said at last. "Go on."

He offered her some complicated directions, which she insisted upon his repeating twice. Still no Beam. She thanked the truck driver profusely and walked rapidly up the street.

The engine was gunned and the truck rolled up alongside her. "Hey," the driver called, "I said go back."

"Well," she told him, smiling gaily, "I figured I'd do a little sightseeing as long as I'm here." She waved goodbye and went rapidly to the end of the block, turning and waving again. If Tom Beam was following her, it was in one of his invisible guises. He knew where Rick lived and had possession of the lane that led onto Rick's street, but she had an advantage over him. She had the keys to the building and to Rick's apartment; Beam didn't. Still, it wouldn't do to rush in.

There was a small grocery store on the corner. Molly went in and found a pay phone at the rear. She dialed the district attorney and was put through to his secretary.

"This is Molly Ryder. May I speak with Mr. Creedon?"

"Sorry, he's out. Can I help?"

"I wanted to explain why I never called for a car and driver."

"We have one waiting for you, Miss Ryder."

"I don't need it now. When do you expect him?"

"In about an hour. Anything I can do?"

Molly hesitated. "Yes. Tell him I've found Thomas Beam."

"You've found Thomas Beam. I didn't know he was lost."

"Lost and found."

"Am I to tell Mr. Creedon where you found him?"

"No, it would take too long to explain," Molly said.

"Any other message, Miss Ryder?"

"That's it. You don't know if Rick Boulter is back?"

"Sorry, I don't. I can ring his office if you'd like."

"No, no, just tell Mr. Creedon that I'll call again."

His secretary laughed. "And not to worry."

"Right." Then Molly added, "On second thought, tell him to worry."

She hung up and peered out of the grocery-store window, which gave a view of the lane opposite; no sign of Thomas Beam.

"Can I help you?" The proprietor smiled at her as she came up front. Another couple of minutes might make the difference.

"A French bread," she said, and also ordered some cold cuts and cheese. Back outside she decided the block was a safe and busy one with children playing and mothers chatting over fences. Beam couldn't try anything there. She left the sweet-smelling sanctuary of the store and went quickly up the gently sloping hill to Rick's building. Another tenant was at the front door, struggling with packages. He gave Molly an apologetic smile. She helped him in and then raced past him up the stairs to Rick's apartment on the third floor. The door was slightly ajar. Rick wasn't expected home and Molly wanted no surprises. She could hear the tenant below struggling with his packages and thought of running back to him for help.

There wasn't a sound, not even Beam's uncontrollable wheezing. A door opened below and then slammed shut. She stood listening and then, when she could bear to wait no longer, pushed the door open.

Rick was there, all right, sprawled facedown on the flokati rug, an ugly red stain beneath his head.

Chapter Thirteen

"Ready to talk?"

They were in the bathroom, Rick sitting on the rim of the tub and letting Molly dab gently at his head wound with peroxide-soaked cotton. She had calmed down after the first heart-stopping moment when she had found him out cold on the living-room floor.

He winced at her touch. "Will I live?"

"You were caught broadside. I think it feels worse than it looks, now that I've cleaned it up."

"Molly, I was slammed by a sledgehammer."

"You're a baby. I was knocked out on my aunt's terrace and I haven't even thought about it since."

"I have." He checked the spot over her brow, which was still discolored and kept hidden under a lock of hair. "The bottom line is you have a far better character than I. Besides, I remember kissing you and making it better."

She bent over and planted her lips against the bruise and then his mouth. "There, the magic spell."

"The magic spell tastes like peroxide."

"Rick, would you mind telling me what you were doing here when you were supposed to be in court?"

"I know what *I* was doing here. How come you're here? I thought we were meeting at your apartment."

She placed his hand against the wet cotton. "Hold this while I get a bandage. Why am I here? That's a long story, too. I'm here because the fates willed it. Your story first." She found a tin of plastic bandages in the medicine cabinet and picked out one wide enough to cover the wound.

"Nothing to my story," Rick said. "I can tell it in fifty words or less. Court let out early—right after I spoke to you, as a matter of fact—so I figured I'd come home, get out of my uncomfortable, go-to-meeting suit, take the car and pick you up at five. On the way here, I had an itch for the latest news. I stopped off at the corner store for a newspaper and a bar of chocolate, which I ate coming down the street. When I arrived home, I unlocked the downstairs door, took my mail, came upstairs reading it, and as soon as I opened my apartment door, everything went black-and-blue."

Molly shook her head. "And to think I figured I was ahead of Tom Beam because I had the key to your apartment."

"Beam? You mean Thomas Beam, the fellow on our long list of suspects?"

"That Thomas Beam. Rick, you didn't hear or see anything?"

"Only stars," he said.

"I don't think we can count Beam out as the man who attacked you, then."

"Why do you say that? Mind telling me what you're doing here and what happened?"

"Except," Molly said, "whether it was Thomas Beam or no, we haven't settled the matter of why he or someone else would come here, wait for you to show up and then attack you. Just an attack with no follow-through."

"Molly, pet, begin at the beginning."

"Hold still. I'm now in an applying-bandage mode."

Rick removed the cotton and said, with a worried, boyish grin, "Take it easy."

"What a baby you are. There," Molly said, sticking on the bandage with a deft touch. "Don't think about it."

Rick stood up, a little wobbly at first, his hand tentatively testing the bandage. "Ryder to the rescue. I'll find a way to thank you that won't disappoint you." Then, with his arm around her shoulder, he directed Molly back into the living room.

"Do you think it was a simple attempt at burglary?" she asked.

He checked around and shook his head. "Nothing touched from the look of things, so for the moment we'll discount the possibility of my interrupting a burglar stealing the family silverware. What I *am* going to do is pour myself a double shot of my best Scotch. Care to join me?"

"I," said Molly, heading for the kitchen, "am going to brew a big pot of coffee for the occasion."

When Rick came to the kitchen door a few minutes later, he had a glass of Scotch in his hand. "I checked the bedroom, but it looks untouched. I wouldn't count on robbery for a motive, particularly because of the time. Your average burglar doesn't practice his profession when the master of the house might be expected home any minute."

"But you were early," Molly reminded him.

"Not by a burglar's standards."

"Whoever he was, he wanted to put you out of commission but not kill you. When Beam saw me at GBC, he was genuinely shocked. I mean, he bolted and ran."

"The beginning, Molly."

"Right, the beginning, the very beginning." She sucked in a deep breath, trying to recall exactly what had happened. "After you called me from court, I worked at my desk for a half hour or so, but I began to get a little antsy.

There were no other visitors scheduled for me to check out. With Lawrence in the manager's office along with a couple of GBC foremen, I couldn't see any trouble on the horizon. I decided to pack up and go home before Lawrence came out. I left through the reception room, certain I wouldn't run into anyone. I was busy congratulating myself when I ran smack into Tom Beam coming off the elevator. I froze and might have cracked into tiny bits of ice except for his reaction.''

"Which was?''

"He backed up and bolted for the stairs.''

"I'm afraid to think of what happened next. You didn't try calling Creedon.''

"No,'' she said and then added, "Look, Rick, I didn't have time. I had to choose: bringing the receptionist in on it, or going back to my office, unlocking the door and calling Creedon and maybe not finding him in, or keeping on Beam's trail. The elevator was very accommodating at that moment of indecision. I was playing detective,'' she remarked after a pause, "but it seemed to me I ought to follow him, ought to find out if he was in collusion with my uncle, ought to—'' She stopped and shrugged. "I don't know, it seemed like a good idea at the time,'' she finished lamely.

Rick grinned and touched the bandage. "It was, in its way.''

"I decided there wasn't much that Creedon or the police could do, so I took the elevator down to the lobby, and when Thomas Beam came along I followed him.''

"Without once believing he saw you, a beautiful woman with a mop of shining hair.''

She ignored his remark and went on. "It was a little hair-raising when he went into the phone booth next to the one I was hiding in.''

Gazing at her with an expression of wonder, Rick said, "You've been a busy little beaver, haven't you?"

"Well, I figured I beat him to the lobby. I had to wait somewhere for him, so I slid into a phone booth. I called your office but didn't dare ask for you, since Beam was right there next to me."

"And of course he missed noticing the beautiful brunette next door."

"Will you stop that 'beautiful brunette' nonsense? He must have been aware of the booth being occupied, but I kept my face hidden. Obviously he didn't know it was I, since he made a phone call, which I heard quite clearly, catarrh and all. He called Elliott Lawrence at GBC and had the nerve to tell him to play it cool, there was trouble. I slipped out of the phone booth, so I missed what else he said. Once in the street, I ran into the stationery store next door and waited for him to appear. He came out and hailed a cab."

"And Beam, who seems to make a living shadowing people, never knew you were shadowing him."

"He's made a few mistakes in his life, like not finishing me off at Windward or on my aunt's terrace."

Rick gave her a skeptical smile. "Go on."

"I commandeered a cab and followed him."

"I suppose you said to the driver, 'Follow that cab. There's a twenty in it if you don't lose him.'"

She laughed. "Okay, okay, it was dangerous and stupid, but I was on a roll. I don't remember, but maybe I even said 'Step on it,' although you couldn't, not in that traffic. Beam *is* the man I bumped into outside my uncle's library. When he saw me at the GBC elevator, he bolted. That should prove it."

"Or he wanted to draw you away to where he could dispose of you."

She flushed, because what Rick said was true. "Well, I followed him, but after a while he turned the tables and caught up with me and we had a contretemps. Apparently I won, because he hasn't shown his face yet." She stopped and stared hard at the coffeemaker as the first hot drops came through. "Unless—" She turned to Rick, her eyes reflecting sudden understanding. "There's a pattern to what happened this afternoon, after all, and it leads to something diabolically clever." She released a nervous laugh.

Rick came over to her and gathered her into his arms. "What, Molly? What is this pattern?"

They stood quietly for a while, Molly encased in his warm touch. She felt as if she'd been running for a long time, and now the end, if not in sight, if not even explicable, had to be close.

"I don't know, maybe my imagination is working overtime."

"I'll pay overtime," Rick said dryly. "Go ahead, give it a run-through."

"The reason Tom Beam didn't arrive with Elliott Lawrence at GBC," Molly said, articulating her words carefully and slowly, as if each one had a special meaning, "was that he was here, waiting for you."

"He'd have to be a mind reader in order to know I'd come back home after court. I'm not that regular in my habits."

"Precisely. He was at the courtroom when you were, and then he followed you and beat you home by minutes."

"Which meant he had to read my mind about stopping off for the newspaper."

"Oh, he's smart. He knew you were headed home and if you'd gone there first, he'd have followed you. People are very obliging about letting in strangers. I saw that for myself. I didn't even have to fumble for the key. Beam looks extremely respectable, and in this case he either picked the downstairs lock or was let in and waited in the hall until you came up.''

''And why go through all that trouble just to put me out of commission for a couple of hours?''

''Because they knew I went to the GBC building every day,'' Molly said patiently, ''although I'm sure they think it was to the offices of the American Society of Linguists.''

''Damn. I was a fool not to insist—''

Molly broke in. ''That I have police protection? I kept thinking I was safe because my uncle doesn't want me killed. Beam is acting on his own, I'm sure of it.''

''Beam is the only one we've smoked out so far, and unless you swear out a warrant... Damn, Operation S.N.A.R.E is down the tubes.''

''What do you mean? That call to GBC? Yes, of course, you're right.''

''I ought to get on to Creedon.''

But Molly stayed him for a moment, wanting to pursue the matter of Thomas Beam. ''Rick, we still haven't figured out what happened to you and why.''

''I'm willing to agree that somebody wanted me down *and* out for a couple of hours. Whoever it was had to be as certain of my whereabouts as yours.''

''If Beam knew I was following him, then why did he turn the tables on me and come back?''

''Take it backward,'' Rick said. ''What was the last thing that happened to you?''

Molly went to the open kitchen window and looked out into the garden below. Some children were playing, and she noticed a fresh clump of daffodils around a shade tree.

''I was on my way here, cutting through a lane that joins this street with the one where I ditched the cab. I ran into

Beam in the lane.'' She stopped and laughed at the memory and her boldness. ''I threw a garbage can at him, you know, one of those plastic things, empty. It caught him off balance. I ran back the way I had come and got myself a garbage-truck escort to the end of the block. Beam must have gotten discouraged and retreated.''

''Any other adventures I'm supposed to know about before I call Creedon?''

''I think it was all a setup of sorts, and I, in my infinite wisdom, just went along. Beam wanted me here.'' She paused, then went past Rick into the living room and over to the window. The street was innocent and deserted at dinnertime in a quiet, ancient section of the city that conjured up hansom cabs and horses and ladies in crinolines.

''He put me out with the idea of forcing you up here,'' Rick said, ''and sooner or later someone would come across the assistant D.A. and the judge's niece in a mysterious, if rather obvious murder-suicide, orchestrated by our friend Thomas Beam.''

Molly rubbed her arms to stop herself from shivering. ''Is it possible, Rick?''

''Everything's possible. I'm getting Creedon on the phone. GBC is in big trouble. I want to make certain our man on the wiretap caught the meaning of Beam's call to Elliott Lawrence.'' Just then the telephone rang, the sound abrupt and unexpectedly loud in the quiet apartment. Rick picked up the receiver. His expression, lively at first, suddenly turned cold. ''I'll be right there,'' he said and hung up. Without a word of explanation, he went for his jacket and was already at the door when Molly stopped him.

''Rick, what's the matter?''

''The offices of GBC—'' his lips were tight, his face drawn, ''—just pipe-bombed. The manager was killed. Damn, they didn't waste a minute, did they?''

"Rick."

"Don't say anything, Molly." He came back into the room and picked up the telephone receiver. "I'm arranging protection for you right now. Stay here and don't move until I get back. Don't answer the door for anyone."

"Rick, it's all my fault."

He spoke into the receiver and then carefully wrote down the name of the policeman who would be posted to the apartment. "Don't let anyone else in."

She nodded, and as he pulled her into his arms, she said, "I have the message, Rick. Beam's call to Elliott Lawrence told him it was a setup and so they ordered the place pipe-bombed. Quick workers. It was done in no time flat. If Beam hadn't seen me . . ."

"Hush, I don't want you blaming yourself." Rick held her for a long moment and then gently released her and made his way out of the apartment. "Don't blame yourself. We had a man on a wiretap. We don't think in terms of blasting your way out of a problem. And there's something else," he told Molly. "It was Alex's secretary, Fran, who tripped us up. Beam gave her the heave-ho, and she came crying to Alex to confess she'd erased the tapes." Rick remembered now why Beam had looked familiar. He was the man standing boldly at the water fountain with Fran.

"Stay put," he said to Molly, "and keep the door locked. Beam has a way of being everywhere at once." He kissed her again and left, closing the door carefully behind him.

Molly listened to his tread on the stairs and after a while went over to the window and watched as he came out and went briskly over to his car. Except for some children racing down the brick sidewalk and a cab rolling by, the street was empty. Rick glanced up and she waved at him. He shook his head, meaning that she should stay away from the window, as well. When the Camaro pulled away from the curb, Molly reached for her bag and jacket and let herself quietly out of the apartment. She locked the door behind her and made her way down the stairs. Then she stepped out into the cool early-evening air.

THE HOUSEKEEPER LET MOLLY into the apartment on Arlington. "The Judge is in the library, Molly. Go right in. He'll be happy to see you."

"And my aunt?"

"Off at one of her meetings."

"You wouldn't know when she's expected back."

The housekeeper shook her head. "Sometimes very late. Can I get you anything?"

"No, thanks," Molly said. "I'll just visit with my uncle for a bit." The housekeeper helped Molly with her jacket and hung it up for her. Molly waited until the woman was back in her room and her door shut with a final click. After that the apartment seemed shrouded in silence. Molly remained very still, suddenly unable to explain to herself why she had come, what had drawn her to her uncle's apartment when it might be where she was least safe.

She had no idea how long she stood there, and it was only the sound of the telephone ringing in the library that at last brought her head up. She heard her uncle on the phone discussing some legal matter in a pleasant, measured voice. At that moment, Molly understood why she had come and understood it with complete clarity. Judge William Ryder was the man she had always known him to be: kind, thoughtful, fair, a loving husband and an adoring uncle. That was why she had been able to get through the past two weeks, why she had been able to smile, to joke, to allow herself to feel something wonderful for Rick.

She was positive that her uncle was guilty of nothing more than generously opening Windward to all and sundry. These included Serena's friends—people with money and power who might, unfortunately, have attained both through unsavory means.

From inside the library she heard her uncle's laugh and the receiver replaced with a little clap. She managed to fix a smile on her face. Beam's actions—whatever their intent had really been—had nothing to do with her uncle, and that was her final word on the subject.

The library was a square, friendly room off the entry hall. Its doors led out onto the terrace where she had been accosted by someone that Saturday night, almost certainly Thomas Beam. The room was lit by a small green desk-lamp and a fire, which took off some of the evening chill. She stepped into the sweet scent of pipe tobacco and wood smoke and found her uncle sitting at his desk, bent over some work. He was wearing his cherished maroon smoking jacket; a lock of white hair fell over his forehead. A wave of nostalgia rolled over Molly and she found herself holding onto the doorjamb for support. It was, she thought, her favorite picture of the man—a pipe smoldering in an ashtray close by, his glasses low on his nose, his air of intense preoccupation, and goodness surrounding him like a golden aura.

"Hi," she said from the doorway, keeping her voice light.

He looked up and gave her a pleased, surprised smile. "Molly. I thought I heard somebody come in." He jumped to his feet and came around the desk to envelop her in a bear hug. "Well, what are you doing here? Serena and I were wondering what's going on in your life. Thinking of moving back with us? You know we never liked the idea of your going back to that apartment after what happened."

"No, everything's all right, I promise. I just came by to talk. Where's Serena?"

"Off on one of her pet fund-raising projects. The symphony this time, if I remember. Talk? Splendid. We haven't had an old-fashioned uncle-to-niece talk in a long time."

He was cheerful, delighted to see her and unscheming. Molly put her bag down and went over to a brown leather couch that faced the fireplace. She slipped her shoes off and bunched herself comfortably into a corner of the couch.

"Molly, all scrunched up on the couch," her uncle remarked. "Just the way you used to sit with a book on your lap when you were in your teens." He retrieved his pipe and took up a seat in a Queen Anne wing chair, which was his favorite.

"How are you feeling?" Molly asked.

"You mean my heart." He smiled. "A small murmur, that's all it is, and we have it under control. Serena makes too much of the whole business. I'm a willing listener," he went on. "What do you want to talk about?"

Molly realized that he was waiting for her to bring up Rick's name, but before she could put her thoughts together, he said it for her. "Your aunt has had a lot of nice things to say about Rick Boulter."

"And you?" Molly asked. "What do you think?"

"I prefer to keep a judicial silence in cases like this. Is Boulter what you wanted to talk about?"

"Yes. No, no, not really. Did you know that the offices of Georgia Boston Construction were pipe-bombed this evening?" she asked. "The manager died. That's the building Ryder Realty manages on Tremont, you know, where my society of linguists has its offices."

He stared at her openmouthed. "When the devil did it happen? I didn't catch the late news." He sucked in his breath. "Your aunt—" He stopped. "Well, I imagine she has found out, even at a fund-raiser."

"Rick is there now," Molly told him. "That's how I learned."

Absentmindedly he reached for an ashtray and tapped the dying ashes from his pipe. "Georgia Boston, did you say?"

She nodded.

"Anyone else besides the manager?"

"I don't think so, but I don't know for sure." She longed to tell him how responsible she felt but couldn't find the words.

"Georgia Boston. It won the sewer extension bid that had Gent Perot screaming foul in the press." He shook his head. "I hope Gent hasn't bitten off a lot more than he can chew. I always thought he was a bit of a fool."

Molly held her breath for a fraction of a second. "Why? He couldn't go public and then solve his problems with that kind of violence." When her uncle didn't respond, she said, "Willy, if you think he's capable of even entertaining such a notion, why do you have him as a friend?"

His face seemed to crumple and he shrugged. "He's young and he amuses your aunt. I can't expect her to enjoy the company of my old cronies as much as I do."

"Oh, Uncle." Molly got to her feet and went over to him and hugged him. "Is that what it all comes down to? Amusing Serena?"

He didn't look at her, but kept his gaze instead on the dying embers in the fireplace. She couldn't go on trying to find out the truth. The case was a police matter. Molly reached for her bag, put on her shoes and went silently out of the library.

However, while she was slipping into her jacket, her uncle called out, "Molly, are you leaving?"

"I'm sorry, Uncle Willy. I suddenly need to be by myself and to get some country air. I'll come back, I promise."

"See you later, my darling."

In the street she hailed a cab and gave the driver the address of the garage where she stored her car. A bare half hour later she was on the highway, heading north. The night was black, clouded over, and the chill in the air reminded Molly that a Massachusetts spring was capricious at best. Still, a drive along the coast would fit the bill. She'd stop at the first public beach she came to for some fresh ocean breezes and ponder her next move.

She tried to keep her mind clear of painful and conflicting thoughts, but lost the battle. Once more she found herself speculating about Willy. He had always been the authoritative figure in her life, strong but loving and a little remote from his wife's fussing over that unexpected arrival in their lives. Little things drew Molly back in time. The wallpaper Serena had chosen for her room when Molly came to live with them—feminine garlands of pink roses, which were comforting through those first, tearful nights. Visits to the dentist's office for braces, when Serena and Willy were all assurance that the sheath of silver would one day turn into a golden smile. She remembered Serena's excitement over helping her pick out a dress for her high-school prom and all the thoughtful, extravagant presents given by them both over the years. Willy's sense of balance when she had cried bitter tears over losing her first boyfriend. She had to hold on to her memories; she was their child and would have to be as nonjudgmental as a child.

Falling for the assistant district attorney hadn't been a clever move on her part. As for Rick, whatever feelings he had for her couldn't possibly stand the test of her loyalty to

Willy and Serena. She lapsed further and further into thoughts of Rick, of the love they had made and what the future might hold for them. She couldn't stop herself from experiencing these abrupt swings of her emotions and beliefs.

Molly had hit the turnoff for Marblehead before she realized how far up the coast she had traveled without even knowing it. She checked her rearview mirror. A dozen cars swooped past her as she edged over to the ramp. She hadn't been followed and hadn't even thought about the possibility. Well, then, Windward it would be. She'd call Rick from the house and ask him to meet her there. She had no idea what she would say to him then. Perhaps goodbye was all it would amount to. She drove cautiously along the harbor road with no one behind her and slowed down to make the left-hand turn into the driveway at Windward, where it had all begun.

As Molly gazed up at the house with its backdrop of sky, she felt herself pale. Something was decidedly wrong.

Although the living-room windows were protected by heavy draperies, she caught a seepage of light around the edges. But even odder was the small sports car, a Porsche, that was parked in the driveway. Molly had never seen it before.

Chapter Fourteen

Molly turned her car lights down and, putting the engine into first gear, slowed to a crawl. She drew up quietly next to the Porsche and sat there utterly exhausted, unable to ponder her next move clearly.

The black sky offered no relief to the dense, silent darkness of the night. If she had let common sense rule her mind, she would have headed for the police station. Instead, she stepped out of her car and stood for a moment in the cool, fresh breeze coming off the harbor. There were no cars on the road, although a strange feeling of menace—perhaps merely a shadow left over from her previous visit—still seemed to hang in the air.

She dropped her keys into her bag, then in a panic changed her mind. She began to dig for her keys but stopped when her fingers grasped her tape recorder. She lifted it out and stared at it. What a curious weapon the little machine was.

In that moment of indecision she heard a high-pitched laugh from inside the house, a woman's laugh. It was Serena's. Good; that would make going in easier. Molly didn't stop to wonder why her aunt was here and not at the fundraiser.

At the front door she hesitated, debating what she would say to Serena to explain her presence at Windward. Perhaps there was nothing *to* say. They were aunt and niece, older sister and younger sister, with years of understanding between them.

She reached for the door. Unlocked and smoothly oiled, it opened at a touch. From the direction of the living room Molly heard Serena talking in a rapid, elevated voice that was new to her. She closed the door quietly and was about to call out when she was stopped by Serena's laugh, a brittle sound that made clear that her aunt was angry in a way Molly had never heard before.

"You really thought it was your brains I was buying? Your contacts in the construction industry?" Her tone bordered on the hysterical. "Gent, if I wanted to buy brains, I can think of a good dozen others that would have suited my purposes far better. What a complete fool you are."

Gent Perot. Her heart skipped a beat. Molly held on to the foyer table for support. Her uncle's words came back to her, and the sad look on his face. *He's young and he amuses your aunt.* It struck Molly with a terrible force that she had come in on a lovers' quarrel and that she should leave at once without hearing another word. But it was Perot's remark that stopped her, that made Molly move closer to the living-room door to listen quite openly. Impulsively she slid the tape recorder from her bag onto the foyer table, switching it on in the process.

"I was, wasn't I?" Perot was saying. "A damn fool, and now I'm as deep in this mess as you are. Pipe-bombing GBC when I was already on record as saying the contract should have gone to Halloway Construction."

"I had nothing to do with that, I said."

"Serena, you supplied the money and set me up as Halloway's partner with the proviso that I kept your role secret, and all you were doing was using me as a patsy. Then you had your friends put a bullet in Halloway's heart, poor bastard, so I could take his place and do your bidding."

Serena's voice was contemptuous. "You really fell for that business about Halloway gambling in Monte Carlo. Well, that's what we wanted and that's what we got, a good-looking man who believes his own publicity."

"I can think of a number of times when you believed my publicity, too."

Serena was silent. Molly could hear the sound of a glass thumped on a table. "I thought maybe we had something going for us," Serena said dully.

"What did we have going for us? I've got a wife and four kids. I wasn't about to dump them, not for you."

"Of all the self-satisfied, self-centered remarks! You just might have to. But if we stick together, things can still work out. There's not one single shred of evidence that ties me to Elliott Lawrence and Buzz, not a shred."

"Dan Halloway would have come around to seeing things my way," Perot said. "I ought to kill you for that."

In the darkened foyer, Molly gasped and in her excitement hit the tape recorder, sending it skittering along the table.

"What the hell's that?"

Molly grabbed the recorder and flattened herself against the wall. If they turned the light on, they'd find her. Gent came to the doorway and stood there for a moment, frowning. She could see him quite clearly, framed by the light issuing from the living room. Her heart beat so strenuously and so loud that she was certain he'd hear it, but he remained very quiet, looking toward the front door.

"It's nothing," Serena said. "Nothing except your nerves. You're jumpy as a cat."

Gent waited a second or two and then went slowly back into the living room.

"You won't kill me, Gent. You need me now as much as I need you."

"Do I really?" His voice had turned cold. "I'm clean, Serena, and if I have to throw you to the wolves, I will."

"I had nothing to do with what happened to Daniel Halloway."

"Or the cop killed in your niece's apartment," Perot said. "Or Jason Loring."

"Loring called and said he had a photograph of you and me in the Bahamas. Buzz was going to meet him, get the picture and deliver it to me. As for the cop, he was killed because he surprised Buzz looking for that damn tape."

"Thomas 'Buzz' Beam of the Construction Workers' Union. Handy man to have around to do your dirty work."

"He wasn't supposed to kill Loring," Serena said. "He was supposed to mug him and grab the photo—make it look like a robbery. The scuffle got out of hand. And by some clever maneuvering on his part, he managed to persuade the D.A.'s secretary to destroy Molly's tape. Fran thought Buzz was in love with her, just the way I thought you loved me."

"We're not talking about love," Perot said, "we're talking about your pal Buzz."

"He's clever, but there's nothing that ties me up with him or with Elliott Lawrence," Serena said.

Nothing but a tape recorder, Molly wanted to shout. *Oh, Serena, nothing but a tape recorder.* She moved cautiously closer, still keeping herself flat against the wall but allowing herself a clear view of what was going on inside.

The room was painted in celadon and decorated with English provincial furniture covered in white satin. Her aunt stood near the fireplace, which was cold and had been swept clean. It was an elegant room, not much used, and her aunt, wearing a slim, dark-blue dress and a dark bow in her blond hair, appeared equally cold, pale and inaccessible. Molly gazed hard at her, scarcely able to recognize the woman she had loved all those years. "It all got out of hand," Serena was saying.

Perot was in the act of pouring himself a drink from a crystal decanter. "It got out of hand," he said and then repeated the words as though unable to believe the folly of Serena's pronouncing them. "It got out of hand. Well, well, tell that to the judge; maybe he'll go soft on you."

"Molly's tape recorder," Serena said. "Something as simple and stupid as that. Buzz and Elliott and their indiscretion, taped by my niece." She moved over to the couch, sat down, and then got up again only to return restlessly to the fireplace, as though she might find some warmth there. "I was a fool to bring them to Windward, to believe they'd fit in. Willy found out that Elliott played poker and took him to his heart, poor, dear Willy."

"Too bad you didn't think of poor, dear Willy when you bought into Halloway and installed me as front man."

She turned on Perot. "I didn't see you objecting. Oh, dammit, Gent." She went quickly over to him and put her arms around him. "I only did it because I love you."

Perot pushed her roughly away. "Did you? Do you? Daniel Halloway made a big mistake turning in an honest bid on the sewer construction job. He had to be taught a lesson for cutting you and your pals out. Sweet real-estate deals, corrupt unions, extortion, racketeering, payoffs—the D.A. is going to go down the glory road on this one, Serena. And the headlines won't look pretty. JUDGE'S WIFE

QUEEN OF CORRUPTION. Beautiful. Did you really think I'd give up my life-style for you? You were a temporary amusement. You threw yourself at me and I did what any man would do: I took what was offered.''

"Damn you, damn you." Serena went for him, slapping her hand across his face. "You said you loved me. I was willing to leave my husband for you."

"That does it." Perot grabbed her arm and twisted it behind her back. "I've had about everything I care to take."

Serena screamed and Molly, without stopping to consider the consequences, ran into the room. "Gent, let her go."

Perot turned, his expression unbelieving. "What the hell are you doing here?"

"I said let her go."

He made a brave attempt at a laugh. "Sure, she's all yours. I'm getting out of here." He let go of Serena's arm. Molly ran over to her as Serena crumpled to the floor.

"Come on," Molly said, holding out her hands and helping her aunt to her feet as the front door slammed shut.

"He tried to kill me," Serena said, clinging to her desperately. "He's the voice on the tape, your tape, Molly."

"It won't work, Serena, I heard everything."

"Oh, Molly, you don't understand."

"But I do," Molly said softly, "more than you can imagine."

Serena held tightly to Molly, fingers digging into her niece's flesh. "Molly, I did everything I could to save your life. They wanted to kill you, you see that, don't you? You'd be dead if it weren't for me." She took in a deep sob. "You won't say anything, will you, to anyone? It would ruin your uncle. If we both get our stories straight, we can put the blame where it rests, on Gent, acting in collusion with Elliott Lawrence and Thomas Beam."

There came the sound of the front door opening and closing once again. Serena looked past Molly, her face lit in the hope that Gent had come back, but then Molly saw her expression turn to one of horror.

"She's not going to listen to you, Serena, because she's not going to live any longer than you are."

Molly turned swiftly and found him framed in the doorway, the raspy-voiced man with the round eyeglasses, Thomas Beam. A gun glistened in his hand.

"Buzz," Serena breathed. "I'm glad you're here. You've got to find Gent Perot. He knows everything."

He shook his head, wearing a hard, eager smile on his face. "Your plan to pin everything on Elliott and me just won't wash. I have Perot out front, hog-tied and unconscious. Elliott's going to love this when I tell him. After I get through with the both of you, it's going to look like a love triangle that got out of hand."

"I wouldn't try anything if I were you," Molly said. "The D.A.'s office knows all about you. I wrote and signed a deposition that you're the man who tried to kill me on a couple of occasions."

Beam laughed out loud. "Should make good reading in the Sunday supplements. Maybe I'll even subscribe from my retirement in the Bahamas." He raised his gun and pointed it straight at Molly. Serena screamed and rushed at him, and in the moment it took to turn the .38 on her, she managed to throw herself against him. A shot rang out and they tumbled to the floor. Molly leaped forward and kicked the gun from his hand. She scrambled across the floor and picked it up, aiming it straight at Beam's heart as he got to his feet.

"Don't move, Mr. Beam."

There was a heavy silence as Beam stood stock-still, staring at the gun in her hand. His face was still twisted into a smile, as if the gun in Molly's hand were only a minor inconvenience. Serena lay on the floor, moaning and holding her hand to her shoulder and a seepage of blood.

Molly found herself viewing the scene as though from a great distance. Serena had saved her life. She knew that whatever Serena had done, she wasn't going to hand her to the police. "Serena, how bad is it?"

"My shoulder. It hurts, but—no, it—it isn't serious." Her aunt got shakily to her feet. "Molly, help me."

"Run, Serena, get away from here. I'm going to call the police now and I don't want you here when they come."

Serena threw her a grateful smile, but with a shake of her head let Molly know it was too late.

"It won't work, Molly." Rick came up behind her and deftly took the gun out of her hand.

She turned swiftly, a feeling of relief flooding through her. "How did you find me?"

"I called Willy and he said you had left, talking about needing some country air."

Her uncle came in at that moment, his face pale and drawn. Serena raised her head, uttered a little cry and met his gaze straight on.

"We've just found Perot out back," Willy said, his voice expressionless. "He told us everything."

THE HOT JULY SUN BEAT DOWN mercilessly on the small patio. Intermingled with the sounds of the city was the extraordinarily pleasant tinkle of ice cubes settling into tall glasses. Molly yawned and looked up from the work she was certain she'd been studying, to greet Rick.

"Ready for lunch?" He balanced a tray holding two crystal glasses and a board with cheese and bread on it.

"Haven't we just had breakfast?"

"Molly, you're in big trouble." He bent over and kissed the top of her head. "That was hours ago. You fell asleep and now you've begun to sizzle. Come on, only mad dogs and linguists stay out in the midday sun."

"Oh, sit down and stop fussing," Molly said. She reached down and plucked a large straw hat from under the chair. "There." She plopped it on top of her thick hair and grinned at him. "I'm out of the midday sun. Is that a wine spritzer?"

"So rumor has it." He put the tray down on a small table and removed the papers from her lap. "Your uncle called. I said you'd get back to him after lunch. I think he just wanted to hear the sound of your voice."

Molly took up a glass and put it to her lips. The drink was cool and a little tart. She took a moment to examine the contents through the crystal facets and put the glass down on the tray. "Rick, do you suppose what happened will ever go away? I mean, gear down in our minds so that it will turn into the kind of history we won't even bother telling our children about?"

Rick motioned Molly to move her legs and then sat on the lounge chair facing her. "That's not really what you want, is it? To hide some terrible facts from the next generation?"

"I suppose the power of love is the good part. Willy's staying around for Serena's sake, helping in her defense. I didn't think he'd forgive me for taping that terrible scene."

Rick, his expression never more serious, said, "You'd have destroyed the tape if I hadn't instinctively known what you were up to."

"I wanted her to escape. She saved my life. If you hadn't shown up..." She let the notion of what might have ensued fall away.

"Talk it out, Molly," Rick said. "I want you to keep talking it out until there's nothing left."

"Nothing left," she murmured, "except a broken man who committed no crime but that of loving his wife and believing in her. Nothing left but the shell of a woman who wanted so much that she thought herself above the law. Ruined lives—it's a terrible legacy."

"Willy fell in love once with a beautiful, ambitious woman half his age, and when he woke up to the fact, she had metamorphosed not, I'm afraid, into a butterfly but into a rare species of creature with a very long sting."

"He carried dignity and justice around with him as if all he had to do was dispense them like the sandman," Molly said. "Justice. Isn't she always depicted with blinders on?"

"Blinders, not cheaters, Molly. Meanwhile, the system has lost two honest men through blinders: your uncle and Alex Creedon—Alex because he thought that his secretary of twelve years had no private life, no desires, no need to be anything but his lackey."

Molly sighed. "Imagine Fran's falling for Thomas Beam."

"He was smooth and he talked money."

"And brought down a district attorney. Is it a job you'll go after, Rick? I mean in the foreseeable future?"

He reached for her. "Right now my foreseeable future is a beautiful brunette in my arms, in my heart." He pressed his lips to hers in a kiss that claimed them both. The future belonged to them, and in a while the past would fade into shadows that would at last be consumed by the sun.

JULIE ELLIS

author of the bestselling
Rich Is Best **rivals the likes of**
Judith Krantz and Belva Plain with

THE ONLY SIN

It sweeps through the glamorous cities of Paris, London, New York and Hollywood. It captures life at the turn of the century and moves to the present day. *The Only Sin* is the triumphant story of Lilli Landau's rise to power, wealth and international fame in the sensational fast-paced world of cosmetics.

What readers say about Harlequin romance fiction...

"I absolutely adore Harlequin romances!
They are fun and relaxing to read, and
each book provides a wonderful escape."
—N.E.,* Pacific Palisades, California

"Harlequin is the best in romantic reading."
—K.G.,* Philadelphia, Pennsylvania

"Harlequins have been my passport to the
world. I have been many places without
ever leaving my doorstep."
—P.Z.,* Belvedere, Illinois

"My praise for the warmth and adventure
your books bring into my life."
—D.F.,* Hicksville, New York

"A pleasant way to relax after a busy day."
—P.W.,* Rector, Arkansas

*Names available on request.